Mara's
Baby

D1521558

Mara's Baby

a novel

DON MARPLE

CreateSpace Independent Publishing Platform
Charlotte, North Carolina

Cover design by Melissa Schropp.
Cover image from Adobe Stock images.
Back cover photo courtesy of the author.

ISBN13: 978-1978009875
ISBN10: 1978009879

This is a work of fiction. Names, characters, places and incidents either are the product of the author's imagination or are used fictitiously. Any resemblance to actual persons, living or dead, events or locales is entirely coincidental.

"Focus more on your desire than on your doubt and the dream will take care of itself."
– Mark Twain

1

WEST VIRGINIA

The silver airliner flashed in the afternoon sun when it lowered a wing and banked left to fly between two long ridges and drop onto the runway at the head of the valley. Its tires chirped and left puffs of blue smoke behind as the low-winged DC-3 bounced past the concrete block terminal. It stopped at the end of the runway and the port propeller slowed and stopped.

The plane spun around and taxied to the gate in the chain-link fence on one engine, sending leaves and twigs tumbling across the runway behind it. It stopped with that engine still running and the passenger door on the opposite side facing the gate.

The door swung out. A blue-uniformed stewardess knelt in the opening and lowered a set of steps to the ground. A slim young man wearing a dark blue windbreaker came to the door, hoisted an overnight bag onto his shoulder, and bounced down the steps. He stopped on the tarmac and scanned the hills above the Hartsburg airport.

The sun was above Union Hill, where he used to play in the grassed-over emplacements for the Federal cannons that guarded the town and its railroad junction during the Civil War, and its red-orange glow was brightening the western slope of Trouserleg Ridge across the valley. He stepped aside to let the man boarding the plane go by him and walked slowly into the terminal.

The agent at the ticket counter was stuffing papers into a brown envelope, and a janitor was sweeping the floor with a push broom. The woman at the rental car counter waved a red envelope over her head. "Over here, Alan."

He walked up to the counter and dropped his bag. She put a rental agreement in front of him. "Haven't seen you since Hec was a pup."

"Well, hello, Mrs. Queen," he said. "How long you been out here?"

"About six months," she said. "You here for the reunion?" She put her finger on the form. "Sign right there."

"Yes, ma'am." Alan took a pen from the counter and scrawled his signature.

Mrs. Queen stuffed the agreement in the red envelope and handed it to him. "Go out the exit over there and I'll fetch the car." She started to walk away, then stopped and turned back to him. "Nice to see you here again, young man."

A few minutes later, she brought the car to the walkway where Alan was waiting and handed him the keys.

He threw his bag on the back seat and drove out of the parking lot on to Route 83. Ten miles from the airport, he slowed down to drive past the Jewel City Drive-in Theater and around the sharp curve half a mile beyond it. Just past the curve, he pulled off the road, climbed over the guardrail and knelt beside a small white cross standing in the field. He bowed his head, pressed his fingers to his lips and touched them to the cross.

He stood, got back in his car and accelerated up the long grade, turned on to Route 30, and drove to the Holiday Inn just across the town line.

The desk clerk, a balding man in his fifties with suspenders running over a white shirt with a frayed collar, studied Alan's American Express card, then peered up at him over half-moon reading glasses.

"Alan Cottrill—Wes's boy, aren't you? I'm Clarence Goff. Your daddy loaned me and Eleanor the money to buy our house in forty-seven, after the war." He put a sheet of paper on the counter. "There's a special rate for your bunch from the fifty-five class reunion. Twelve dollars a night." He gave Alan a pen. "Sign there."

As Alan signed, the clerk asked, "Seem like it's been five years to you?"

"It's been a long five years for me, Mister Goff." Alan handed the paper back.

As he took it, the clerk said, "Your father was a good man. This town misses him. Misses you, too. Too many good sons gone away."

Alan shook his head. *Not much to stay for.*

"Here's your key," said the clerk. "School's closed, you know. Boarded up. A shame."

"It sure is. We were the last class."

Alan picked up his luggage and trudged down the long hall to his room. He went in, threw his bag on the bed, washed his hands and face, and walked across the road to Marino's restaurant for a Budweiser, some garlic bread and a plate of manicotti.

He trotted back across the road in the twilight. In his room, he closed the thin curtains that only partially darkened it, took a copy of *The Four Loves* out of his bag and slipped into bed, but he could neither read nor sleep. A flow of memories rushed through his consciousness as the eighteen-wheelers rumbled by on the interstate outside.

The final hundred yards of the mile run when his legs cramped under him and he bloodied his knees on the cinder track, lying there in pain as his competitors crunched past him to the finish line. Standing between Virgil and Fred and bowing his head to receive the medallion of honor from the Grand Councilor while his father watched. Coming off the bench and scoring eight points in the semi-final game of the state basketball tournament his senior year. Projecting the final lines of the senior class play into the darkness above the footlights, all that he could see.

His father's last words to him: "Look after your mother, son." Sitting beside her as she drove the three of them home from the hospital in Morgantown, his tears blurring the view of the oncoming headlights on the dark, narrow road . . . The call at 3 a.m., "I'm sorry to tell you that John Wesley Cottrill . . ."

Mara. Bright, lively Mara. Pressing her body against his, her dark eyes sparkling as she gazed up at him.

—◦◦◦—

HE GOT UP AT seven and ran along the interstate highway for forty minutes with the cool, damp air wiping his face. He showered, shaved, dressed in gray slacks and a short-sleeved shirt and walked through the dim, green-carpeted corridors to the small coffee shop, stopping in the lobby to buy a copy of the *Hartsburg Citizen*.

The paper seemed to carry the same news every time he was here—new service club and Masonic officers, the latest Eagle Scout, bowling league scores. A citizens' group was raising money to restore a downtown hotel to its former glory.

At nine, he was on the bypass highway around the town, on his way to the cemetery. He drove over the East Fork River that flowed through the hills to the Ohio, past the abandoned glass manufacturing plant whose tall stack had spewed a continuous yellow cloud over the town until it was closed ten years ago, putting eight hundred men out of work—the hot, grinding toil that had supported the glassworkers and their families, and enriched the town for fifty years.

The hills outside the town were deformed by the yellow scars and unnatural shapes left by surface mining. Their peaks looked like circular dirt race tracks had been torn out of them halfway up, leaving their tops in the center pointing at the sky like fat, green-tipped spears.

As he drove between the tall stone pillars of the entrance to the cemetery, he saw the uneven white limestone slabs that marked the resting places of the town's first settlers. They had come here in the middle of the eighteenth century, leaving the East Coast for the unknown wilderness of this hill country with its promise of independence and hope.

In the cemetery, Alan took the first fork to the right and drove around the side of a hill until he recognized a red maple tree to the left of the road. He parked behind a faded-blue VW Beetle, got out and walked up the slope toward a light gray stone at the head of two graves:

COTTRILL

JOHN WESLEY   GRACE MATHEW
1897 – 1952   1900 – 1959

The morning sun brightened the faces of the stones he passed and cast shadows behind them. The forest beyond the hill, its leaves stirring in the wind, showed the dark green of mid-summer. The hillside was full now. The cemetery had just opened this section when Alan and Connie picked the spot, halfway up and overlooking the valley, for their father's grave eight years ago. Now his parents were here together.

They had built their lives and raised Alan and Connie in this town. It was far away from the farms where Wes and Grace had been brought up and the parts of the state where their parents, brothers and sisters rested.

He knelt beside the granite stone, head bowed, and thanked the Lord for his parents and all they had given him—a strong family, constant love and acceptance, their beliefs in the power of good and the importance of work. They had shown their children the blessings of sacrifice, how to bear misfortune and, finally, how to face death, as he'd had to do twice in the last two years. They left him all of this, and their good name.

I am alone, Lord Jesus. Guide me.

He rose, wiped his eyes with the sleeves of his shirt and started back down the slope, not noticing a figure standing higher up the hill a few rows away.

"Hello, Alan."

Startled, he turned and saw a petite, dark-haired woman looking down at him. The darkness of her eyes was intensified by their reflection of the sun. She was wearing a cream halter-top sundress with a full skirt cinched at the waist by a brown belt.

His breath left him. He stared at her, dumbfounded. *Where did you come from?*

She raised her right hand to shade her eyes. "Don't you know who I am?"

"Yes." He folded his arms. "What brings you here?"

"My mother's buried just over there." She pointed.

"Is that all?"

"I'm here for the reunion, too. Aren't you?"

He nodded, took a half step backward and shifted his weight to the downhill leg. "Are you still Mara Sabatelli?" He spoke the name as though it were difficult to pronounce.

"Yes."

They stood staring at each other, he on the down slope, she above him.

A puff of air ruffled her dress. The gold cross on her necklace flashed in the sun.

A black-winged butterfly bounced through the air between them.

"You finished here?" she asked.

"Yeah."

"Will you wait a few minutes for me? I want to talk to you."

He stuck his hands to his sides and kicked at the grass. "I guess so. I'll wait down there."

Alan went to his car, climbed in and lowered the windows, and listened to the wind in the trees and the *pop* of the grasshoppers flying among the graves. He took off his glasses and pressed his hands against his face.

Never thought I'd see her again.

Presently, Mara came over the crest of the ridge and walked down the hill, stepping carefully between the markers. The wind was blowing her hair behind her face and her dress against her breasts. He could see a small piece of white tissue in one hand.

Still beautiful.

She walked to the middle of the road and stopped. Not until then did she look at him.

He looked back. "Yes?"

"Down there," she said, tilting her head to the left. "A bench."

Alan opened the door and got out of the car, leaving the windows open. As he straightened, a gust pushed against his back and blew road dust in Mara's face. She cried out and put an arm in front of her face.

"You all right?" he asked.

She took a deep breath and batted her eyes. "Yes, thanks."

They walked around a curve in the road toward a cul-de-sac, he at the edge of the pavement, she in the center. Mara stopped at a concrete bench on her side of the road that faced a family gravestone:

STALNAKER

HENRY CARSON   LOUISE JEFFRIES

1880 – 1953   1886 – 1957

Our Father   *Dearest Mother*

Together for Eternity

She pointed to the bench. "Sit?"

"I'd rather stand."

She sat down and looked up at him, pleading with her eyes.

"Yes?" he said, stone-faced.

"Give an inch, Alan. It's been five years. I came here to see you. Can you say something nice, like, 'How are you, Mara?' Can you?"

His expression did not change. "You look good, Mara. You always looked good to me and you look good now."

"Is it good to see me?"

He walked behind the bench, put his hands on its back and leaned back against them, watching the leaves and small pieces of gravel skittering down the road with the wind.

"You really hurt me, and you had to know it. I may have been immature, but I loved you with all my heart." He watched a pair of crows flying above them and cawing softly to each other.

He turned around. "It would've been different if you'd broken up with me—said we weren't right for each other, that you had to marry a Catholic. I knew how your father felt about that and I might have understood." He opened his palms. "But you vanished. I found out when the store was sold, you all were gone, and your house was for sale. Then the movers came. They told me they were taking everything to Akron, but they wouldn't give me an address."

"You did find my family."

"Were you there? You didn't return my calls, and after a while, whoever answered hung up on me. Then the phone was disconnected. You dropped off the face of the earth, out of my life, and I didn't know why."

"I loved you, Alan, more than anything. But I had to go away." She looked up at him, tears flowing down her cheeks and falling on her dress. "I was pregnant."

Alan turned away, pressed his palms against his temples and cried out to the stones on the hill below. "Jesus Christ—while she was telling me she loved me."

"I did love you, Alan."

He walked behind the bench to the Stalnaker gravestone and leaned forward against it. "God *damn* it. All the time you were telling me you loved me, you were *fucking* someone else."

"Oh, Alan, I'm so sorry. I didn't know what to do. I couldn't tell you. I just couldn't. What would you have done if I told you I was pregnant?"

"Who was it? Sure wasn't me." He slapped the stone. "Who got you to do it?"

"Are you sure you want to know?"

He glared at her.

She swallowed and choked out the words. "Bucky Connor."

Alan lowered his head. "Our all-state halfback."

"Do you want to know how it happened?"

"How could you do that to me? I really loved you."

"Bucky and I were on the stage crew for the class play. You remember?" His head stayed down.

"You went home with your parents after the dress rehearsal. A few of us stayed to work on the props, getting ready for the next night. He started flirting with me and I went along with it a little bit. Just for fun. Then everyone else was gone, the lights were out, and he was chasing me around in the dark. I was in my cheerleader outfit, running around tables, ropes and curtains backstage, laughing and teasing him, and he was trying to catch me.

"He caught me and pinned me against the arm of a couch. He tried to kiss me and I turned my cheek to him. Then his hand was up my skirt. I screamed and struggled, but he held me against him. I couldn't do anything to stop him, he was too strong! He was in me before I knew it. It took no time at all for him to finish. I felt it.

"I didn't want to do it with him." She pounded her thighs. "I was *just playing.* I didn't want to do it with anyone." She put her face in her hands. "I ran to my car and drove home in a panic. Didn't tell anyone. I couldn't say he raped me, no one would believe it. I missed two periods, my breasts swelled up, and Mama knew I was pregnant. She took me to our doctor and our priest, and then she told Papa. He never spoke to me after that. To this day."

He sat down on the bench. "You had to move?"

"Everyone would have known. The homilies would've been about sin and forgiveness, and everyone in the parish would know why. Papa would have to face them in the store every day, those that did come in."

She stared at the hill full of gray and black stones in front of them. "Punishing sin excites people, Alan. Draws them together. It carries more force than forgiveness. You saw what happened to Ginger Hawkins.

Everyone knew she went to New York and had an abortion. I couldn't do that. Frankie would've been taunted at school, just like Tommy Hawkins was. 'Your sister's a whore. Whore, whore, whore. Ha, ha, ha.'"

She wiped her eyes. "Papa knew what it would be like. He sold the store to John Perry and moved to Akron. Worked for his brother for a year—it must've been awful, they don't get along—then he moved to Defiance and opened his own store. Mama died not long after that. Her heart was broken."

Mara leaned forward and held the tissue over her eyes again. Her body shuddered. "Papa didn't tell me, Alan. He didn't even tell me. He told Aunt Sophie and she told me."

"Aunt Sophie?"

"Mama's sister. A schoolteacher in Iowa. I went there and had the baby. Gave it up for adoption in Iowa City. Aunt Sophie called Papa to tell him, but he didn't want to know. 'Not mine,' he said."

"Did you see it? The baby."

Mara pulled her head up and back, wailing. "You don't get to. Saddest day of my life." She covered her face with her hands. "I will never see my child."

She had compressed the tissue into a ball smaller than a marble. Alan took a handkerchief from his hip pocket, flicked it open and held it out to her. Mara stared at the white cloth for a second, then up at him. She took the handkerchief, murmured, "Thank you," and held it over her face.

A brown DeSoto sedan came down the road, turned into the cul-de-sac, and parked across from them. A couple and two young children got out of the car and walked through the grass to a black grave marker. The man knelt on one knee while the woman put a vase of white flowers on the base of the stone. The children, little girls in blue skirts, white blouses and black shoes, skipped across the road holding hands and stood in the grass watching Mara and Alan.

Mara stared at them, her eyes glistening. "How old, do you think?"

Alan put his elbow over the back of the bench and studied them.

"Little one's three, I'd guess. The other one's five."

"So's mine." Mara turned away.

The man across the road got up, backed away from the grave marker and started toward their car. His wife put her arm around his waist and leaned against him. She called to the girls and they ran back across the road and got in the car, clambering in through a back door. The DeSoto went around the cul-de-sac and drove away.

Alan leaned back and watched the clouds above them drift into the sun. "I'm sorry, Dark Eyes."

Her eyes sparkled. "Oh, Alan, I'm going to cry again."

"Please don't," he said, smiling. "That 'kerchief will only hold so much."

She put her arm toward him along the top of the bench. "Should I have told you?"

"Did you tell them who it was?"

"Only Mama. We didn't dare tell Papa."

He looked at the horizon. "Then he thought it was me."

"I guess he did. I'm sorry." She clasped her hands together. "Blessed Mother, will this never end?"

He reached out and took her hands. "I would have married you."

She shook her head. "No, Alan. It would have ruined your life, too. We would still be in this town. We'd have two or three kids. One of them would not be yours, and everyone would know it. You'd be working split shifts for the power company and I'd be working Friday nights and weekends at Woolworth's. Your parents would be gone and mine would not speak to us. We'd both be unhappy. We'd fight a lot."

"You're a pessimist," he said. "I don't fight."

"You didn't use to cuss, either." Mara refolded the handkerchief. "Here."

He took it in his open hands and pushed his hands between his knees. "Alan . . ."

"Hmm?"

"No one here knows."

"I won't." He leaned forward and put the handkerchief in his hip pocket. "Where's your father now?"

"Defiance. Remarried. She has two kids."

"Huh. How do you know?"

"Frankie," she said. "My buddy."

"I remember him. Little Frankie. Where is he now?"

"San Diego. In the Navy." She took a small wallet from the pocket in her dress and pulled out a snapshot of a smiling, dark-haired sailor with a blonde woman leaning on his shoulder. "Little Frankie is six foot two."

"Wow." He squinted. "She Catholic?"

"Nice Catholic girl. Papa approves."

"You?"

"Still." She crossed herself. "It's in my genes."

"I mean, do you have pictures of yourself with someone?"

"Oh, no." She put the picture back and closed her wallet. "It's hard. I can't let anyone get close."

He squeezed his eyebrows together. "Where d'you live?"

"Cedar Rapids. I'm a dental hygienist. You?"

"Boston. I've just started on a master's in accounting."

She studied his face. "Pictures?"

"Huh-unh. Hard for me, too."

They sat—silent—staring at the cold stones rising from the grass and the trees swaying in the gusts.

After a while, Mara said, "You have an older sister, don't you? I remember her looking me over at your house one time when she was home from college."

"Connie. Three years older. She wanted to know what a beautiful girl like you was doing with a twerp like me."

"Kid brothers are all twerps. Where is she now?"

He drew in a breath and exhaled. "Connie was killed in a car wreck two years ago."

"Oh, Alan." She held him close—a sister's hug—and pressed her cheek against his. "I'm so sorry."

He stared over her shoulder into space. "Thank you."

A red riding mower came clattering around the curve in the road and turned up the hill into a row of grass between graves. Its motor coughed as the cutting decks were lowered and began to spit grass behind them. The machine and driver climbed the slope and disappeared over the ridge. The growl of the motor faded.

When it was quiet, Alan said, "Buy you a cup of coffee?"

"I'd like that. Want to go to the Brooklyn? It's still there."

They walked together down the middle of the road to their cars. Alan followed Mara's Beetle to the center of town.

Main Street had some small shops—two restaurants, a dress shop, a drug store—and two banks, a courthouse and its plaza, amid dark storefronts and a rubble-strewn lot. Half a dozen men sat on the wall of the courthouse plaza, several wearing overalls, some in straw hats or baseball caps, idly talking. In a corner of the plaza was a small statue of the local Civil War hero, his horse at a gallop, urging his men forward.

A bakery truck was parked at the curb, its blue-uniformed driver carrying a tray of cellophane-wrapped pastries into the Brooklyn Restaurant. Mara and Alan followed him in.

The Brooklyn had not aged well. A faded red Formica counter ran along its left side with a dozen round red Naugahyde-covered stools affixed to the floor beside it, padding showing through tears in their surfaces. A row of dark plywood booths ran along the right wall, coat hooks sticking out from the posts between them. The restaurant was dimly lit, dark even on this bright morning, its stale air telling of decades of smoking.

Two men sat at the counter, sucking on red-tipped cigarettes and drinking from coffee mugs. A couple was eating breakfast in the first booth. Mara and Alan took the second.

A waitress in dungarees and a wrinkled white shirt carrying a pot of coffee and two mugs pushed silverware wrapped in paper napkins in front of them.

"Hi, kids. Coffee?"

"Please," said Alan. The waitress dropped a mug on the table and sloshed it full.

"What kind of tea do you have?" asked Mara.

"The kind in bags, sweetie."

"That'll be fine," said Mara. "How about doughnuts?"

"On the counter, sweetheart. What kind ya want?"

They were on a plate sitting on the counter, covered with a tall plastic lid labeled "Eat Tamara's Bread Today." Mara peered at the selections—glazed, cream-filled, chocolate-covered—and said, "Two glazed ones, please."

After the waitress brought them on a plate, Mara cut the doughnuts into quarters and picked up a piece with her fork. "I shouldn't eat these things, but I do love them." She put the piece in her mouth. "The downtown isn't like I remember it. Was it this way when we were growing up, or has it gone downhill?"

"It's been going downhill since we were in high school. I probably noticed it more than you because my dad worked downtown. The good stores on Main and Park are gone. No one comes here to shop anymore. The malls outside of town are busy—even the big grocery stores are out there. Our classmates who are still here live in Adamsport or the country club development out past Lost Valley. All the schools are consolidated now. The new high school is outside of town—everyone is bused there. It's bigger than the two we knew combined."

"Is it any good?"

"There are lots of complaints; discipline, lower standards, that kind of thing. Too much interference from Charleston. People say the schools are very different. They're not connected to the neighborhoods anymore." He shook his head. "The neighborhood schools you and I went to are gone."

Alan looked through the plate glass window at two men standing on the sidewalk, smoking. A large cockroach was on the back of the white shirt of one of them, its antennae flailing.

He put his chin on his cupped hand. "This used to be a town of neighborhoods. Connie and I grew up and went to elementary school in Northside. The neighbors knew all of us kids, and they watched out for us. Everyone wanted you to be good and do well." He raised his head. "I didn't realize it, but that neighborhood was a powerful force in my life."

"That's what it was like in the East End, too. And if you weren't good, you suffered, didn't you?"

"Especially girls. Those who did it were considered trash by the good ones. Ginger sure was."

"Like I would have been."

"For sure."

She nodded. "What did they say about me?"

"Not much. Most of it was about your father."

"Really?"

"Lots of rumors. He murdered that couple in Meadow View, he was in a witness protection program and the Mafia found him and killed him. I forget what else."

Mara shook her head. "You didn't say anything? After all the mostacholi Mama fed you?"

"I didn't know anything. Didn't care about him."

"Coward."

"That, too."

"Mafia," she said. "The curse on all Italians. My family's from the north. Bologna. We hate the Sicilians." She stabbed the last piece of doughnut with her fork. "What else did they say?"

"I don't remember much else. Some did wonder how you two and your mom were getting along. Then something else must have happened and you were forgotten, except by me." He grimaced, slapped the back of his neck and examined his hand. "You stay in touch with anyone?"

"Oh, no. Couldn't."

"How'd you hear about the reunion?"

"Frankie. Jerry Skinner told him Drusie Wallace was organizing it. I called Drusie and told her I might come. She told me who all would be here and said you would, so I came." She rubbed her hands together. "I'm having lunch with them today at Abelli's."

He raised his eyebrows. "With who?"

"Drusie and Joanne Davis. Jo's coming in from Texas. She's Jo Baker now. Drusie says her husband's an oil millionaire. I don't know about Barb Hamilton."

"Your high school buddies. What was it you used to call yourselves?"

"The Famous Fabulous Four."

"What are you going to tell them?" He took a sip of coffee.

"Papa moved us to Ohio and opened a new store. I went to school in Iowa and live there now. Apologize for not keeping in touch."

"You and me?"

"We broke up. You're not Catholic." She tilted her head and studied his face. "Okay?"

"I guess."

"It's important to me, Alan. I want to come back."

"Yeah?" He lowered his brows. "Why?"

Mara looked at the top of the table, then up at him. "Ever been to Iowa? They love it, but I'm not one of them. And it's flat—no hills. . . . No . . ." She made a circle above the table with her arms. "Nothing around you, nothing to climb and see what's up there. It's poor country to me, there's no strength in it. People here have teeth." She smiled, showing hers. "Most of them. I can make a living here. Am I nuts?"

"You could be. Where's Bucky?"

"Gone. Shot by accident last year when he was deer hunting. Drusie told me. It's so sad. His wife was expecting their first."

She put her arms on the table and leaned toward him. "I came here this weekend to see you, Alan. I have to work on Monday, and it's a two-day drive to Cedar Rapids, so I need to start back tomorrow. I'll miss the party tomorrow night." She caressed the table. "But I got to see you, and tell you, and that's why I came."

Alan put his hands over his cheeks and wiped the moisture from them with his fingertips. "Oh, Mara." He choked, and had to clear his throat before he could speak. "I loved you so much."

Mara reached across the table and touched his arm. "I loved you too, Alan. You will always be my hero."

The light outside had faded. Alan stared out the water-streaked window of the Brooklyn at the splotches of gray spreading on the sidewalk. "The good guy in the white hat who rides off into the sunset."

"Yes."

"He never gets the girl." Alan took her hand. "It's not fair."

Mara squeezed. "You're right," she said. "It's not fair."

2

Barbara Hamilton was meandering through the Pittsburgh airport, waiting for the last flight to Hartsburg, and went to the newsstand off the concourse to get something to read. She stopped at the rack of magazines near the entrance and rotated it to see the covers that had pictures of celebrities and headlines shouting about their affairs, divorces and babies.

Who reads this crap?

She walked past the checkout counter, where a teenage attendant was leafing through one of the magazines and cracking a mouthful of gum, to a wall of bookshelves at the back of the newsstand. Looking for a book of detective stories, she reached around a tall blonde wearing a Longhorns T-shirt and reading a hardcover book to pull a copy of *Three for the Chair* from the shelf. They touched. Barbara said, "'Scuse me."

The blonde said, "Sure," and took a step away.

"Rex Stout," said Barbara, half to herself. "Wonder if these are any good."

"Not for me," said the Texan. "William McGivern is much better." She looked up. "Read anything of his?"

Barbara froze. "Jo?"

The woman opened her arms. "Oh, my God! Barbie! Barbie Hamilton!" They hugged. Jo dropped her book on the counter and held Barbara's shoulders. "How are you? You have to be going to the reunion. Dru didn't tell me! This is wonderful!"

"I just decided the other day, and I didn't call Drusie. She'll kill me."

Jo leaned forward. "Barb . . ."

"Hmm?"

"Mara's coming."

Barbara's eyes widened. "You're shitting me! Mara? Where's she been?" She pitched Three for the Chair into an empty space in the shelves. "My God—Mara."

"Dru said she's driving here from Iowa, that's all I know. The three of us are having lunch tomorrow at Abelli's." Jo nodded. "You can come, can't you? It'll be the four of us together again."

"Yes, oh, yes. I can't wait to hear what Mara's been up to." Barbara paused. "Does anyone know why she left?"

"Not that I know of." Jo tapped the counter with a manicured fingernail and glanced sideways at Barbara. "But you know . . ."

"Mara? That's hard to believe. She wasn't that kind."

"I guess not," said Jo. "Maybe she'll tell us."

The boarding announcement for the flight interrupted their conversation. They hurried down the concourse, stood in line and boarded the small airliner for the flight to their hometown.

When they were settled in—they had arranged aisle seats across from each other with the stewardess—Jo leaned over the aisle and said, "Guess who else is coming." She pumped her eyebrows. "Will Evans, your heartthrob. I can't wait to see the two of you together again. Of course"—she raised her head and looked down at Barbara—"that may not matter now."

"Why's that?"

"Dru thinks he's gone homosexual."

"Pfft," said Barbara. "I doubt that."

"So do I. But stranger things have happened."

Jo's mother was waiting for her inside the terminal and drove Barbara to the Holiday Inn on their way home. As Barbara got out of the car, Jo put her elbow outside the front window and said, "It's going to be a wonderful weekend, Barb. The Founders' class of 'fifty-five and the Famous Fabulous Four—together again after five years." She waved as the car drove off. "See you tomorrow at Abelli's."

—⁓—

BARBARA SLEPT LATE. SHE had just ordered breakfast in the motel's coffee shop when a stocky, sandy-haired man wearing a pressed khaki shirt and trousers came to the entrance. The teenage waitress left Barbara and went up to the man, handed him a menu, and said, "Sit anywhere you like, sugar." She pushed the door to the kitchen open and disappeared as it swung shut.

He stood between the cash register and the chalkboard advertising breakfast specials and scanned the room. A solitary man was eating at the counter. A couple sat in a booth at the far end of the shop, holding hands and talking softly. His mouth opened slightly when he saw Barbara watching him. He mouthed her name. "Barbara."

She nodded.

He stepped carefully between tables to stand a few feet from the booth where she was sitting.

"How are you, Barbara?"

"Fine, Will."

A plate crashed and shattered in the kitchen. The waitress screamed, "God dammit!" Then there was only the murmur of the couple across the room talking.

"You look good," he said, fingering his menu. "I didn't know you were coming."

"I decided at the last minute, and I didn't call Drusie."

"Oh, she'll like that."

The waitress delivered Barbara's breakfast—cereal, toast and milk—and said, "You sittin' here?" to Will.

He said, "I don't know," and watched Barbara pick up her napkin.

She put it in her lap and smoothed it with both hands. "Sit where you like."

The waitress left.

Will said, "Jesus, Barbara . . ."

She looked up.

"I would like to talk a little bit," he said, "but I guess not." He tapped the menu against his leg, said, "Excuse me," and started away.

She called, "Will." He stopped. "Will, I'm sorry. Come back, please. Sit down." He did. "I don't know why I can't let go after five years," she said, "but I can't. I think about us and everything goes kaflooey inside. I see you after all that time, and it blows out. I act like a mule, turn around and kick at something I can't see but I know is there." She rubbed her eyes with her thumb and index finger. "I'm sorry."

"Don't be." He pushed his menu aside. "I'm sorry for what I put you through and how much it hurt you."

"You never said that before."

"I should have. I'm sorry for that, too."

The waitress dropped a mug of coffee in front of Will. "You goin' to order?" He asked for scrambled eggs and toast. She gave the door to the kitchen a hard shove as she went back through it.

They watched the door swung back and forth. Barbara said, "You're not a bad guy, Will. A bad guy would have been prepared."

"Then we wouldn't have had to worry."

She pressed her lips together. "Then it wouldn't have happened."

"It shouldn't have."

"Our hormones were raging, and we were inexperienced."

"We sure were."

She leaned back. "And it's not like I tried to fight you off."

"Still, I should have stopped."

"I hurt you, too," she said. "I wanted to hurt you—for what I let happen, and for what it did to Mom." She put her hands over her cheeks. "She knew, Will. I could never hide anything from her. She knew, and she was hurt."

Will didn't know what to say next. He wanted to know about Barbara's mother, Lois, who had worked as a secretary to support herself and Barbara after Barbara's father left them when she was ten, but he was afraid to ask. Barbara was staying at the Holiday Inn, so Lois was not living in town, or not living.

Lois had liked him. She had encouraged Barbara to make up with him when they had a serious falling-out early in their senior year. He had betrayed the trust Lois had given him. His tongue felt like it was made of lead. He took a sip of coffee.

"What is it?" asked Barbara.

"I have to ask." He winced. "Your mother?"

"She's remarried. Lives in Charleston. He has two grown children."

"She was always good to me. Would—uh—would it be okay for you to tell her hello from me?"

"Yes. She'll like that."

"So will I."

The waitress slammed a plate of soft scrambled eggs and toast on the table. "Anything else?" Will shook his head. She stomped back into the kitchen.

He lifted a bite of eggs with his fork and the slippery mass slid between the tines and spread across his plate. He grimaced. "These aren't cooked."

Barbara smiled. "Don't complain. She'll clobber you." They laughed.

"You've filled out," she said. "You used to be skinny."

"The Army does that to you."

"Seeing the world?"

"That's the Navy. All I see is hills at Fort Benning. Georgia. You?"

"Chicago. I see the lake."

"Like it?"

"I do. It's a nice city." She paused. "What do you do in the Army?"

"Drive a tank up and down hills and shoot at targets."

The waitress came back. "Separate checks, I suppose?"

They both nodded. Barbara said, "Did you bring it here?"

"Sorry?"

"Your tank. I need a ride to Abelli's at noon. Can you take me?"

"I'd be glad to."

"Can I shoot at some targets?"

Barbara was early—Will told her it was unacceptable to be late in the Army—and greeted Jo Baker and Dru Wallace when they arrived at Abelli's. The hostess said, "Your table will be ready in a few minutes." They stood in front of the hostess station and reminisced about their times together at Washington-Jefferson High.

They and Mara had been best friends and accomplices until Mara disappeared late in their senior year. Barbara and Dru played in the band, Jo and Mara sang in the choir. Dru, Barbara and Jo were in the same sorority and belonged to the same Methodist church. Mara was a cheerleader. The four of them had pulled off pranks together—smoking in their tents at night on camping trips, running from the police after they broke into the local haunted house and setting off firecrackers inside garbage cans on Halloween. The boys got the blame for the firecrackers.

The three of them dated the same boys and talked about them when they got together—what their parents were like, whether they smoked or drank, where they went to park and make out, the lines they used on them and what kind of kissers they were.

Jo leaned toward Barbara and put her forehead on her friend's shoulder. "Do you remember the list we kept?"

"List?" said Barbara. "No. What list?"

"You know. *That* list. You kept it."

Barbara's face reddened. "Oh, my God, that list." She stared at Jo. "Of the guys we dated and how big we thought . . ." She bent over, laughing.

"That's it!" said Jo, her eyes sparkling. "And do you remember who the champion was?"

Jo and Barbara nodded at Dru and chanted, "Rick-ee!"

"Oh, shut up," said Dru.

"What's the matter?" asked Jo. "Not there anymore?"

The outside door opened and Mara came in. After hugs and exclamations of happiness about seeing each other again, they moved out of the entryway and stood just inside the empty, semi-dark barroom.

Dru, always the chief inquisitor of the four, took Mara by the shoulders. She was six inches taller than the petite brunette, and towered over her. "Okay, Miss Mara Sabatelli," she said, forcing a frown. "Time to 'fess up. Why'd you leave? Where'd you go?" She shook Mara gently. "Why didn't you write?"

Mara said, "I'm sorry, I'm so sorry. I should have written or called, I know. There's no excuse for that. I hope you'll forgive me. I loved you all so much." She wiped her eyes and took a deep breath. "What happened was, Papa decided we had to move just before the end of my senior year. And when Papa decides in my family, that's what we do."

"Why'd he do that to you?" asked Dru.

"He got in a big fight over something that happened, and he couldn't get over it. He said there would never be peace for us as long as we lived here, so he moved us to Akron and worked with his brother for a year. Then they moved to Defiance and he opened a store there."

"Oh, Mara baby, what was the fight about?" asked Jo. "Alan?"

Quickly. "Nothing to do with Alan."

"I see," said Jo. She glanced at Barbara.

Dru stepped in. "How'd you get to Iowa?"

"I was miserable in Akron and I made everyone else so miserable that Papa sent me off to Iowa to live with Mama's sister. I finished high school there and went to a community college to be a dental hygienist. I've been working for a dentist in Cedar Rapids for three years. It's nice and the money's good, but I miss this place. I miss the people and I miss the hills.

I want to come back."

"I wouldn't," said Dru. "This town ain't what it used to be, honey, believe me. You got a good job in a good town, you better stay there."

"Well, maybe I should. I don't know." Mara sighed. "I was unhappy for so long, and I didn't call or write anyone. I should have. I'm sorry." She started to cry, and opened her hands to them.

They put their arms around her. "It's okay, Mara, it's okay. You're here now and we love you. We're so glad to see you."

Dru stepped back. "Okay, one more question."

"You're heartless," said Barbara.

"What about Alan Cottrill? He nearly went crazy after you left. He tried hard to find you but he never could. No one could." Dru took Mara's hand. "He's here. What are you going to say to him?"

"I was born and raised a Catholic. It's in my genes. I could never marry a Methodist." Mara patted Dru's hand. "I ran into Alan this morning. He understands. I'm glad I got to see him, too, 'cause I won't be at the dinner tomorrow night. I have to work on Monday, and it's a two-day drive to Cedar Rapids. I have to start back tomorrow."

"Who do you work for?" asked Jo. "Simon Legree?"

"He's a good boss," said Mara. "He gave me three days off, but he needs me on Monday."

"Barb," said Dru, "you and Alan were buddies. Have you seen him?"

"Not since we graduated. I saw Ollie Nutter at Marshall a couple of times when he came to see Eve Carter, and he said Alan was doing okay. I've missed him. I can't wait to see him tomorrow."

The hostess came up to them. "Your table is ready."

Abelli's was a small Italian restaurant with booths along three walls and tables in the center covered with red and white checkered cloths. Pictures of Papa and Mama Abelli, who started the hot dog stand that grew to become this popular restaurant, hung on the walls alongside autographed portraits of beaming entertainers and politicians. The hostess seated them at one of the tables.

All of them ordered salads except Jo, who asked for pepperoni rolls. "I miss these so much," she said. "You can't get them in Houston."

As they ate, they talked about vacation trips they had taken and shared some experiences they'd had in the five years since graduation. Jo and her husband, Jake, had been to London and Paris; Barbara had taken the Canadian Railway through the Rockies to the West Coast.

Dru and Rick had a boy and a girl. "That's where our travel money went."

Then the talk turned to their high school days—teachers, students, classes, football games, band and choir trips. They talked about the romances in their school years, who dated whom, what happened to couples after they graduated, who married locals and who did not, and what had become of them.

Dru turned to Barbara. "Barb, whatever happened between you and Will Evans? You two seemed so much in love, and all of a sudden you broke up."

"Oh, I don't know," said Barbara. "We probably had a spat of some kind, got mad over nothing, and didn't get back together."

"Oh, really?" said Jo, shaking her head. "Well, I saw Will today. He's one handsome guy. Is he married?"

"No, he isn't," said Barbara. "I had breakfast with him this morning."

"Single these five years?" asked Dru. "I bet he's queer."

"He's not," said Jo.

"Is that so?" said Dru. "How do you know?"

"I dated him when we were juniors at WVU. He is very good at not being queer."

Dru lowered her eyebrows. "What do you mean, 'very good'? At what?"

"Never you mind, honey." They all laughed.

Dru returned to questioning Barbara. "What about you, Barb? Can you vouch for him?"

"Oh," said Barbara, "it was a long time ago."

"You mean you didn't?" said Jo. "No wonder he broke up with you!"

The women exploded in laughter. Barbara put on her sweetest smile and waited for them to quiet down. "He loved me for my intellect."

More laughter. Mara stomped her foot under the table, Jo buried her face in a napkin.

Dru kept going. "Oh, Barb, you and Will were the straightest arrows that ever lived."

"He wasn't a straight arrow when I dated him," said Jo, raising a glass of water to her lips.

"Oh, really," said Mara, finally joining in. She leaned in over the table and lowered her voice. "How do you do it with a bent arrow?"

"Mara!" Their shrieks of laughter filled the small restaurant. Jo spilled some water before she could get her glass to the table. The other patrons were glaring at them. The hostess came to the table and asked them to please not be so loud.

"Okay," they said, "we're sorry." They were laughed out.

Their waitress delivered the check to the table. Dru picked it up and said, "Seven dollars apiece, girls. That'll leave her a nice tip."

Dru looked across the table at Barbara. "How long has it been? Five years? And he's still single? He's gone homo."

Barbara shook her head.

Seeing that they were not going to get any more from Barbara about her high school boyfriend, the women turned the conversation to other topics—who would be at the reunion, who would not, and what anyone knew about them.

When it was time to go, Dru, Jo and Barbara took turns embracing Mara and thanking her for making the long drive to see them. They made her promise to keep in touch.

The three of them stood side by side and waved to Mara as she got into her Beetle and jerked it through the gears driving out of the parking lot. It turned right onto the side road and waited for the light at Route 30. When the light changed, the little blue bug went right again, accelerated down the highway and disappeared over the crest of Trouserleg Ridge.

Barbara murmured, "Bye, Mara."

"Bye." The other two echoed her.

Dru went into the restaurant to retrieve her wallet. Jo and Barbara waited outside.

"Why'd she say she left, back then?" asked Jo.

"Her father decided."

"Why'd he decide?"

"She said he got in a big fight over something."

"Her old man was one tough wop." Jo pressed her lips together. "You s'pose she fought with him about Alan, and that's why he sent her away?"

"She said it had nothing to do with—"

"I heard what she said."

"We'll never know, will we?" Barbara stared at the crest of the hill where Mara's car had gone. "Poor Mara."

On the way back to the Holiday Inn, Jo said, "Barb, how about coming over for dinner tonight? Mom and Dad would love to see you. It'll be informal, just cornbread and soup beans." She winked. "Unless you and Will are . . . doing something."

"Oooh, cornbread and soup beans. They don't know what that is in Chicago," said Barbara. "Will's going bowling with his buddies. At Fair Lanes. Alan Cottrill and Ed Stewart are here, and Rickie's going. Will said Dru gave him a pass."

"Army talk," said Jo. "So I'll pick you up. Six?"

"That's so nice of you," said Barbara, stepping out of the car. "I'll see you then."

———❧———

WILL AND A MAN fondling a martini glass were sitting at the bar in the Holiday Inn when Barbara came in after dinner. The bartender was reading something he held low, out of sight. Barbara came up behind Will and hugged him.

"Well, Mister Don Carter, did you sweep the lanes clean tonight?" She sat on the stool beside him.

"Not quite, but we had a good time. How about you?"

"I had dinner with the Davises. Cornbread and soup beans. Yummy." She picked up a thick paper coaster and tapped it lightly on the bar, staring at it. "What're you drinking?"

"I just got here. Bourbon and water."

Barbara raised her hand to the bartender and ordered that for Will and a glass of sherry for herself. When they came, she said "Cheers" to Will and asked for the check.

"Are you limiting me to one?"

She nodded. The man beside the martini glass got up and left, unsteady on his feet. The bartender wiped the bar and went back to his reading. Barbara put an arm on the bar and eyed Will's face.

He raised his brows. "Yes?"

"I don't know how to do this delicately, so I'll just jump in. You were quite the topic of conversation at lunch today. My friends wondered why you're still single. Some of them thought you might not be"—she pulled some air through her lips—"interested in women anymore."

"Your friends. The Famous Fabulous Four?"

"That's us. Jo, Dru, Mara and me."

Will raised his right knee and held it with his clasped hands. "Huh. What did Jo think?"

"She says you weren't that way at WVU."

"And you?"

"Five years is a long time. It won't bother me if you are, Will," she lied.

He scanned the partly full bottles of brown whisky sitting on glass shelves behind the bar. The bartender looked up, and Will shook his head.

"I don't know why they would think that. Believe me, I'm only interested in women." He put his hand over hers and leaned toward her. "Barb Hamilton, I haven't changed since I loved you in the twelfth grade. It's still me—Will."

She turned her hand over and gripped his. "And it's still me, Will—Barbara, who loved you." She took his hand between hers, lifted it to her lips and kissed it. "Will you come with me?"

Barbara led him to her room, where she pressed herself into him, her head high, as he kissed her neck at the shoulder. "Oh, Will, let's not hurry this time."

They didn't.

—⁓⁓⁓—

IN THE MORNING TWILIGHT, she pushed away the blankets, got astride him and kissed his chest until he woke up. She lifted her head and raised her eyebrows; he compressed his, questioning. She lowered herself and kissed the hollow at the base of his neck, then bent her shoulder and reached for him.

"I bet you can," she said.

He could.

Later, they walked out of the motel, across the road and down to a park where the East Fork flowed through wooded hills that were being uncovered by the rising mist, and sat on a wooden bench beside the water. He put his arm around her and she leaned against him. They watched leaves flutter down to the stream and float quickly by them, spots of green and yellow spinning on the water's gray surface.

He raised her chin. "I've never gotten over you, Barb." He pulled her closer. "I hope it's not too late."

"It's not too late, Will."

3

MASSACHUSETTS

The volunteers at the Interfaith Soup Kitchen were gathered around the night captain, a slim, blonde nurse wearing soft white shoes and a light blue, calf-length dress with a white Peter Pan collar and "B.C.S.N." embroidered above the left breast. She was parceling out assignments for the evening.

"Let's see—the cooking's done so you, Mark, Allie, Julie, and—I'm sorry, I've forgotten your name."

"Billie."

"Thank you, Billie. You all can serve. Divvy it up any way you want. There are six trays and the salad bowl."

The four of them spread out behind the trays of food in the serving counter.

"Ruth, will you and Jim bus the tables for us? You know where the cans are, don't you?"

The couple went among the tables in the center of the room and put napkins and condiments on them.

A young man came through the entryway from the church basement and hung an umbrella on one of the coat hooks along the wall. He was medium height and slim—no bulges front or back—with deep-set brown eyes and a thin nose and lips, wearing a checkered brown sweater and khaki trousers. He brushed a shock of dark hair from his forehead, cleaned his glasses with a handkerchief and scanned the room, observing, until he spotted the nurse studying him.

The corners of his eyes crinkled. "Are you in charge?" A low-pitched, friendly voice.

She nodded, still taking him in. "Do I know you?"

"I haven't been here before. I'm Alan Cottrill."

She glanced at the umbrella. "You think it's going to rain?"

"Likely."

She said, "Excuse me," and turned away from him as a line of people—men, women and children—came in the door from Cherry Street and shuffled along a wall decorated with banners of the Calvary Methodist Church to the serving line, where the volunteers were making a clatter pulling metal spoons and spatulas out of drawers and dropping them beside the trays of food.

The people were quiet, dressed in shabby, nondescript clothing, most of it dirty gray or black. The men were wearing T-shirts, dungarees and canvas shoes or sandals. A few had on baseball caps whose bills were separating in the front, white threads hanging down from them, or knit caps that covered their heads down to their ears. The women wore tank tops or sweatshirts. Some were in skirts, some in short pants.

Two children went up to the serving line and pulled themselves up on the bars of the tray platform to see the steaming meats and vegetables on the other side of the counter and smile at the servers.

The nurse scanned the crowd queuing up. "Just a minute, please," she said. "We aren't quite ready. When we are, it's women with children first. The rest of you can get coffee over there"—she pointed to the urns at the end of the room—"while you wait."

A new line formed. Several men poured themselves coffee and sat down.

She went back to the new volunteer. "We're short two tonight—cleanup. How are you at washing pots and pans?"

"I can do that."

"Good. It's all back there in the sink. You're behind already."

He walked with a slight limp past the serving counters to the sink in the rear.

"All right," the nurse announced, "we're open for business." She took the arm of a middle-aged, bearded man in the front of the line. "Sorry, sir, it's women with children first, if you don't mind."

"And if I do?" He glared at her with hostile, red-rimmed eyes.

"It's still women with children first." She put herself between him and the line. "Have some coffee."

The man shook his head, sat down and muttered, "Bitch," loudly enough to be heard around the room.

The nurse dragged a chair across the floor and sat down facing him with her back straight, elbows on her knees. She spoke to him for a few seconds, so softly that no one could hear what she said, then reached out and patted his knee.

"All right?" she asked.

"All right."

She pulled the chair back to its table and walked along the line of people getting food. "Take all you want. There's plenty for everyone. We don't want you to go away hungry." She stepped to the kitchen and stood behind the servers, watching the people in the line.

Alan was taking dirty pots and pans from the stainless counter next to the deep sink in the back of the kitchen, dousing them in soapy water, scrubbing their insides with a stiff brush or steel wool, rinsing them with a movable spray head suspended above the sink and putting them on the counter on the other side of the sink to drain. A pair of elbow-length yellow gloves was slapped on the counter.

"Here," said the nurse, "use these."

The basement room quieted down to a murmur as people took their plates to the tables and began to eat. As some finished, the table servers started loading empty plates and utensils into the dishwashers under the rear counters.

Alan was clasping one handle of a large cooking pot and scrubbing the inside, his elbow deep in the soapy water. He splashed some on his face, stood back and wiped the foam from his nose with his sleeve. When his head came up, the captain was facing him. She was not quite as tall as he, with strawberry blond hair and light blue eyes.

"You doin' all right?" She put a hand on his shoulder. "We usually have two back here, so you'll get paid double tonight." She winked.

He smiled. "Good. I could use it."

"That's a nice smile. Can you be here next week?" She was charming him.

It was working. "Yeah, I think so."

"All right. See you then."

When the meal was over and everyone was gone, Alan helped Ruth and Jim load the dishwasher, then he rinsed and washed the serving trays brought to him by the other volunteers. Everyone pitched in to wipe the counters and tables, empty the coffee urns and rinse them out.

That done, they stood around in the center of the kitchen until Mark said, "Well, that's it. Let's go."

The nurse was standing by the desk at the passageway to the downstairs hall of the church, talking on the telephone. She waved goodbye as they passed through the outside door and started up the steps to Cherry Street. Still on the phone, she took a marker from the desk and put another black "X," this one through the day's date—September 28, 1960—on the calendar tacked to the wall. She hung up, switched off the lights and walked through the dark room and out the outside door. She closed it, twisted the doorknob to be sure it was locked, and walked up the steps to the street.

It was starting to rain. She inhaled through mostly closed lips and looked around at the dark streets. A red neon Miller High Life sign shone above the sidewalk outside Pokey's Tavern in the next block.

It was five blocks to the bus stop on Moody Street. She lowered her head and started walking.

Something snapped. "Miss . . ."

"Aah!" She jumped as a figure shadowed by an open umbrella stepped out from beneath the overhang of the church building. "What?"

The figure lowered the umbrella, taking the shadow away. It was Alan, the pot washer. "Sorry, but I don't know your name."

"You—you startled me."

He stood there.

She drew a deep breath and exhaled slowly. "Sara. No 'h.' O'Brien. I'm glad it's you."

"Alan Cottrill. I thought you might be going to the downtown bus stop. Want to walk?" He held the umbrella over her. They went around the corner to Moody Street and walked in the rain, stepping around the puddles spreading on the sidewalk, both of them under his umbrella.

After half a block, she said, "You're not from around here."

"I'm in school at BC. Just started."

"Really? You're a freshman?"

Quickly. "Oh, no. I'm in the MSA program."

"An accountant."

"Yes."

Sara stepped back to let a man holding a suit jacket over his head run by. "Belong to the church?"

"Not yet. I visit."

"What brought you here tonight?"

"The minister asked for volunteers on Sunday, and I used to help at a Salvation Army kitchen back home. There's a lot of hungry people there, too."

"Huh. Where you from?"

"West Virginia."

"A country boy."

"Small town, really." He spun the umbrella. "You are from here."

"Easy to tell, isn't it?" She looked up at him. "Why'd you come here to go to graduate school?"

"I got a scholarship here. It beats digging coal."

They walked another half block in silence—just the patter of the rain on the umbrella and the splashing when a car drove by, its headlights flashing in the water. They moved away from the curb every time one came down the street.

After a while, he asked, "What did you say to that man?"

"Poor Gus. He's in terrible shape. Alcohol. It's an awful dependency. He's always angry—hoping for a fight, so he can be driven out again—and you mustn't give him one."

She pulled on a tree branch hanging over the sidewalk, sending a small shower spattering onto the sidewalk behind them. "I tell him I'm glad to see him, I know he'll feel better after he's eaten, and I want to see him next week. I make him promise to come back."

He stopped, and stood looking at her. "That is so good. How do you know—?"

She stopped and stared at him, her blue eyes gleaming in the light of a street lamp. "Don't ask."

"Okay," he said. "Where do you do your nursing?"

"I'm a senior at BC. I work at Children's Hospital downtown and spend Saturdays at a children's clinic in the South End."

As they came to the bus stop at Moody and Spruce, a white and yellow MBTA bus with "548 Downtown" shining above the driver appeared out of the gloom. It stopped at the curb and opened its door.

"Good night, Sara O'Brien."

She put a foot on the first step. "You're not getting on?"

"I live near here."

She lowered her eyebrows. "No one lives around here."

"Pleasant dreams."

Sara stood on the first step of the bus and watched him walk into the darkness between the street lamps, stepping lightly around the puddles in the steady rain, until the hiss of air brakes told her to climb up the steps and take a seat. She sat by a window on the curb side, leaned toward it and looked out ahead. As the bus splattered by the moving umbrella, a hand came out from under it and waved.

She watched the umbrella and the figure beneath it dissolve in the rain. *Good night, Country Boy.*

4

The crowd at the soup kitchen was unusually large on the Wednesday before Thanksgiving. It was nearly eight-thirty when the volunteers finished cleaning up and left, bounding out the door and up the steps on their way home for the holiday weekend.

Alan was the last of them. Sara was still there, talking to the minister. They waved to him and he lingered at the door for a few seconds, reluctant to leave. He closed the door behind him, climbed slowly up the concrete steps and crossed Cherry Street. His shadow from the corner street lamp wheeled around him as he walked past the lamppost and down Moody Street. Halfway down the block he stopped at the red neon Miller High Life sign buzzing in the window of Pokey's Tavern and looked inside. It was nearly deserted. He pulled open the wooden door and stepped into a dim barroom that smelled of cigarettes and stale beer.

A dozen pale wall sconces lit the tavern's interior. Autographed pictures of Pete Runnels and Ted Williams in action—Runnels catching a ball on the run, Williams swinging for the fences—hung above the bar. Empty four-person booths ran along wood-paneled walls across from the bar and down an aisle to its right.

A woman was sitting between two men at the bar. The three of them were listening to the bartender tell a story. When he finished, the woman's hoarse laugh cut through the room. She took a drag on her cigarette, pushed a stream of smoke from the corner of her mouth toward the ceiling and laughed some more. The men kept their eyes on her.

The bartender came over to Alan. "H'lo, professor. Bud draft?"

Alan nodded.

The barman took a glass from the counter, put it under a tap and pulled down on the Budweiser handle above it.

As the glass filled, Alan said, "Quiet night, Ike."

"Yeah. No one's out tonight." Ike slid the foam-topped glass across the bar and grinned. "Sit anywhere." He wiped his hands on a rag hanging from a metal ring below the counter and went back to the threesome.

Alan took his beer to a booth halfway down the deserted aisle and sat down. He flipped through the tunes displayed in the wall box in the booth, put in a quarter and punched the tabs for "Only the Lonely." He lowered his head and listened to Roy Orbison's lament of separation and loneliness. When the song ended, he went to the men's room that was down a corridor across from the bar.

He finished, filled his cupped hands with water, buried his face in them and dried it on a fabric towel hanging from a white metal container on the wall. He studied his face in the mirror and thought of the joyful Thanksgivings with his parents and Connie. He missed them so much. He put his hands on the wall beside the towel dispenser, leaned on them and bowed his head.

O Lord Jesus . . . stand by me.

He dried his face again and went back down the corridor toward the bar.

Sara was standing there. Ike tipped his head toward Alan. "That him?"

Alan thought he was going to melt. He took a step back as Sara, smiling, came toward him.

"Buy me a drink?" she asked.

"Anything you want."

"I already ordered."

They went to his booth and sat down opposite each other. Sara put her purse on the seat. A waitress brought her a bottle of Coca-Cola and a glass of ice.

"That'll be all, thanks." Sara poured the Coke into the glass and the foam overflowed. "You're not going to West Virginia for the holiday?"

"No."

She lifted her glass and wiped up the spilled foam with a napkin. "No hometown honey?"

"Huh-unh."

"Family?"

He shook his head.

"I'm trying to talk to you, Alan." She looked across at him, her head tilted to one side.

"Sorry. I'm still in shock."

She nodded.

He clasped his hands together and put his chin on them. "My parents are gone. I had an older sister. I lost her two years ago."

She winced. "Oh."

"I went back for my high school class reunion in August." He took a drink. "And I go to a Cottrill family reunion on Memorial Day. See my cousins."

"In West Virginia?"

"A farm in Braxton County."

"How do you get there?"

He smiled. "By boat."

"A boat to West Virginia?" She laughed. "You're kidding."

"I'll fly to Hartsburg and stay with my Aunt Lil in Weston. On Memorial Day we'll drive down to the Elk River and Ken Cottrill will pole us across to the farm in a johnboat."

She narrowed her eyes. "What do you do there?"

"We eat. Country food, most of it from the farm. We sing hymns in the cemetery and decorate the graves. Uncle Harvey tells us about the family members who have gone to be with Jesus, and we remember them." He inhaled unevenly. "We thank the Lord for our blessings."

He lowered his head, put his glasses on the table and wiped his eyes with his fingers.

"It must be wonderful there."

"It is."

"You are a country boy."

"I guess I am."

"Tell me about that."

"There's a strong spirit of independence there—and hope. We have faith in God, but He expects us to take care of ourselves and our neighbors. We take care of each other in a way I haven't seen here yet."

"What do you miss the most?"

"My parents. But I have what they gave me, and their good name to live up to."

He watched the bartender pouring liquor into three glasses on a serving tray. "Sounds perfect, doesn't it? But there's rivalries and bickering and a few bad apples in there, too—we just don't talk about them." He scratched his chin. "And the hills. I miss the hills." He tapped his chin with his cupped hand. "How's that for talking?"

"Pretty good."

"You're a saint, you know that?"

"Careful. You don't know me, either."

A frazzled waitress with a strand of dark hair hanging in front of her face came to the table. "Anything else?"

Sara said, "No, thanks," and glanced at her watch.

"Do you have to go?"

"Pretty soon." She swallowed. "Since you're not going away this weekend, would you like to come to my mother's house for dinner tomorrow? My family and I would like to have you join us."

His eyes widened. "I don't know what to say."

"Try 'Yes.'"

"That would be wonderful. Are you sure I won't get in the way?"

"You'll give my brother-in-law some company. His name's Cal Jackson. My boyfriend's gone home to Illinois, so Cal will be the only other man there. I warn you, he loves to talk about the Red Sox."

"Isn't baseball over?"

She shook her head slowly. "Never."

"I'll bone up on them. Who else?"

"My sister Mary Clare, Cal's wife. They have a daughter, Erin, and a boy, Ryan. Eight and four. They live with Mom. My other sister, Cassidy—Cass. She's a legal secretary downtown." Sara tapped the table. "Be careful with her, she likes men."

He squinted at her. "What's wrong with that?"

"Just be careful."

She pulled her purse into her lap. "Mom is Marie." She patted her chest. "I'm the baby."

He thought for a second. "Your father?"

"He won't be there."

"Oh?" Alan raised his glass and took a drink, watching her.

"All right," she said. "We don't know where he is, and we don't talk about it."

She slapped the table and stood. "So, 386 Concord Avenue, two o'clock tomorrow. It's in west Cambridge. Don't dress up, and bring your appetite."

"I'll be there." He stood. "Are you going to the bus?"

"I drove tonight. Parked right outside. See you tomorrow."

The threesome from the bar went out together. The closing door cut off the woman's mirthless laughter.

Sara pushed the door open and disappeared as it closed behind her.

A blanket of warmth enveloped Alan as he stood by the booth and gazed at the door. Sara was an angel, sent to deliver him from his loneliness and sorrow on Thanksgiving.

A lovely angel.

5

The next afternoon, Alan walked from the bus stop through a neighborhood of white clapboard houses and stopped in front of number 386 on Concord Avenue. A gray Chevrolet Impala sat in the driveway. He went through the gate in the unpainted picket fence, up the wooden steps, and rang the doorbell. A girl in a green dress opened the door and smiled at him.

"Hello," he said. "I'm Alan Cottrill, here to see Sara."

She ran away, her heels flying, leaving the door half open. "He's here!"

A redheaded little boy clamped the door between his hands and peered at Alan with dark, questioning eyes. "Are you the hillbilly?"

Alan squatted to the boy's eye level and said, "Can you keep a secret?"

His head bounced up and down.

"Well," said Alan, "I'm a Mountaineer."

The boy used his small hand to push Alan's head to one side and examined his ear. "What's a mountain ear?"

"Mountaineers are strong and brave."

Someone scooped the boy off his feet, and Alan stood. A young woman with auburn hair and Sara's blue eyes was holding the boy on her hip. She wore a pale yellow blouse and a green plaid skirt.

"You must be Alan," she said. "I'm Mary Clare Jackson, Sara's sister."

The boy took Mary Clare's face in his hands and twisted it toward him. "He has mountain ears. They're strong." He pulled her head in front of his. "It's a secret."

"I see," she said, and freed her face. "Come on in. Sara's upstairs. She'll be down in a minute."

"She's getting gorgeous!"

"Ryan here is our keeper of secrets." Mary Clare rubbed the boy's head. "Say hello to Mr. Cottrill, Ryan."

"Hello." Ryan squirmed in his mother's arms and she let him slide to the floor. He ran into the house.

A pudgy man in a Red Sox sweatshirt came up behind Mary Clare. "Alan, this is my husband, Cal," she said. "And this is our Erin." The girl who had answered the door was smiling at Alan around her father's substantial belly.

Cal said, "Hello, Alan. Mrs. O'Brien's finishing up in the kitchen and Sara's upstairs. What can I get you to drink?"

"A beer would be nice."

"I'll get you one."

Mary Clare and Alan walked into the carpeted living room. A couch against the back wall faced two high-backed chairs covered with flowered fabric and three tables with porcelain figurines on them. Paintings of New England scenes—churches, forests, cottages in the snow—were on the walls. A crucifix hung above the entryway.

Cal came back with a bottle of Michelob. "Would you like a glass?"

"This is fine."

Before Alan could take a drink, Sara's voice behind him said, "Is this the mountain man?"

He spun around, drawing breath to say, "Hello," and stopped.

A tall woman with flowing, copper-colored hair was looking down at him, her wide-apart green eyes sparkling with amusement. "Close your mouth."

"You—you sound just like Sara."

"She sounds like me. I was here first." The redhead put out her hand. "I'm Cass."

"Alan Cottrill."

"So I heard," she said, her eyes appraising him, "but I think I missed something."

"Pardon?"

Cass looked over his shoulder. "Well, here she is, our Irish princess." She put a large hand on Alan's chest. "Sara, you didn't tell us your mountain man was this handsome."

Alan turned around and saw Sara, her arms akimbo, giving Cass a look of mock disapproval.

"I see you've met the bouncer, Alan," said Sara. "Be nice, or she'll kick you down the stairs."

"Hello, Sara. Thanks for inviting me. I'll try to stay on Cass's good side."

Cass gave his upper arm a soft squeeze—almost a caress. "You better, mountain man." She strode away.

Sara was wearing a high-collared white blouse knotted at the waist and a tan, knee-length pleated skirt. Her hair was in a ponytail cinched by a green ribbon, from which a few strands had escaped. Alan stared at her, speechless again.

Her face softened to a slight smile. "Say something."

"Whoo. Ryan was right."

"What'd he say?"

"You were getting gorgeous."

"Thank you. Did you meet everyone?"

"I haven't met your mother."

Sara took his hand. "Come on." She led him through the dining room where the dishes of the meal sat in the center of a rectangular table surrounded by eight place settings of white dishes and napkins.

"Those are my scalloped potatoes," she said, "and Mary Clare made the rolls. The broccoli is Cass's. Mom and I fixed the ham." He closed his eyes and took in the odors of the baked ham and bread. They reminded him of Thanksgiving at home in West Virginia.

Mrs. O'Brien, short and stout with graying red hair, was closing the oven door. She pulled a green-checkered apron over her head and hung it on a hook in the open pantry, took a deep breath and slowly wiped her face.

She saw the two of them. "Sara?"

"Mom, this is my friend Alan Cottrill. He's in the Master of Accounting program at BC and helps me at the soup kitchen."

"Welcome, Alan. Sara's told us all about you. I'm glad you could come today."

"I'm happy to be here, thanks."

Well, Sara," said Mrs. O'Brien, "everything's ready and our guest is here."

Sara walked into the dining room. "Come on, everyone. Dinner."

The sound of moving feet came from the living room. In a minute or so, eight people surrounded the dining table. Cal held Mrs. O'Brien's chair for her as she sat at the head, then took the chair opposite her. Sara sat on her mother's left and directed Alan to sit beside her. Cass took the seat next to him. Mary Clare sat on her mother's right. The children clambered into chairs between her and Cal, Ryan next to Mary Clare and Erin next to her father.

When they had settled in and put napkins in their laps, Sara said, "Mom," and everyone bowed their heads.

Mrs. O'Brien began, "Bless, O Lord, this food we are about to eat; and we pray you, O God, that it may be good for our body and soul. If there be any poor creature hungry or thirsty walking along the road, send them in to us so that we can share the food with them, just as you share your gifts with us."

She took a deep breath. "And please, dear Father, watch over our poor Padraig in his loneliness, and if it be Your will, send him back to us."

Sara touched her mother's arm. "Mom . . ."

Mrs. O'Brien looked at Sara, tears in her eyes. "We'll see him again someday, God willing."

Cass pushed her chair away from the table with such force that water spilled from the glasses and the silverware rattled. "He left us, Mom. Left you and the three of us to starve, for all he cared. I never want to see him again. I want God to make him pay for what he did to us."

"No, Cassidy. We must pray for God to help him find his way home."

Cass lowered her head. "This isn't his home." She stormed from the room.

The children stared at their parents. Erin cried, "Daddy!" Cal took her in his arms and carried her out of the room, his face dark with anger. Mary Clare picked Ryan up, hugged him and went into the living room where Cal was talking quietly to Erin. The Jacksons sat with their arms around their children, rocking them gently.

Sara went to one knee beside her mother's chair. "It'll be all right, Mom. We'll see him again someday. We know he loves us. He just didn't want to hurt us anymore."

Alan walked through the living room and into the den, where Cass was sitting on a dark leather sofa, staring into the middle of the room.

She patted the pillow next to her. "Come in. Sit."

He did.

"Did Sara tell you about our father?"

"She said you didn't talk about him."

Cass peered obliquely at him. "Made a liar out of her, didn't we?"

"Oh, no."

Cass clenched her fists and raised her head. "The *bastard*. He ran out on us owing a ton of money. We'd have been in foster homes if the Diocese hadn't saved us. They helped support us for almost four years—kept us together. We can never repay them."

"When did he leave?"

"Twelve years ago. I was twelve and Mary Clare was sixteen. Sara was only nine. Mom got a call from the Charles Street Jail. He'd been arrested for drunkenness and brawling at some whorehouse in Scollay Square. She went there right away. When he saw her, he cursed her for smothering him and said he wanted no part of her anymore. 'I want my freedom,' he said. 'I want to be with men.'

"She could hardly make it up the steps when she came home, and we didn't know why. She got weepy one night years later and spilled it all out. She wanted to know what she'd done to make him leave." Cass stared at Alan, her eyes shining. "Do you wonder why I hate him? She's the dearest person in the world."

"What happened after that?"

"He was released the next day and he disappeared. We haven't heard from him since. Then the bill collectors started calling and the sharks he'd borrowed from came to the door. They scared the hell out of us. Mom couldn't talk to them, so Sara and I faced them down. That's why she calls me the bouncer. Even they wouldn't hit a little girl."

She crossed her arms. "The Diocese appointed someone to help us, and she did. Mrs. Harris. A fat, middle-aged lady who backed down to nobody. She made sure things were taken care of and that we had enough to pay the bills and the rent. She got Mary Clare a job waitressing till she finished high school, then one at the Water and Sewer Commission when she graduated. She met Cal there. Mom and I cleaned houses till I was sixteen and could get a job as a waitress. Then Sara helped her."

"What about the loan sharks?"

"I don't know what Mrs. Harris did, but they quit. She probably got the Diocese to call or buy them off. No one in Boston wants to get on the wrong side of us or the Catholics."

He wrinkled his forehead. "You're not Catholic? I thought all Irish were."

"Not us. The O'Briens have been Anglicans since Henry the Eighth."

"Huh." He put his hand on her arm. She looked at him, surprised. "Tough times," he said, patting her. "So hard. But the rest of you are here, and together. You can be thankful for that."

"There you are." Sara was standing at the entrance to the room, eyeing the two of them. "Come on back," she said. "It's Thanksgiving, and we do have things to be thankful for."

Cass pressed Alan's hand. "That's your line."

When everyone was seated again, Alan tried to heal the sullen silence. "Cal, how do you think the Red Sox will do next year without Williams?"

"Who knows?"

"Do you think they'll keep Pinky Higgins on?"

Cal shrugged and stuffed a forkful of potatoes into his mouth. Mary Clare glowered at him. Alan felt Sara's foot pressing on his. Her eyes told him to quit trying to get a conversation going.

Everyone ate with their heads down until they were finished. Erin and Ryan got down from their chairs and waited until Mary Clare told them they were excused. They left the room and tramped up the steps to the second floor.

Mary Clare leaned forward and glared at Cal. "Don't you think someone should check on them?"

"All right, I'll go." He pushed on the table and grunted as he lifted his weight out of the chair. He followed the children up the stairs.

Cass left the room, keeping her head low. The silence returned.

Mrs. O'Brien looked at Alan. "I'm so sorry," she said, dabbing her cheeks with an embroidered handkerchief.

"Please don't feel bad, Mrs. O'Brien. It was a delicious meal. I'm very grateful."

Sara got up, stood behind her mother and patted her shoulders. "You should lie down, Mom. You've worked hard all day."

"But someone has to clean up."

Alan jumped to his feet. "I'll do that, Mrs. O'Brien. I'm good at it. Ask Sara."

Sara put an arm around her mother and led her from the room, leaving Mary Clare and Alan standing at the table covered by half full plates, glasses and serving dishes. She stacked four plates, took them to the kitchen and started running water over them. "I'll help you."

"Oh, no, please. Don't you think you should help Cal with the children?"

"I suppose so." She touched him on the arm and walked out of the kitchen.

Alan took off his sweater, threw it over the back of a chair, rolled up his sleeves and started clearing the table. He carried the dinner plates and glasses to one side of the sink and the serving dishes with food in them to the other. He washed the plates, silverware and glasses and put them in the drainage rack, then filled the sink again and washed and dried the pots and pans, whistling softly as he worked. He dried his hands on a dishtowel when he finished half an hour later.

He heard the *rip* of Saran Wrap tearing. Sara was beside him, trying to cover the leftovers but sobbing so hard her hands were shaking. She stopped, gripped the counter and leaned over it.

"Sara."

She came to him. He wrapped his arms around her. "Oh, Sara."

She put her arms inside his. "I'm sorry. I'm so sorry."

"It's all right."

She pressed her hands against his chest. "You're the saint today."

"I wish there was something I could do."

Sara shook her head. "Don't try to help us. We're Irish. We never know what we want, but we're always ready to fight over it."

He compressed his eyebrows. "What does that mean?"

"You'd have to be Irish." She went back to the counter and the Saran Wrap.

"Okay." His arms wanted her again, but he put them in his sweater and pulled it over his head. When it popped out, the sadness was gone from her face. She had regained her self-control.

"Would this be a good time for me to go?" he asked.

"I think it would. Thanks for all you've done today."

"Thank your mother for me and say goodbye to everyone. Maybe I'll see them again."

"Maybe you will."

He walked out the door, down the whitewashed steps and through the gate to Concord Avenue. A blast of air blowing in from the Bay pierced his light jacket and crawled inside his sweater. He shivered, stopped and zipped the jacket up to his neck, put his hands in his pockets and leaned into the wind, walking slowly toward the bus stop at Fayerweather, shaking his head to clear it after the turmoil he had witnessed.

The O'Briens were a family in torment, each of them burning from the abandonment by Padraig O'Brien a dozen years ago. Sara had tried to hold them together, but once their wounds were opened they could not be re-covered, and the Thanksgiving celebration blew apart. Sara held herself together until the meal was over, then she grieved for either her father or her family—he couldn't tell which.

Alan stopped in the middle of the street and watched the dry leaves scratching past him in the wind. He closed his eyes to remember how good it felt to have Sara pressed against him.

He tried to think about what it would have done to his family if his father had deserted them—but he couldn't imagine it. It took death to separate them.

He saw the bus approaching Fayerweather up ahead and sprinted to catch it.

6

Alan was studying in his room the next Tuesday when Mrs. Evans knocked on the door.

"Telephone call for you, Alan. Someone named Cassidy."

He went to the telephone at the end of the upstairs hall. "Hello."

"What's doin', Alan? It's Cass. I hope we didn't ruin your Thanksgiving."

"Oh, no. It was nice meeting everyone." He thought for a second. "How'd you get my number?"

"From the church. Sara said they probably had it. I told them I was your Aunt Pearl from West Virginia."

"That's clever."

"I called to see if you could come to our after-work party this week. The gang from Wardell Longman gets together every Friday to drink, gossip and flirt. We have a good time, and invited outsiders are welcome. Can you join us?"

"Yeah, I'd like to."

"We go to the Top Hat on Bowdoin Street downtown. It's between Cambridge and Derne. There's a bus stop at Cambridge and Bowdoin, and it's a block from the T."

"I know where that is. What time?"

"I'll be there by six. We usually eat there, too. It's pretty good food, but after a couple of drinks, who cares?" She laughed.

"Thanks. I'll be there by seven and I'll look for you."

"Terrific! See you then. Bye."

———❦———

A BLAST OF NOISE and smoke struck Alan in the face when he opened the door to the Top Hat at seven on Friday. He stopped inside the door, took out his handkerchief and wiped the moisture from his stinging eyes. He was standing amid round cocktail tables and high stools filled with men in dark suits, vests and loosened ties.

One of them said, "You all right, pally?"

"I think so." Alan put the handkerchief in his hip pocket and looked down the long aisle that ran along the bar, filled with people—jostling, drinking and laughing. "Where would I find Cassidy O'Brien?"

The man shook his head and asked his companion at the table. "You know her?"

"Oh, yes. Redheaded Irish gal. Tall." The man held his cupped hands, palms up, below his chest. "Stacked." He saw Cass coming toward them, waving her hand in the air. "There she is—see?"

Cass took Alan's hand. "Glad you could make it. Come meet my friends." She led him along the crowded bar where bartenders were scurrying between customers, registers and the shelves of bottles hung from the glass walls behind them. They went single file, Cass leading, stepping aside as waitresses went by and squeezing through clusters of drinkers that filled the aisle in places, to the other end of the room, where four well-dressed women sat at a rectangular table.

She put her arm around Alan. "Gals, this is my friend Alan Cottrill. He's from West Virginia and goes to BC." She pointed around the table. "Ellie, Mary, Jane and Leslie."

"Hello, Alan."

"Hi, gals. How are you all?" They laughed.

Cass let go of him. "Keep an eye on this gent while I get him a beer."

"Wait," he said, "I can buy my own."

"From now on," said Cass. She slid into the crowd at the bar.

Ellie, a stout brunette, asked, "How long you been in town, Alan?"

"About four months. I'm still learning my way around."

Leslie, a long-faced blonde with crooked teeth, asked, "How do you like it so far?"

"I like it a lot. I'm even starting to understand the accent."

"Accent?" they cried, laughing. "What accent? We don't have an accent. You do!"

"Of course!" His fist punched the air. "How could anyone think you all had an accent?" More laughter.

"How'd you meet Cass?" asked Ellie.

"Through her sister Sara."

"Oh, yes," she said. "The nurse."

"Do all of you work at Wardell?" he asked.

"We do," said Leslie and Mary.

"I'm with the State Attorney's office," said Ellie.

Cass put a glass of beer on the table. "Here you are, Mountain Man." The other women went back to talking among themselves, and Cass pulled up a stool. She was wearing a knee-length green skirt and a revealing silk crossover blouse. If her eyes had not been so commanding, he would have had a hard time looking at them instead of her cleavage.

"Thanks for inviting me," he said.

"I just wanted to show my sister's friend a good time. Besides, you ran away last week without saying goodbye." She smiled and took a drink of her old-fashioned. "You rascal."

"It seemed like a good time to go."

She put her glass on the table. "It was."

Alan waved toward the front door. "Tell me something. The men are at that end of the bar and the women are down here. Why's that?"

"It's the legal caste system. The partners and associates sit down there, drink scotch and martinis and talk about Supreme Court decisions. The little people sit down here, drink wine and whisky sours, and talk about them."

"Who talks about the Red Sox?"

"The peasants at Buzzy's sports bar down the street." She tapped the table beside his glass. "They drink beer there, too."

"So I should go down there?"

"No." She grabbed his arm. "I'm kidding you. You should stay right here." She lowered her face. "By the way, what did Sara tell you about me?"

"Not much."

"Did she tell you to watch out for me?"

"What?"

"Did she?"

"Why would she do that?"

She pulled him to her and whispered in his ear, "Liar." She kissed him on the cheek. "Watch out for me, Mountain Man."

Looking to get away from Cass for a minute, he saw that their glasses were nearly empty, said, "My turn," and started toward the bar.

Cass called, "An old-fashioned with Old Forester."

When he came back with their drinks, Cass said, "I put us in for a booth. It'll be about five minutes. All right?"

"Sure. I'm ready."

They were shown to a booth in a few minutes and took seats across from each other. Cass eyed him over her menu. "So," she said, "tell me about yourself. All I know is you're studying accounting at BC and you're from West Virginia. What else?"

"Not much, really." He folded his menu and dropped it on the table. "I grew up and went to school there, but my parents are gone, and I only go back once a year."

"You lost a sister? Sara told me."

"Two years ago."

She waited, but he did not say more.

The waitress came to the table with glasses of water and two sets of silverware wrapped in napkins. They ordered hamburger platters.

Cass watched her walk away. "I see. That's why you think we should be thankful."

"I'd give anything—"

"I bet you would," she said, her eyes studying him. "We O'Briens may fight, but we're never lonely."

When they had finished eating, Cass picked up her check and said, "A few of us gals and guys are getting together at Mary's after this. A nice, quiet time. Would you like to come?"

"I'd better not. Maybe some other time."

She read him—cautious, reluctant—and said, "Want to come again next week?" She took a business card from her purse and handed it to him. "Call me if you do." She leaned toward him and lowered her head. "I'd like to see you again, Alan, but I don't want to crowd you."

———⟡⟡⟡———

THE NEXT DAY, ALAN tried to study the assigned cases in International Tax Strategies, but he kept thinking about Cass.

Heck with being careful. I want to see more of her.

———⟡⟡⟡———

ALAN DID NOT GO to the soup kitchen the next Wednesday. He called the church and left a message for Sara saying he was sorry, but he had to study for an exam. Then he called Cass and said he would see her Friday night.

He was sitting at the bar Friday evening with his hand around a cold Bud when Cass wrapped her arms around his shoulders from behind.

"Buy me a drink, mister?" She pressed her body between the bar chairs and stood close to him. "I really need one."

The woman in the chair next to her got up and told Cass she was leaving. Cass put her foot on the bar rail, lifted herself into the seat and handed a half-full ashtray to the bartender.

"Get rid of this and bring me an old-fashioned with Old Forester." She put her arm on the bar and turned to Alan. "And he'd better be quick about it."

He leaned on his elbows. "Bad day?"

"Bad week—a week in hell." She puffed. "I need to blow off some steam. May I cry on your shoulder tonight?"

"Sure."

In a few minutes, the bartender put the old-fashioned in front of her. She threw it down and put her hand on Alan's arm. "I can't do it in this place. The noise drives me nuts. How about I buy you dinner? There's a nice little Italian restaurant a couple of blocks from here. It's good, and it's cheap. A little red wine and some pasta will do us both good." She patted his arm. "It won't destroy your independence to have a pretty girl buy you dinner, will it?" She lowered her voice. "I can afford it, I make a good buck. You can pay me back some day. Buy me dinner at Locke-Ober's when you're a financial hotshot and rolling in money."

"I can't say no to that."

They put on their coats and walked through the crowd and out to the sidewalk. They walked south on Bowdoin, the cold wind in their faces, then right on Derne, where the buildings shielded them, and right again on Temple, a brick-paved pedestrian street with plane trees in its center. She put her arm around his waist and pulled him close. "I appreciate this, Alan. I need someone to listen to me tonight, and you're easy to talk to."

Mancini's restaurant was halfway down the first block. They went through two heavy glass doors and down a curved stairway to a subterranean room with exposed brick walls covered with garish paintings of distorted bodies and angry faces.

The hostess, a short woman dressed in black, said, "Table for two? Right this way, please," and led them to a corner table.

Alan looked around at the paintings. "What's all this?"

"Why, it's modern art, can't you tell?" she said, grinning. "From local creative types."

"Ghastly." He picked up the menu. "So, tell me about your week in hell."

"My guys at Wardell do industry stuff. Companies squabbling over rights and patents. And they almost always settle. There are no Perry Masons at Wardell."

She took the silverware out of her napkin and put it on the table. "But one of them blew up on Tuesday. The partners thought they had an agreement until some big shot at the client decided he wanted more—money, I think—and it fell apart. Our partners went running from one meeting to another all week and there was a lot of shouting going on behind closed doors. Everyone's running around pointing fingers. They're scared shitless we'll lose the client. They want this done right now and that done right now, and 'why can't you find my file on that?' It's probably in the pile on his desk the size of Mount Everest. My guy was so nervous I think he wet his pants in the men's room. Couldn't find his pecker."

"What happened?"

"Nothing yet. We might know next week." She rubbed her forehead with her fingers. "At times like this, I'm glad I'm a grunt. I do what they tell me and keep my head down. Survival." She blew out a breath. "Whew."

The waiter had been standing just out of earshot. Cass raised her hand. "An old-fashioned with Old Forester, and a Nastro Azzurro for the gentleman." She put her hand back on the table. "You are a gentleman, Mountain Man."

"Alan."

Green eyes swept his face. "All right—Alan. How was your week? Study, study, study?"

"I'm studied out. Had an exam this morning on international tax strategies."

"Oog! How'd you do?"

"I don't know. At least it's over."

The waiter brought their drinks and they ordered—ravioli for Cass, lasagna for Alan.

"And two glasses of your house Chianti," said Cass.

"Are you trying to get me drunk?"

"I always try to get my dates drunk. Then I can have my way with them. Sara tells me you're unattached, so . . ." She paused. "Am I crowding you?"

"A little."

"Sorry, I don't want to do that." She leaned her forehead on the tips of her fingers. "I'm on edge tonight. There's a lot going on . . ."

"More than the mess at Wardell?"

"Oh, that's just one of my many messes." She raised her head. "So, tell me some more about Alan Cottrill. You're one handsome man, well educated, on your way to big things. And no girlfriend?"

"No girlfriend. I did love a girl in high school, my junior and senior year. But she moved away, and we didn't reconnect till it was too late."

"Do you still love her?"

"Maybe."

Cass clamped her hands together. "What do you mean, 'maybe'? Do you or don't you?"

"I don't know. I did. There were problems. It's over."

"Problems?"

"She's Catholic. I'm a Methodist."

"Damned religion. Where is she now?"

"Iowa."

"No wonder it's over. You wouldn't want to marry a milkmaid, would you?"

He put his head in his hands.

She reached across the table, took his hand and pulled it to her lips. "I'm sorry. I've hurt you, and I didn't mean to."

He touched her cheek with his fingertips. "You didn't hurt me. I think you just woke me up." He waved to their waiter. "Let's have some more wine." Cass pressed his hand into her cheek.

When the wine came, Alan raised his glass to her. "Look at us. Two people dancing around what to say to each other. What are we afraid of?" He tilted his glass toward her. "Here's my story. I loved the girl I told you about. In high school, six, seven years ago. Her family was Catholic, and her father wanted her to marry some nice Catholic boy. When she wouldn't, he sent her to Iowa to live with her aunt, and we lost touch. I saw her last August at the fifth reunion of our high school class. We talked a little while and agreed it's over. So it's over."

He drank some wine. "I'm here studying accounting because I like to figure things out using numbers. It's valuable work, the jobs pay well and I'm good at it. When I graduate, I'd like to work for an accounting firm doing consulting for a few years, and then start my own business. I like being independent."

"After that?"

"Somewhere in there, find the right girl, get married and raise a couple of kids."

"Where would you like to live?"

"Where I get the best job offer, and I know it won't be West Virginia."

"Hmm. Where do you live here?"

"I rent a room on Cushing Street in Waltham. Behind Saint Charles school."

"A room? That's all?"

"It's enough. I don't cook, anyway."

"What do you do for fun?"

He watched the hostess lead three men through the room to a table. "Not much, I guess."

"Could you live in Boston?"

"Sure, if I get the right offer."

"I just might make you one." Mischief in her eyes.

He ignored that. "Okay, now it's your turn. Tell me about Miss Cassidy O'Brien."

"I've wanted to be a paralegal since high school. I like to read words and dates to figure things out, and I'm good at what I do, too."

"Where'd you learn how to do it?"

"Fisher College, here in town. I got an Associate's Degree in Criminal Justice. It's very good, but it's expensive. Cal, Mary Clare's husband, loaned me what I needed to get through." She looked away. "I'm still paying him back." She folded her arms, gripped her elbows and twisted her shoulders, then leaned on the table and gazed at him.

"Is that a problem?"

She nodded.

He shook his head. "But you make good money."

Green eyes bored into his. "That's not what he's collecting."

His mouth opened.

"Yes," she said.

"God in heaven." He closed his eyes. "Who knows?"

"Mary Clare's told me she suspects something. She won't say who." Cass ran her fingers through her hair. "They don't get along that well."

"Sara?"

"She's never said anything."

"How long?"

"He caught me in my bedroom alone during my second year at Fisher. He started by complaining about Mary Clare, how she'd trapped him, how cold she was, how she didn't appreciate all he had done for her— bought the house, kept her family together, kept her out of poverty. The usual crap a married man gives you. I hadn't heard it before."

"Mary Clare trapped him?"

"She was expecting when they were married." Cass drank a mouthful of wine. "Then he told me I should be grateful for what he was doing for me, making me an independent woman, as well as a desirable one, and he hoped I wanted to show him some appreciation." She patted her cheeks. "He grabbed me and pushed me down on my bed. The next thing I knew, he had pulled my pants down and was on top of me, sweating and breathing hard. I didn't dare scream—Mom and Ryan were in the house—and he was too heavy for me to push off. I couldn't do anything but lie there till he finished."

She looked down at the table. "I've tried to stay away from him ever since, but he forced me two more times while I lived in the house. Came into my bedroom at night. Said if I'd didn't go along, he'd tell Mary Clare and Mom I seduced him."

"Would they believe him?"

"I don't know what would happen, but I was afraid it would tear us apart, so I gave in and didn't say anything." She covered her face. "I've stayed away from him since I moved into my apartment a year ago. I won't go near him unless someone's around, like Thanksgiving. But he cornered me in the kitchen that day and said he wanted to see me again, soon. I called his bluff—told him to go ahead and tell everybody right then, and I'd take my chances. I haven't heard from him since, but I'm afraid he'll do something that'll hurt us all. He's an evil man."

"Could you talk to your lawyer guys about it?"

"Huh-unh. The male consensus at the firm is that it's the woman's fault—for making herself available or for tempting the man. It would hurt me there if management thought I was a temptress."

He slapped his fist. "And they tell stories about what goes on in the hills of West Virginia."

"Hypocrites, all of them." Her eyes grew wide. She reached across the table and gripped his arm. "I shouldn't have told you, Alan. I don't know what got into me. There's nothing you can do. Promise me you won't say anything to anyone about this." She lowered her face to the table and shook his arm. "Promise me."

"I promise."

She sighed, took out her wallet and put some bills on top of the check. "Let's book outta here."

They walked to Derne Street, where Cass hailed a taxicab. As it stopped, she put her arms around his neck and stared down at him with those commanding eyes. "Now that you know all about me, will I see you again?"

"You sure will."

"Good. Here." She pulled his head up to hers, put her open mouth over his lips and caressed them with her tongue, inviting his in. Her mouth was warm and sweet. He lingered.

The cabbie rapped on the window. She pulled her mouth away slowly. "Are you sure I'm not too tall for you?"

"I'm sure."

She opened the door of the cab. "Good night, Mountain—" she caught herself. "Alan."

7

Alan was almost finished wiping the rear counters in the church basement on the Wednesday before Christmas when the lights went out.

"Hey!" *Click.* They came back on.

Sara stuck her head through the entryway. "Sorry. I didn't know you were still here."

"I'm almost done."

She laughed. "Do you always stay with something till you're finished?"

"Pretty much. It's a curse."

She came toward him—erect, arms crossed over her chest, laying her feet down slowly—and stood beside him. She had a distant look in her eyes. They were aimed at him, but unfocused.

He stopped wiping. She blinked.

He said, "Yes?"

"If you have a few minutes, maybe we could talk."

"Sure. About what?"

She walked to the other side of the serving counter where she stopped, put her hands on the tray rail and leaned toward him. "Us. You and me."

His throat tightened. "Okay." He leaned back on the rear counter.

"I want to thank you for all you've done for me since you came. You've done the dirtiest job here every time without complaining." She drew a small "s" on the display window. "You've always been cheerful— fun to have around. Everyone appreciates that."

He nodded.

"You've been wicked good company for me, too. On our walks. And you were so good to me on Thanksgiving. Some men would have run away from a scene like that." She stepped over to the outside door and stood staring out its top-half window. The beam of light pouring through the glass from the street lamp across the street surrounded her body and sent a long shadow across the floor.

"It's too bad Richard wasn't there," she said. "You two would get along. Richard's from a family of doctors in a small town in Illinois. Galesburg. He'll go back there and practice medicine with his father and his brother who's in med school at Vanderbilt. I'll get to see what a small town is like."

"You haven't been there?"

"Not yet. Richard says the time isn't right. His mother has some health problems." She took off her cap. "It'll be so nice to be part of a doctor's family in a small town."

"I'm sure you'll like it. When's the wedding?"

"Richard doesn't want to set the date just yet. He will, though. Soon." She turned to him. "I have my ways."

Alan lowered his eyes so she could not see the alarm in them. *Sara! Don't do something foolish.* He wanted to warn her, but the words would not come out.

"We're good friends, Alan, and I hope we can be friends till I'm married and move to Galesburg. I can't wait to belong to a loving family with strong Midwestern values. You know what that's like."

"Yeah."

She walked out of the light, around the counter, and put a hand on his arm. "I admire you, Alan, but I'm committed." Her pale blue eyes held his. "You understand, don't you?"

They stood facing each other, their eyes open wide, until something gave way inside him. He moistened his lips and took a half step toward her. When she did not retreat, he raised her chin with his fingers, turned his head and pressed his lips onto hers. She tightened her grip, made a soft noise in her throat and turned her head the other way, twisting her lips on his. He pulled his head back, she dropped her hand and they stood, not quite touching, in the quiet kitchen—still, eyes locked, afraid to move or speak.

Beams from the headlights of a car driving into the church parking lot punched through three small upper windows of the basement in succession, sweeping the room. The car's engine roared, subsided, roared again. A horn blasted.

"There he is." She ran to the door, shaking her head and fluffing her hair with her fingers. "Good night. Turn out the lights and lock up when you leave."

Then she was gone.

Alan went to the electrical panel, threw the light switch and stopped in the entryway for several seconds, staring at the rectangle of light on the floor where Sara had stood.

What a jerk. Sits in his car and blows the horn. She's too good for that.

Alan lowered his head and walked out of the dark, silent basement.

Standing in the cold winter night, he checked the door to make sure it was locked, shivered, and started the long trudge to his empty room.

8

Mrs. Evans handed Alan a note when he came in from class a few weeks after Christmas.

"A Calvin Jackson called," she said. "He'd like you to call him during business hours at this number. He said it was important. Who is he?"

"I don't know him very well."

Alan called the number the next afternoon. Cal answered. "Mechanical Engineering, Jackson."

"Alan Cottrill, Cal, returning your call."

"What's doin', Alan? Are you in school?"

"I just finished for the day." He waited.

Cal cleared his throat. "Alan, I was thinking maybe you and I could have a little talk sometime."

"What about?"

"I thought I might help you understand some of the things you've seen at the house."

Alan thought for a few seconds. "Okay. When would you like to do it?"

"I can't do it tonight," said Cal. "Tomorrow? We could meet someplace down where you are. Warwick, isn't it?" Alan heard him breathing into the phone. "What's a good place? About seven? A place you could walk to."

"How about Pokey's Tavern? It's on Moody Street, near Cherry. Do you know where it is?"

"I'll find it." Cal's breathing came through the phone again. "See you down there at seven tomorrow. And, uh . . ."

"Yes?"

"Let's not tell anyone about this right now."

Alan wondered why Cal was doing this, and what it was he wanted Alan to know. Something about the family? He couldn't imagine Cal talking about him and Cass. The father? Maybe, but Cal had never met him. He'd have to wait and see, and do a lot of listening tomorrow.

ALAN PULLED THE DOOR open and stepped into Pokey's Tavern a few minutes before seven the next day. Cal was facing him from a booth across from the bar, his nearly bald head shining from the light above it. He showed his palm to Alan. The bartender drew a Budweiser and pushed it out on the bar between two patrons for Alan to take as he walked by.

Cal took a drink from a lowball glass as Alan sat down across from him.

"Did you have class today?" asked Cal.

"Yeah. Till six. A long day."

"What're you taking?"

"International Tax Strategies and Strategic Consulting. Tough ones this semester."

"How ya doin'? All right?"

"So far." Alan looked past Cal at the TV screen at the end of the room, where the dark-haired newscaster David Brinkley was scowling at America. "Cass told me you work for the Sanitary District. What do you do there?"

"I'm a mechanical engineer for the Water and Sewer Commission. I write specs for the pumps, valves and air compressors that move water and air in the wastewater plants in Boston Harbor. Then I evaluate the bids to see if they meet the specs so purchasing can buy them."

"Sounds like important work."

"If my equipment doesn't work, the sewage goes in the harbor."

"Ouch!"

"Yeah."

The waiter delivered a plate of potato skins filled with cheese and onions. "Here you are, gents."

Cal took half of one, dipped it in sour cream, pushed it into his mouth and spoke through it. "I thought you'd like something." He swallowed. "What else did Cass tell you?" His eyelids were at half-mast.

"Not much."

"She didn't tell you anything about the family?"

"A little."

"And the old man leaving? What did she say about that?"

"Let me think." Alan raised his glass and drank a mouthful. "He left ten or twelve years ago and they had a pretty hard time. The Diocese helped them out. Mary Clare got a job at the Water and Sewer Commission and met you there."

"Is that it?"

"I think so," said Alan, reaching for a skin and avoiding Cal's stare.

Cal tilted his face down and looked up at Alan from under his brows. "Nothing about what she's doing these days?"

Alan shook his head.

"Have you seen her since Thanksgiving?"

Alan wanted to tell Cal it was none of his business, but he didn't. "I saw her one Friday after work at a bar on Bowdoin. Why?"

"I just wondered. I thought you were really taken by her that day."

"What made you think that?"

"Just the way you looked."

"I see," said Alan. "And Cass?"

"She looks that way at every man."

"Really!"

"You may not like to hear this, pal, but she's not very discriminating." Cal put another half a skin in his mouth and eyed Alan.

Alan looked up to the TV screen again. The Bruins were skating around on the ice at Boston Gardens. He pursed his lips, determined to keep his feelings away from his face.

"How do you know that?" he asked.

Cal washed down his mouthful. "You promise not to say anything? I wouldn't want what I know to get around."

"Sure."

Cal stroked his mustache with his thumb and index finger. "Well, I paid most of her tuition at Fisher College here in town so she could get a good job, and get out of the house. After I did that, she got really 'friendly,' you know what I mean? Little winks and touches when no one was watching. I tried to stay away from her, I'm not that kind of a man. Mary Clare's not the warmest woman in the world, but we *are* married." He crushed a napkin. "Anyway, one afternoon she cornered me in her bedroom. She put her arms around my neck, pushed herself against me and said she wanted to show her appreciation for all I'd done for her. I tell you, she's a strong woman. Next thing I know, she's on top of me on the bed with her hand in my pants."

Cal put his face in his hands and spoke through them. "Well, I hadn't done anything for a while, and I gave in. I let her. I shouldn't have, but I did. She did it without taking anything off. That woman's got the guts of a burglar—Mrs. O. and Ryan were downstairs. I couldn't wait for her to get off of me. Then she told me we'd have to do it again sometime." He put his hands down. "I tell you, there's something wrong with that woman. She can't get enough."

Alan put his chin on his fist. "And since then?"

"I've avoided her like the plague. I'm scared to death any time she comes in the house. On Thanksgiving she cornered me in the kitchen and told me I had to call her." He hit the table with his fist. "I won't do it. I don't dare be alone with her again. It would tear the family apart if anyone knew."

"That's quite a story."

"It's awful. I'd pay for her to move out of Boston, but she won't do it. I think she stays around to torment me. She's threatened to tell Mary Clare if I don't do what she wants, but I won't do it. It's blackmail."

Cal's brown eyes studied Alan's face. Alan hoped his disbelief was not in it.

Cal went on. "Cass is all screwed up. I think her father took advantage of her when she was a little girl, and then he left her. She needs a shrink." He waved to the waiter. "An order of curly fries and another round, pal."

Alan struggled to think of something to say that would keep Cal talking. Finally, he said, "You've helped them a lot."

"I have, and this is my thanks. If a man can be raped, I was, and now blackmail. I wasn't all that hot to get married and move in, either, but here I am with a mortgage, a wife, two kids, their aunties and gramma, all of them moaning and groaning about some Irish drunk who left a dozen years ago. It's fried."

He eyed Alan over the rim of his glass as he took a drink. "Sometimes I don't blame him."

"What about Sara?"

"She's a nice girl. A real help to Mrs. O., but she may not be around much longer."

"Oh?"

"She's got this boyfriend. A rich kid from some little town in Illinois. He's going to be a doctor, and she wants to marry him and go there. I hope she likes it."

"Have you met him?"

"He's come to the house a couple of times in his souped-up 'Vette." Cal stroked his mustache again. "He's going to go back home to mom and pop when he's through here. I wouldn't be surprised if he has a girl back there, too, or a hometown sweetheart in college somewhere. He doesn't strike me as a one-girl guy." He shrugged. "But what do I know?"

The waiter put two drinks and a wicker basket of steaming fried potatoes covered with yellow cheese on the table. Cal put half a handful in his mouth and spoke through it. "Hot."

"You're not going home for dinner?"

"I told 'em I'd be working late tonight and I'd grab a bite downtown." Cal wiped his hands with a brown paper napkin. "Have some."

The whole room moaned. People at the bar turned away from the television screen and shook their heads. The red-clad Montreal Canadiens were skating around the goal and hugging their center, who had just scored.

Cal turned around as far as he could. "What happened?"

"The Canadiens scored."

Cal turned back around and reached for more potatoes. "They're no good this year." He looked up and down the aisle and mumbled, "Where's the john?"

"That way, past the end of the bar."

Cal pushed himself to his feet and waddled away toward the men's room.

Alan twisted around and watched, his brow wrinkled. *Why's he doing this?*

A few minutes later, Cal returned to the booth, drying his hands on his trousers.

"I've been thinking," said Alan, "and I have a question for you."

Cal studied him. "Yes?"

"I appreciate your telling me all this, but I'm not sure why you're doing it."

"I almost didn't. But I saw what they did to you on Thanksgiving and it worried me. You're a real gentleman, Al, but if you don't mind my saying, you're just a little naïve. I've seen these O'Briens draw in people who think they can help the family, then suck 'em dry and spit 'em out. And when I saw Cass put the moves on you, I thought you ought to know about her before she gets the hooks in. It hurts when she pulls 'em out."

"I see."

Cal picked up the check, stuffed one copy in his shirt pocket and dropped the other and two twenty-dollar bills on the table. He waved off Alan's ten. "No need. I'll get reimbursed."

Cal stood. "Time for me to book it. Be careful, pal."

He waved to the bartender as he wove his way down the aisle and out the door.

Alan put his glasses on the table and pulled his fingers down his face. His feelings toward Cal were ambivalent. The man had been trapped by Mary Clare into a life he did not want to live, but what he had done to Cass was unforgivable.

9

Alan called Cass the next week and asked if she could go with him to see *The Apartment* on Saturday.

"I hear it's a killer," she said, "but I can't go Saturday. How about Friday?"

Alan agreed, although he had a paper due and an exam that day.

BITS OF SNOW CURLED around Cass and Alan as they hurried through the streets of the North End toward her apartment after the movie. Arm in arm, they hunched their shoulders and leaned into the blasts of wind that roared down the narrow streets and slammed into them.

During a lull, he said, "I absolutely adore Shirley MacLaine."

"Shut up and deal." They laughed.

The wind steadied, and the air filled with snow that stuck in their hair and on their coats. They brushed it off in the lobby of her apartment building.

"I'd better go before this gets worse," he said. "I didn't get much sleep last night."

"Come up for a minute and get warm. I'll make some tea for you."

In her apartment, Alan opened his coat and sat down heavily on the couch. Cass went into the kitchen. She filled a teakettle, put it over a gas flame and looked back at him. His head was dropping and rising. She took two cups from the cupboard, put teabags in them and looked again. His chin was on his chest, his eyes shut.

She switched off the gas, went behind him and pulled on his coat sleeves to free his arms.

"I have to catch the bus," he muttered.

"Calm your liver." She took him by the shoulders and laid his head on the pillow at one end of the couch, picked up his feet and put them on the other. She took off his shoes and rubbed his feet.

"I gotta go."

"Don't be a chowderhead. It's a blizzard out there."

She covered him with a blanket from her bedroom closet and tucked it under his shoulders and hips. "There you go."

"Thank you." A whisper.

She kissed his forehead, said, "Sleep tight," turned out the lights and went to bed.

—✺—

Two a.m. A string of light coming in under the window blind stretched across the floor of the living room, softening the darkness.

"Alan." Connie's sweet voice, clear and close by.

Alan sat up.

"Connie!" His head shook, then jerked to the right. "Where are you?"
Silence.

A faint shadow came over his face. "It's me, Alan." Cass laid a hand on his shoulder. "Are you all right?"

They came again. Blinding beams of light sweeping across Connie's face and the windshield. Her eyes filled with horror. Her scream. The crashes. The blackness.

His body stiffened. "No!"

Cass sat beside him, wrapping her arms around him and pressing his head to her shoulder. "It's all right, Alan, it's all right. You've had a bad dream." She ran her hand through his hair. "Want to tell me?"

"The headlights were bearing down on us. We hit the guardrail and bounced back into the truck. It tipped over on us." He moaned. "Connie didn't make it to the hospital. Mom told me the next day."

"Your sister." Cass tightened her grip. "I'm so sorry."

He buried his face in her bathrobe.

"Let go, Alan, let go." She held him and rocked him while he trembled and cried. "It's all right. It was a terrible thing, but you did all you could."

When his crying receded, she laid him back on the couch and brushed the hair from his forehead. "Think you can sleep now?"

She saw the pain in his blank eyes. "Want me to stay with you?"

Cass lay alongside him with her arm over his chest until his muscles relaxed and he was breathing deeply. Then she slid off the couch and tiptoed back to her bedroom, leaving its door open.

<hr />

ALAN WOKE AT EIGHT and looked around the living room. It took him a few seconds to remember where he was and how he got there. Cass, barefoot and wearing a deep red bathrobe, was in the kitchen, cutting up bananas and peaches and dropping the pieces into a glass bowl.

The coffee pot was bubbling. He closed his eyes and inhaled the sweet smell of the fresh brew.

He stood in the entryway to the kitchen in his socks, sweater and wrinkled slacks. "Morning." He rubbed his cheeks. "Sorry I crapped out on you last night."

"Don't be sorry." She filled a cup and held it out to him, watching his face. "How did you sleep—on that couch?"

"Like a log. I was shot." He took the cup. "Did I bother you?"

"Oh, no." She went back to the counter. "I'm glad you stayed."

"I have to call my landlady. She'll be worried."

She went past him sideways in the entryway, the bathrobe loose around her breasts. Her hair was unkempt and she wore no makeup. He thought she looked more natural this morning, and was prettier for it. The hard edge he had seen in her before was gone.

"There's a phone on the end table."

He called the house and told Mrs. Evans's teenage daughter that he had decided late last night to stay with a friend because of the weather, and he would be home later that day.

He hung up. "I hope she remembers to tell her mother."

Cass leaned on the frame of the entryway. "There's a washcloth and towel and a toothbrush for you in the bathroom, and a bathrobe on the door. Leave your underclothes and socks on the counter and I'll wash 'em."

In the bathroom, he undressed, stepped into the pebbled glass stall that held the shower and stood under its soft stream. The tension in his body flowed down his legs and away with the warm water.

The bathroom door opened. He turned his back.

The shower door swung out. Cass, carrying a washcloth and a bar of soap, stepped in and closed it. She was an authentic redhead.

Before he could say anything, her arms were around his neck. She held the washcloth above their heads and twisted it, wringing out warm water that found its way between them.

"Turn around," she said, "and I'll wash your back."

She scrubbed his back, neck to thighs, then put her forearm around his neck and started on his chest, washing down. She whispered in his ear, "Ooh, I see they grow 'em big down the mountains."

She knelt and washed his legs, then handed him the washcloth. "Your turn."

He took it eagerly and turned her around. "They grow 'em big up here, too."

They came out of the shower and toweled each other off. He pressed her against the counter and kissed her.

She pressed back. "It'll be better in the bed."

It was.

Later, they sat in the kitchen, sipping coffee and nibbling on the fruit. The dryer in the hall closet rumbled as it tossed his underclothes around.

"Well?" she said. "What d'you think? Am I?"

"Are you what?"

"Too tall for you."

He shook his head slowly. "And me?"

"Oh, no. Your height fits me nicely."

"So," he said, "what's next?"

The telephone on the counter rang. Cass snatched the receiver from its cradle, picked up the base and turned away. "Hello. . . . Yes. I'll call you back. . . . Before long. . . . Yes. . . . Bye."

She hung up the phone and put it back on the counter. "Well, we like each other a lot, and we want to keep seeing each other. So we keep going."

"And see where it takes us?"

"And go where it takes us. But I don't own you, and you don't own me. All right?"

"Fair enough."

She put her hands under his arms, lifted him up and pulled his body to her. "But man, do I like having you here." She kissed him for a long time, then pushed him back. "Time for you to go. Your landlady will start worrying before long." Her eyes held him again. "Call me."

"I will."

He dressed and left.

Snick. Half an hour later, the deadbolt on the outside door turned. The door opened and Ellie peered into the living room. She put her overnight bag on the couch and tiptoed into the kitchen, where two fruit plates and coffee mugs sat in the sink. She went down the short hall, tapped on the door to Cass's bedroom with her index finger and pushed it open. Cass was pulling a tan sweater over her arms.

"'Morning, Red."

"Hiya, Punch. Everything go all right?"

"Yeah. The Top Hat was full. Horace was half in the bag and tried to put the make on Mary. He was soft for trying it there." She watched Cass pull the sweater over her head and fluff out her hair. "You?"

"He zonked out on me. Slept on the divan last night."

"No sir!"

Cass grinned. "He made up for it this morning."

"Did he?" Ellie studied her fingernails. "What about that other man? Tony."

"He called this morning. I'll see him tonight."

Ellie shook her head. "Sometimes I worry about you, Red. All those men."

"Calm your liver, little friend. The redhead knows how to handle 'em."

"I hope you're right," said Ellie.

"Don't worry your pretty little head about Miss Cassidy. She can take care of herself." Cass mussed the shorter woman's dark hair. "Come on, Punch. Let's go to Prospero's and get some lunch. I need a Bloody Mary."

10

Sara graduated from Boston College with a bachelor of science in nursing in the spring of 1961 and went to work as a nurse at Boston Children's Hospital, where she had been an intern for two years. She was promoted to floor nurse in mid-1962. Alan graduated from the Masters of Accounting program at BC that summer and went to work for Moran, Hass and Haverty, a regional accounting firm.

Alan called Sara when he graduated and told her that he would not be returning to the soup kitchen. He asked her to say goodbye to the crew. They agreed to keep in touch, but, because they were both busy and had other priorities, they didn't.

Alan traveled constantly. He was paid well by his firm and saved most of what he made because the clients paid his travel and living expenses, but he did not have much of a social life, and had no time to develop close relationships. The firm frowned on romance or affairs between partners and associates.

He did have a six-month covert affair with the first female partner in the firm, a divorcee seven years older than he who had a four-year-old daughter. Little Margie adored Alan. She would be waiting for him, hiding behind the door or a couch with her arms full of books for him to read to her when he came to see her mother. She would laugh with delight and pound the book with her palm when he missed a word—she knew the books by heart. She would sit beside him and listen until her mother turned her over to the au pair and went out for the night with Alan.

He rarely spent the night at Judith's apartment, but when he did, he had to leave early the next morning. She wanted him out of the house when Margie got up and came into her bedroom. If Margie cried out in the night, Judith would go to her, but she would not let Margie leave her room.

Alan finally broke off the relationship. Judith earned five times his salary and he was afraid that the senior partners would learn of the affair and force him out. Judith was driven by a lust for power and wealth, and he knew she would abandon him if he put her position at risk.

Judith understood, but little Margie was heartbroken. Both Judith and Alan said that he could visit the little girl from time to time, but they knew it would not be so. He resolved that he would never put himself in that position again, and that he would never get involved like that with someone else's child.

Alan and Cass had an intense, but on-and-off, relationship during 1961 and early 1962. They would call each other and date from time to time. They spent a week together in Bermuda in May of 1962, riding motorbikes around the island, shopping for woolens in Hamilton, singing "Maybe It's Because I'm a Londoner" in the bars, and lying on the beaches. They made love there, in the nighttime breezes that cooled them afterward.

Cass told Alan that Richard would finish his residence in December and return to Galesburg to join his father's medical practice. Sara continued to assume that they would be married that summer, but no date had been set and there was no engagement ring. She had not visited Galesburg, and his family had not come to Boston.

"I don't like it, but what can I do?" said Cass. "She's so defensive when I try to talk about it. She may be frightened herself. I can't tell."

"There's not much you can do," said Alan. "You don't want to make her doubt him unless you're sure."

"My little sister is so wrapped up with marrying that man and moving to Illinois that it scares me."

———◦◦◦———

A NEW PARTNER BROUGHT clients in the Midwest to Moran, Hass in mid-1962, and Alan spent July and August of that year in Cleveland and Akron. He worked constantly, leading his team of accountants, and thought about little besides work.

On his final flight home, Alan reflected on his relationship with Cass. They had known each other for almost three years, and, while Cass said she loved him, he knew she did not love him alone. She enjoyed other men and kept that part of her life secret from him. After their periods of intimacy, the barrier of her other lovers came back between them.

He could not continue in this kind of a relationship; it would have to grow into a permanent one or be dissolved. Ending it would be heart-wrenching for both of them, but it had to be done. Putting it off would only make the separating more difficult.

He called her the next day.

"What's doin', stranger? How's the great state of Ohio?"

"Over, thank goodness."

"What's next?"

"I'll be here for a while," he said. "Can we get together?"

"I'd love to. Sunday?"

"How about a walk in the Garden? The weather's supposed to be nice."

"Terrific. I live not far from there and I haven't seen it this summer." She paused. "Would one o'clock be all right? After church?"

"One it is. Where?"

"The Arlington Street gate, by the statue."

"I'll see you there."

THE WEATHER ON SUNDAY was sunny and humid, with a feel of rain in the air. Alan came out of the Arlington T station at a quarter to one and walked through the gate to the Garden where George Washington, riding through a gap in the city skyline, looked out over him.

Cass, her head down, stood beside the pedestal, dressed in a calf-length plaid skirt, a white silk blouse and a red scarf. He gave her a wolf's whistle and she ran to him.

"Hiya, handsome." She hugged him, then pulled back. "You're a wreck."

"I'll recover."

She took his hand. "Let's go see the swans."

They strolled past willow and cherry trees to the short suspension bridge over the lagoon and stopped by the stone columns in its center. Alan put his hand flat against the cold stones and watched the swan boats, full of tourists, being paddled around by guides who sat in the stern and pointed out the different kinds of trees—yellow-green willows, red maples and pink cherries—that spread over the water from the stone-lined shores.

"Want to take a ride?" she asked.

"Maybe some other time. They're pretty crowded."

They went back across the bridge and took the first path to the right on the other side. They walked along the path, sat on the wooden planks of the third bench they came to, and looked out over a narrow arm of the lagoon.

Four swans swam left to right in front of them, their necks swaying. The weeping willow across the lagoon waved as a puff of air blew through it. The moving air roughened the water and brushed their faces.

Cass leaned on Alan's shoulder and patted his chest. "This is lovely, isn't it? Too bad it won't last."

He pulled away. "Yes, it is too bad. But I'm afraid we can't go on, either."

She drew back. "What do you mean?"

"Cass, I have to hold myself back from falling in love with you, and I'm not going to be able to do it much longer."

She twisted around, put her feet on the bench and her head in his lap. "Go ahead," she said. "What's wrong with that?" She put an arm around his neck, pulled herself up and kissed him. "Hmm?"

He took her face in his hands. "Cassidy O'Brien, you are a temptress."

She pulled him down to her and whispered in his ear. "Give in."

"I can't."

She sat up and faced him. "Why not?"

"It's not right for us to go on like this."

She narrowed her eyes. "What do you mean, it's not right? What isn't?"

"What we're doing."

She stiffened. "You can't do this to me! I love you. I've never loved anyone this much." She glowered at him. "Who is it?"

"There's no one else."

"What do you want that I haven't given you?" She took his shoulders in her hands and shook him. "Tell me! When have you called that I haven't come running?"

"Could you marry me?"

"Is that a proposal?"

"It's a question. Could you?"

She dropped her hands. "I don't know."

"You said once, a long time ago, that you don't own me and I don't own you. Has that changed?"

She got up and strode away.

He followed. "I want someone to own me, and I want to own her. We'll both give ourselves up to each other. You won't do that."

She spun around. "What the hell are you talking about?"

"I'm a one-woman guy, Cass. I want one woman forever. What do you want?"

"I love you and I want you." She stamped the ground. "Are you listening to me? I don't know what I'll do if you leave me. What more can I say?"

"Only me? Forever?"

"Damn you! Listen to me! I want you more than I want anyone else. Don't you understand English?"

He closed his eyes. "Yeah. I understand." He walked away.

"Come back here! What has gotten into you?"

He dropped to the bench so hard that it creaked. "Reality."

She stood beside him, hands on her hips. "Reality? I'll give you some reality." She drew her foot back and kicked him in the calf.

"Ow!" He stood and grabbed his leg, bending and straightening it, then limped around the bench into the grass. "Okay, that's enough." He held his hand out toward her. "I'm sorry. I was warned, and I didn't listen." He raised his foot to the bench and massaged his calf. "We want different things. Can't you see that?"

"No. That's baloney. You can't have Sara so you tried me on, and now you're dumping me because I'm not her. Well, I never will be. She's an Irish princess and Richard is her Prince Charming. If anything happens with him, she'll get to a nunnery and be a virgin forever. Not me. Nobody's going to hold me like that. I've seen what it's done to my mother and my sister and I want no part of it."

"I just wish I could—"

"Oh, shut up. You talk in riddles. If you want to dump me, do it and be damned. The hell with you!"

He waited, watching her.

She clutched his arm. "Oh God, Alan, I didn't mean that. I love you so much. Don't do this to me! Can't we keep what we have? We have such good times . . ."

"We do," he said, "but we aren't going anywhere and I can't go on like that. I don't want to take advantage—"

She snorted. "I can take care of myself, buster."

They sat in silence, watching the swans' return.

After a minute, he said, "I wish you could see—"

"There's nothing to see. You're dumping me. I don't believe you. There is someone else."

"There isn't."

"Bullshit! What are you going to do, follow Sara to Galesburg and wash pots and pans for her? You're an idiot."

"We can agree on that."

Her eyes flashed. "All right, little boy. Have it your way. But you'll be back. When Princess Sara's in Galesburg pushing out babies you'll come crawling back." She jabbed him in the chest. "And I'll kick your goddamn teeth down your throat."

Cass stood. "Don't get up." She spun around, hiding her tears, and strode away.

Alan sat for a few minutes, studying the grass between his feet. Then he got up, walked slowly out of the park and into the Albemarle station.

11

Anthony Biggi had Cass pressed against the wall of the elevator as it rose to her floor in the apartment building. His hands were moving over her breasts and pushing them upward.

"Easy, my man," she said, taking hold of his wrists. "You don't know your own strength."

He took her face in his hands with his thumbs under her chin and growled, "Where'd you say Ellie was?"

"Spending the night with a friend."

"Who's scooping on her?"

The elevator door opened. Cass shoved him back and laughed. "None of your business, Tony-boy." She took a key from her purse.

In the hallway, she unlocked the apartment door, pushed it partway open with her hip, and stopped. Ellie's overnight bag was just inside the door.

"What's this?" said Cass. She put a hand on Tony's chest, said, "Just a second," and thrust the door open.

Ellie was standing in the middle of the living room and Sara was sitting cross-legged on the couch.

Cass looked from one to the other. "What? What's happened?"

Ellie shook her head. Sara stared at Cass, owl-eyed.

Cass patted Tony's chest. "Sorry, my man, but you'll have to leave. Something's happened to my sister." She put a finger across his open mouth. "I'll make it up to you."

"Okay, Red." He looked past her into the room. "I don't know what's going on, but if you need anything done, you call me, understand?"

"I will." She held his face in her hands, kissed him on the lips and eased him out the door.

Cass eyed Sara, then shifted her gaze to Ellie. "When did she get here?"

"An hour ago. I was just leaving."

"What happened?"

"I walked in on him in bed with a med student," said Sara.

Cass curled her upper lip. "I'll kill him."

"I was bringing a paper I'd typed for him," said Sara. "It was pretty technical, and I knew I hadn't gotten all the terms right, so I wanted him to check them." She sniffled. "He didn't answer when I knocked on his door, so I unlocked it and went in, thinking I'd leave it for him. The bedroom door was partway open, and I heard him moaning in there. For a second I thought he was sick, but it wasn't that kind of a moan. I could see his head through the door but I couldn't see her." She swallowed. "Then I went to the door and saw her. Monica Henderson."

Ellie said, "Who—" but Cass held out her hand.

"I couldn't breathe," said Sara. "I thought I was going to choke to death right there. I kicked the door open and threw the paper at him— fifty-seven loose pages. I yelled, 'You shit-head! I hope she bites it off,' and ran out." She wiped her eyes. "I came right here. I hope it's all right. I've messed up your evening."

"Don't worry about that. You did the right thing." Cass knelt on one knee and put an arm around Sara's shoulders. "I'm glad you're here."

"So am I," said Ellie.

"You're so good to me," said Sara. "I don't know what I would have done—"

"You don't have to think about that," said Cass. "You're in the right place. Can I get you anything?"

Sara rubbed her arms. "I'm cold. Could I borrow a sweater or something?"

"You sure can." Cass went into the bedroom and came back with her red bathrobe. "Here, put this on. Nice and warm." Sara stood and put her arms in the sleeves. Cass wrapped it around her and knotted the fabric belt in the front. "Anything else, sweetie?"

"Do you have any whisky?"

Cass stepped back. "Well, yes, we do." She frowned. "Are you sure that's what you want?"

"Yes!"

Cass went into the kitchen, took a bottle of Old Forester out of the cabinet over the refrigerator and dropped it on the kitchen counter. "What do you want in it?"

"I don't know," said Sara. "Ice?"

Cass cracked an ice tray and dropped cubes into two eight-ounce old-fashioned glasses. She poured the whisky over the ice until the glasses were full, gave one to Sara and kept the other. "Let it melt a little."

Ellie said, "I'll have a Heinie." She opened the refrigerator door, took out a green bottle and levered it open.

Cass and Ellie sat down, one on either side of Sara. She sucked in a mouthful of Old Forester and her eyes popped wide open. She closed them and forced the whisky down. Her face reddened.

"Take it easy," said Cass.

"Why?" Sara swigged some more.

"Who's Monica what's-her-name?" asked Ellie. "Do you know her?"

"Henderson," said Sara. "A med student. Third-year, I think. From Georgia." She slurped some more Old Forester. "Not bad, Cass." She held the glass up and shook it. The cubes rattled. "Not bad at all."

"How does he know her?" said Ellie.

"I don't know. Classes, the hospital, parties. I see her at the hospital.

Maybe he did, too."

"What's she like?" said Ellie.

"Dark hair. Big. Built like a cheerleader." Sara put a hand beneath a breast as though it were holding a melon. "Maybe that's what he saw in her." She poured the rest of the Old Forester into her mouth.

"Huh-unh," said Cass. "That's not what they want."

Sara laughed, spitting a mist of whisky into the room. She wiped her mouth with a sleeve. "How would you know?" she asked. "You've got 'em."

"'S not what they're after, sweetie," said Cass. "Just a stop on the way."

"You tried to warn me, didn't you?" said Sara. "You never liked him."

"A real charmer," said Cass, "and rich. But I didn't trust him."

Sara raised her head and compressed her face. "I am *so stupid*!" To Ellie: "Did you know 'im?" She looked into her empty glass. "I need some more a' this."

Cass went to the kitchen and came back with the bottle. She put it on the coffee table. "In a minute."

"I met him once, when he came to the Top Hat to get you," said Ellie. She went to the refrigerator and took out another Heineken. "Good-looking. I thought he might be a little stuck on himself."

"Yooo got it," slurred Sara.

"A real bastard," said Cass.

Sara stood and untied the belt around the bathrobe. "I'm too hot." She shook her shoulders and the robe fell to the floor. "Thass better." She stepped over it and leaned down to get the bottle of Old Forester.

Cass pulled it away. "Easy, little sis."

"I'm gonna join a nunnery," said Sara. "Might as well."

"They won't let you drink," said Cass.

"Well, you won't either." Sara plopped down on the floor, reached across the coffee table, grabbed the bottle and filled her glass.

Cass took it from her. Sara closed one eye and squinted. "An' I thought you were my frien'."

Cass rolled her eyes. "Okay, sweetie, but let me get you some more ice." She went into the kitchen, held the glass over the sink and dropped a handful of ice into it, spilling half of the whisky. She gave the glass to Sara. "You're going to be sorry."

"I'm arready sorry!"

"You're better off finding out now, honey," said Ellie. "Imagine being in Illinois with a couple of kids and then finding out what a shithead he is. What would you do then?"

Sara took another slug and sputtered, "Call Cass to come 'n' kill 'im."

"You're a coward," said Cass.

"Damn right," said Sara. "You're the muscle in our family. The bouncer. You'd rub 'im out." She hiccupped. "Oops. 'Scuse me."

"What about her?" asked Ellie.

"I won't rub out a woman," said Cass.

"Maybe she'll flunk out from all her extracurricular activities and go back to Georgia," said Ellie. "Marry a peanut farmer."

"Serve her right," said Sara. "Marry a peanut." She drained her glass.

Cass glanced sideways at Ellie and shook her head. Now it was her turn to take care of her sister, and it was going to be a long night.

"She better not fool around down Georgia," said Ellie. "He'd beat her up."

"She'd have it coming," said Cass.

"Lovely," said Sara. "Jus' lovely." She got up, wobbled and collapsed onto the couch. "I'm drunk. Whaddo I do now?"

"Time for bed," said Ellie. "You've had a rough day."

"Yeah," said Sara. "Rough." She blew out a lungful of air. "Arright if I stay here? Prob'ly couldn't find m' car."

"We insist," said Cass.

At 3 a.m., Sara, her face ashen, was lying on the cold tile floor of the bathroom and clutching the toilet bowl.

Cass knelt beside her. "You'll live, sweetie."

Sara pulled her head over the water. Cass reached down and swept up

Sara's dripping hair, squeezed some water out and held it above her head.

Sara heaved and threw up. "I'm a whore. Thassall I am, a whore." She heaved again and retched. Nothing came out. "No one'll want me now. Jus' use me an' leave me. Wish I'ze dead."

Cass pushed the lever down and the toilet flushed. Sara retched again. Cass raised Sara's head and wiped the cold sweat from her forehead. "Don't talk like that, sweetie." She swabbed Sara's lips and chin. "You'll feel better tomorrow."

"When I'm dead."

"Here, take some Alka-Seltzer. It'll help."

Sara forced it down.

—⟨ⱷⱷⱷ⟩—

SARA SLEPT UNTIL TEN Sunday morning. Cass brought her a tray of tea and toast, and more Alka-Seltzer. "Feel better?"

"I think so. How was I last night?"

"Fine, considering."

"Considering what?"

"What the bastard did to you." Cass sat down in front of Sara and brushed a strand of hair away from her face. "This may be hard to take right now, sweetie, but you're better off. The longer you hold on to something that's not going to work out, the harder it is when you have to let go." She held Sara close. "It took me way too long to learn that."

"I had such hopes."

Cass kissed her hair. "They were imaginings, and you held on to them too long. I hated to see it. The way he treated you wasn't right. Like you were a possession. You couldn't see that."

Sara lowered her head. "No."

"You were in love with Illinois, and Galesburg, and being away from here as much as you were in love with Richard. You saw him as your ticket out from under this misbegotten family, and there isn't one."

She held Sara's face and kissed her forehead. "You can run away from us, little one, but you can't escape. Mary Clare and I know that. Maybe now you do, too."

12

SAN DIEGO

The restaurant was dimly lit—light enough for the patrons and staff to navigate the spaces between the tables, dark enough to encourage intimate conversation and soft laughter. One row of tables sat along the entire left wall. Another ran along the right wall from the entrance to the bar, a hockey stick–shaped counter with enough seats for a dozen people. One couple and a lone man in gray slacks and a long-sleeved blue shirt sat on chairs at the bar.

Two women and a man came in the front door and stopped at the hostess stand. She hurried to them from the rear of the room.

"Good evening! Reservations?"

"Yes," said the man. "For three. Sabatelli."

The hostess made a mark in a spiral notebook. "It'll be just a minute."

They stepped back. The shorter woman, a brunette, looked around. "Nice."

The other woman, tall and blonde, said, "It's one of our favorite places. Frank likes their steaks."

The brunette patted the man's stomach. "Frankie is a steak and potatoes guy, except when he's gobbling up pasta." Her low-pitched peal of mirthful laughter rolled through the crowded room. "Me, I want some seafood."

To the blonde, Frank said, "Mara and I were raised on Mama's pasta. I didn't know what good steak was till I went to Chicago, on leave from Great Lakes."

"Steaks in Iowa are good," said Mara. "But no Italians, so no good pasta."

"Are you two telling me that only Italians make good pasta?"

"Yes." In unison.

Frank winked at Mara. "She doesn't believe us."

Mara flashed a smile at him. "Now, now, Frankie. Winnie's entitled to her opinion." Mara looked at her. "Winnie, don't you let my little brother"—he put his hands on his hips and leaned over her, a fake scowl on his face—"boss you around."

The hostess said, "Ready now," and started toward the back of the restaurant carrying three menu folders. Halfway back, Winnie stopped, put a hand on Frank's chest and pointed to the man sitting at the bar.

"That's Thomas. Do you think Mara would mind if he joined us?"

"Mara never met a stranger." Frank went to the bar. "Lieutenant?"

"Hello, Frank." Thomas waved to Winnie. "Out for the evening?"

"We're here with my sister from Iowa, Lieutenant. We thought you might like to join us." Frank glanced toward the entrance. "Unless you're waiting for someone."

"We're off-duty, Frank. It's Thomas. Are you sure your sister won't mind? I don't want to butt in."

"You'll even things out. You and I can sit and watch while Winnie and Mara talk."

"I don't think Winnie's a big talker."

Frank smiled. "She isn't."

Thomas chuckled. "Well, okay. Tell me your sister's name again."

"Mara." Frank spelled it.

Winnie and Mara were seated across from each other when Frank and Thomas came up to the table. "Mara," said Frank, "this is Lieutenant Thomas Colombo, my commanding officer. Thomas, my sister, Mara."

Mara shook his hand. It was big, and cool to the touch. "Hello, Lieutenant."

"Thomas, please. Nice to meet you, Mara." He leaned down and kissed Winnie on the cheek.

Mara looked at her brother. "Did you set this up?"

"Would I do something like that to you?"

She laughed. "Yes."

"He didn't," said Thomas. "Believe me."

Mara smiled at him, her dark eyes sparkling. "I believe you."

The waiter approached. "Can I get you something from the bar?"

Winnie ordered white wine and Frank ordered red. Thomas said, "Scotch mist."

"What's that?" asked Mara.

"Scotch and ice, with a lemon peel," said Thomas.

"Yuck," said Mara, laughing. "Red wine for me, too."

"You like red wine?" asked Thomas.

"Oh, yes," said Mara. "Frankie and I were raised on dago red. Papa got some every year from his customers."

"So was I," said Thomas, "in Chicago. But they don't have it here."

"Too bad," said Mara, laughing again. She picked up her menu. "I want some seafood. What's good here?"

"The rockfish," said the waiter. "Caught fresh."

"Okay," said Mara. "I'll have it."

The others ordered—mahi-mahi for Winnie, steak for Frank and abalone for Thomas, who asked for a separate check. Their drinks came. Frank raised his glass. "Here's to Mara, my big sister. Welcome to San Diego."

Thomas drank and put his glass down. "Mara, where do you live in Iowa?"

"Cedar Rapids."

"You were raised in West Virginia, with Frank?"

"Yes. I went to Iowa and lived with my aunt for my last year in high school, and then went to school to be a dental hygienist."

"Your senior year?" asked Thomas.

"Mara and Papa did not get along," said Frank, "so Mara went to live with Mama's sister her senior year."

Frank and Mara exchanged glances. "But Frankie is my buddy," she said. "Little Frankie."

"He's not so little," said Thomas.

"Do you have a big sister?" asked Frank.

"No," said Thomas. "A little brother."

"You know what it's like, then," said Mara. "Having a kid brother." She laughed. "So, tell me about Chicago."

"I grew up on the south side," said Thomas, "in Bridgeport, and went to the De LaSalle Institute."

"That's a high school?" said Mara.

"Yeah. Five of our mayors went there."

"What happened to you?" she laughed.

"I wasn't Irish enough, so I got an appointment to Annapolis and went there."

"Did you always want to be a sailor? Yo ho ho?"

"Not really," said Thomas. "But it was free. My father's a tailor."

Their meals came. After a while, Frank said to Thomas, "Where's your brother?"

"In Chicago. He teaches math in high school. Has two kids."

"Uncle Thomas," said Mara. "I bet they love you."

"They're good kids."

Winnie reached under the table and gripped Frank's thigh. He rolled his eyes at her.

Mara peered at Frank. "What about you, buddy? Any nieces or nephews on the way?"

Frank grinned at her. "Never you mind."

"You're fifth in line to know," said Winnie.

"Guess I'll have to wait." Mara winked at Thomas. "Meantime, tell me what's going on in the Navy. Are you ready to defend our shores?"

"Always."

"Are they going to need defending? Are the Russians about to invade us?"

"One thing we know about the Russians," said Thomas, "they're always probing for an opening. And when they spot one, they go at it."

"Do we have any?" asked Frank.

"Oh, I don't know," said Thomas. "Cuba, maybe."

Mara's eyes widened. "You think so?"

"Nothing to worry about," said Thomas. "If they try anything there, the Navy will take care of them. The Caribbean is our lake."

"Thomas," said Frank, "do you know something you can't tell us?"

Thomas held out his palms. "We're ready for whatever happens, believe me." He picked up a menu card. "Who wants dessert?"

Winnie and Mara asked for flan, Frank ordered apple pie and ice cream and Thomas asked for a dish of strawberries.

The waiter left with their orders. Frank said, "Excuse me," and got up.

"I'll go with you," said Thomas. They went toward the restrooms in the back of the restaurant.

Mara watched them. "Nice guy. Not bad looking, either."

"Frank thinks a lot of him," said Winnie. "He's a good officer."

Mara leaned toward her. "Not married, is he?"

Winnie shook her head. "Single."

"I bet he has girlfriends."

"Probably," said Winnie. "But you never know."

The two of them went to the women's room.

In the men's room, Thomas said, "Your sister is something. Is she attached?"

"No, she isn't."

"How does she like Iowa?"

"So-so," said Frank. "She's alone out there."

"How long will she be here?"

"Till Wednesday. Four more days."

"What do you have planned?"

"Some sightseeing with Winnie." Frank smiled at his commanding officer. "Do you have my phone number?"

"Yeah. Okay if I call her?"

"Sure. Call her if you want to, or ask her now."

"What do you think?"

"She'd like to be shown around."

"I will," said Thomas. "And what's this about Mara and your father? They don't get along?"

"You'll have to talk to her about that."

Frank and Thomas went back to the table and waited for the women. When they returned, Thomas said, "Frank, I have two tickets to see the Chargers play Dallas at Balboa on Sunday. It ought to be a good game. I wonder if Mara would like to come with me." He watched her.

"I'd like that. I love football." Mara raised a fist. "Go, Hawkeyes."

Winnie peered sideways at Frank, who winked at her.

The checks came and the men paid.

On the sidewalk outside, Thomas said, "Mara, I'll pick you up at noon on Sunday. Our seats are in the sun, so you'll need sunglasses and a cap."

"Yes sir, Lieutenant." She saluted and laughed. "Noon it is."

In the car, Frank said, "Mara, I didn't know you liked football."

"It depends on who's playing," said Mara.

"Or who's in play?" asked Winnie.

Mara laughed. "Well, that too."

It's good to hear you laughing and having fun again, sis," said Frank. "Going out."

"I gotta live, Frankie. I gotta live."

—◦◦◦—

Thomas lost sight of Mara in the close-packed crowd on an exit ramp after the game. "Mara! Where are you?"

She raised her hand from a few yards away. "Here I am."

He reached for her. "I didn't see you."

She laughed. "Don't worry. I'm hard to get rid of."

"What did you think of the game?"

"I liked it. San Diego won."

"On a field goal."

"A forty-two-yarder," she said. "Terrific."

"How many football games have you been to?"

"Lots. I was a cheerleader in high school." She put an arm around his waist. "Thomas, I had a wonderful time. Thanks for bringing me and listening to me talk all afternoon. I'm sure you would have rather watched the game."

He tapped her nose with a finger. "I've never enjoyed a game as much as I did this one. Come on, I'll buy you dinner so we can talk some more."

"Y'know," she said, laughing, "I could get to like you."

13

BOSTON

Alan walked slowly down Spring Street on a blustery autumn afternoon, on his way home from a workout at the YMCA, looking up between the three-story row houses on either side of the street to watch dark clouds roll between them on their way to the bay. The crossing wind sent catspaw gusts down to the street between the gray stone buildings, swirling and scattering the leaves piled up at the curb. They would be all over the yards and the street again by morning.

He'd had a bad day. The client had been upset by his report, which showed that their declining returns on investment had been brought about by a lack of controls on capital expenditures for the last five years by the current management.

Alan was as delicate as he could be in explaining this to the client's management team, but delicacy could not sugarcoat the situation. They had let things get out of control, and their company was in for difficult times.

Alan's boss, a senior partner, had not defended him. Instead, he took Alan over the coals in front of the client for the conclusions and how they were presented, even though the partner had made "suggestions" to Alan on how the report should be written and presented, and Alan had followed them.

He was pained and depressed by the abuse, and by the partner's perfidy. The only successful thing in his life since graduation had been his performance in the business, and today that was threatened. Was he finished at Moran?

Nothing else was working, either. He had his long-time buddy Ollie and a few other male friends, but nothing more. He had been attracted to some women, and they to him—Mara, Judith, Cass and now Gia. He had found pleasure in their company—and in sex with Judith and Cass—as they had in his. But no binding love had developed with any of them except Mara, and she had been yanked out of his life before they were mature.

Sara? She was in Illinois, married and raising her family. He wondered what her children were named.

At twenty-seven he should be married and have a family on the way, but his prospects for that were nil. Would he never have a son to name John Wesley, or a daughter to name Constance? His dread of being alone for the rest of his life pressed down on him like giant hands on his shoulders.

He felt some drops of rain, looked up into the dark sky and started to trot toward the house in the next block where he and three of his friends lived.

The four men had different jobs and different interests, but they got along on the things important for living together. Chad Denton was a soft-spoken North Carolinian who had graduated from Boston College and stayed on to get his master's in accounting. He was a tax accountant for Moran, Hass and Haverty. Oliver Nutter and Alan had known each other in high school and stayed in touch when Ollie was at Boston University studying engineering. Bud McNair was a friend of Ollie's from engineering school. He was coming out the door of the house when Alan slowed down, blew out a lungful of air and came up the steps.

"What say, Alan?" asked McNair. "Done for the weekend?"

"Not quite. I have to go in to work tomorrow, but I'll finish before the game."

"Who you playin'?"

"It's a big one. We're playing Pitt in Pittsburgh."

"Do you play Pitt every year?" asked McNair.

"Yeah, in mid-October."

"What are your chances?"

"Good. The Mountaineers are three and oh. We beat you guys last week."

"We stink," said McNair. "Oh, by the way, there's a message for you."

"Who from?"

McNair pointed his index finger at Alan, squinted one eye and cocked his thumb. "A friend of yours." He fired—"Ka-pow!"—and hurried down the street.

Alan went from the pale outside light into the dimly lit vestibule of 142 Spring Street and up the two steps into the living room. The dark carpet on the floor absorbed most of the light that bled through the front windows. A wooden table and four chairs were in the corner closest to the street and a faded blue couch, donated by Chad's parents, sagged against the wall across from the stairs. A bag of golf clubs leaned against one arm.

The front door slammed shut. "That you, Alan?" called Nutter from upstairs. "Check out the message by the phone."

"Who is it?"

Denton's voice came from the kitchen. "The redhead, buddy. She wants you."

"She wants your body," said Nutter.

"Smart-asses." Alan picked up the phone and dialed Cass's number. Ellie answered. "Hello?"

"Hi, El, it's Alan. Is Cass around?"

"What's doin', Alan? No, she's out for the evening, but she wants you to meet her tomorrow at ten at the Dunkies on Mount Vernon.

It's important. Can you do it?"

"What's it about?"

"She'll tell you."

"Come on, Ellie, I need more than that. I was going in to work tomorrow."

"It's about Sara. That's all I can tell you."

"What about Sara?"

"She'll tell you." Ellie paused. "You'll be there tomorrow at ten? The Dunkies on Mount Vernon."

"Okay—yes."

"I'll tell her. Bye."

Alan put his fingers over his lips. *What's happened to Sara?*

—✦✦✦—

ALAN WAS SIPPING COFFEE and munching on a glazed doughnut when Cass came into the Dunkin' Donuts shop the next morning.

"I'll be right there," she said.

Alan eyed her up and down as she walked to the counter and ordered. The clerk drew a cup of coffee, opened the door of the glass cabinet, took out a doughnut with a piece of waxed paper and put it on a small paper plate. "Here you go, honey."

Cass picked up her breakfast and sat down across the Formica-topped table from Alan. "What's doin', Alan? You all right?"

"I'm fine, thanks. Busy as anything. You?"

"Me, too." She took a sip of coffee. "You look good. Better than last time."

"Thanks. You always look good."

She reached across the table and gripped his hand. "I miss you."

"And I miss you." He patted her arm. "It's too bad."

She pulled her lips in between her teeth and nodded.

They eyed each other until Alan said, "So, what's this about Sara? Is she okay?"

"She and Richard broke up."

"Really?" His eyes narrowed. "I haven't seen her in almost two years. I thought she'd be in Illinois by now. What happened?"

"Why don't you ask her?" Cass leaned over the table toward him. "I'm scared, Alan. She's in terrible pain, and I can't help her. I think you could."

"What could I do?"

"Get her to talk. Listen. You're good at that." Cass handed him her business card with a number written on the back. "She's sharing an apartment near the hospital with two other nurses."

He studied the card. "Does she still run that soup kitchen in Waltham? On Wednesdays?"

"That's a good thought. She does."

He snapped the card with his fingers. "Okay." He gazed into those green eyes. "Thank you."

"You're welcome."

He took a sip of coffee. "How's everyone else? Your mom, Mary Clare, the kids?"

"Fine."

He inhaled slowly. "Cal?"

"Fatter. Mary Clare says he's less active, but I still stay away from him." Cass put her fingers on the top of the table. "She got what she wanted, and now she's paying for it. I feel sorry for her."

She slapped the table. "Not for me, my man. But you know that." Her chair scraped the floor as she stood. "You have to go in to work, so I'll go." She gripped the back of the chair and leaned toward him. "Sara's my little sister. You mess with her, I wring your frickin' neck. You savvy?"

"Me savvy, Kemosabe."

—⦿⦿⦿—

THE NEXT WEDNESDAY, ALAN shook the rain out of his umbrella and walked into the basement of the Calvary Methodist Church a few minutes after eight. The crew of volunteers was cleaning up. A woman wiping a table said, "We're closed, sir. Everything's put away."

She waved at someone in the kitchen. "But maybe we could find something for you."

A voice from the kitchen roared, "Nah! Heck with him. Let him starve!"

Alan peered into the kitchen and pointed at a man standing there. "Hi, Mark."

"Besides," said Mark, "he didn't come for dinner." He raised his head. "She's upstairs. Better get her at the front."

Alan bolted from the basement, ran up the steps to Cherry Street and around the corner to Moody, holding his breath. He looked down Moody toward the bus stop and didn't see anyone, so she was still in the church or she was gone. He jumped up the steps from the sidewalk and slid to a stop on the slate walkway to the church. Lights were on inside, so she was still there. He exhaled.

The rain, falling steadily from the dark sky, plastered his hair to his head and poured down his face until he put up the umbrella.

The lights went out and Sara came through the door. She pulled a hood over her head and started toward the street.

"Hello, Sara."

"Alan." She stood still. "What brings you here?"

"I got here too late for dinner, so—"

"Don't be a wise guy. Did you come to pick up the pieces?"

"I came to see you."

"Cass told you," she said.

"Yes."

"What did she say?"

"That you broke up. I was sorry to hear it."

"*Were* you?"

"It sounded so good for you," he said.

"Well, it wasn't, and I couldn't have had it, anyway."

"I *am* sorry."

She nodded.

"Want to walk?" he said. "I can buy you a Coke at Pokey's, or we can go to the bus stop." A gust caught the umbrella and he grabbed the shaft with both hands. "Whoa, Nellie!"

"Walk me to the bus stop. I'm beat."

She came under his umbrella and they started down Moody Street, walking close together to keep out of the rain. He kept holding the umbrella over her far shoulder and she pushed the shaft back between them. After half a block of this, he gave up.

A little farther along, he asked, "How'd it go tonight?"

"Terrible. A woman came in with two little kids, cute as anything. They got in the line, but when they got to the food trays, she said she saw rats crawling around in them. She went crazy. She screamed, 'You want to kill my babies!' One woman tried to calm her down, but she grabbed the kids and ran out with them, still screaming. She must have been on something—either that or she has the D.T.'s."

"Ah! That's horrible."

"If she has them, she needs treatment or it could kill her. I asked if anyone knew her, but no one said they did. I doubt that, and I weep for those kids." She took a deep breath. "There's so much pain out there, so much damage. And never enough help."

"Sara, you do all you can. You mustn't let something like that pull you down."

She stopped, her head down. "It's hard for me right now."

He put his arm around her shoulders. "I know it is, but you mustn't give in, because then you couldn't help. And that's your life—helping."

"I guess so." She pulled away and eyed his face. "What's your life?"

"I want to have my own business, love someone, raise a family, and pass on what I inherited."

"I wish I could want that." She started to walk away. "But what I inherited . . ."

He went after her, holding the umbrella ahead until it was over her.

"You should want to pass on what you are, Sara."

"I'm a damaged woman."

"We're all damaged."

"You really think that?"

"We've all been damaged—by ourselves or someone else—but we can't let it ruin our lives." He saw the blue and yellow MBTA bus coming toward them. "You're such a good person, Sara. I wish I could convince you of that."

They stepped back from the curb until the bus stopped and opened its door. She put her foot on the first step and grasped the vertical bar above it.

He said, "Good night—"

She reached back to him. "Come with me." He sprang up the steps behind her.

They sat down. She pulled off her hood. "What happened between you and Cass?"

"We broke up."

She tilted her head and gave him the "I-*know*-that" look.

"I called it off. She wouldn't commit, so I couldn't," he said.

Sara watched the cars splashing past the bus. "How'd she take it?"

"She kicked me."

"She used to kick me, too, when she was really mad at me. And she had to be mad at you because you broke up with her. No one's ever done that."

"Really?"

"I warned you, remember? Nothing lasts with Cass. She breaks up with everyone. She starts it and she has to be the one that ends it." Sara gripped the bar on the back of the seat in front of her with both hands and lowered her head. "Alan, did you have good times with my sister?" She stared at her feet. "I know you went to Bermuda."

"Cass and I had good times."

"Richard and I had good times, too." She looked up at him. "But he's not your brother."

They turned away from each other and gazed out the windows until the bus stopped. She said, "We change here."

As they stood in the aisle she said, "Do you want to know what happened?"

They stepped down to the sidewalk. "If you want to tell me," he said.

"I walked in on him and a med student. But it was over before that. I just didn't know it."

"Why d'you say that?"

"There was always some reason why I couldn't meet his family, here or there. Maybe they thought the daughter of a Mick from Boston who'd deserted his family wasn't good enough for him." She covered her breasts with her hands. "And look at these. You should have seen hers."

He gripped her shoulders and the canopy of the umbrella dropped behind her. "You look awfully good to me."

She leaned away from him. "Really?"

"Really. Anyone who picks a woman for her cup size is an idiot. They'll hang below her waist by the time she's fifty." He ran a hand over his hair. "That guy's an idiot."

She smiled at him through the drops of rain tapping on her nose and cheeks. "You think so?"

He was so taken by her again—smiling through the raindrops falling on her face and flashing between them—that he could not think or speak. He would not let his arms reach out and pull her to him.

A bus with a "Boston Hospitals" route sign splashed through the intersection and stopped for them to climb on. They rode in silence, Alan wondering how she felt about him now, after almost two years.

He followed her when she got off at the third stop. He put his umbrella over them and they walked down the sidewalk to a gray apartment building in the next block, taking long steps over pools of water between the broken slabs of concrete.

The building's door did not open when he pulled. "Is it locked?" he asked.

"Pull harder."

He put one hand on the frame and jerked the door handle with the other. The door creaked open, and she went by him into the dimly lit vestibule while he shook the umbrella outside. He came in and stood before her—mute, waiting,

She pulled his cold hand to her lips. "Thank you."

The elevator door opened, and Sara started toward it.

Alan found his voice. "May I call you?"

"Not right now."

He took a step back. "Does that mean you want me to go away?"

She stood in the door. "Oh, no—but I need some time." She stepped inside. "I'll call you."

He watched the door close and went back out into the rain.

14

Chad Denton was jumping down the steps from the second floor of 142 Spring Street on a Wednesday afternoon in mid-January, taking them two at a time, when a car horn blared outside. "I'm coming, I'm coming."

The phone rang. "Damn." He dropped his suitcase beside his golf travel bag at the foot of the steps, strode to the phone stand and grabbed the receiver. "Hello?"

"Hello." A woman's voice. "I'm calling for Alan. Is he there?"

"No, he isn't."

"Do you know when he'll be back?"

"Sorry, I don't."

"Is he in town these days?" she asked.

"Yeah."

"Will you ask him to call Sara, please? He has the number."

"Yeah."

"It's important," she said. The horn sounded again.

"Okay." He threw the receiver on its cradle, grabbed his bags and ran out the door.

—⁓⁓⁓—

"WHAT DOES IT TAKE?" screamed Ollie, pounding the pillow on the floor beside him. "Did you see that?" He pointed at the TV screen. "Checkon just *mugged* Thorn. His sorry ass should be thrown out of the game!"

"Easy, Ollie," said Alan. "Rod'll make the foul shots and we'll be ahead by eight with five seconds left in the half."

It was the following Saturday. Alan, Ollie, Bud McNair and two of their girlfriends were in the den, watching the basketball game between West Virginia and George Washington University. Thorn made the two foul shots and the Mountaineers led GW by eight points when the half ended.

The halftime commercials took over—Ford F-150 pickup trucks splashing through brown mud, Coca-Cola, the new film *To Kill a Mockingbird*. McNair got up and stretched, his hands interlocked above his head. "Anybody want another?"

"I'm cold," said Ollie. "I'm going to get me a sweater. You want one, Evie?"

Eve Carter said, "I'm fine." She went to the bathroom.

Alan turned to the buxom woman sitting close to him on the couch. "You okay?"

She mussed his hair. "I'm warm enough." She got up, collected the empty bottles and snack trays and took them into the kitchen, stepping over the pillows on the floor.

McNair skipped across the living room and bounced down the steps to the vestibule. He pulled the closet door open and a tangle of sweaters and jackets tumbled to the floor. He yanked a blue sweatshirt out of the pile by its sleeve, stuck his arms in and pulled it over his head. When his head popped out, the outside door was partway open and a young woman with light blue eyes was smiling at him from under the bill of a baseball cap.

"Is Alan here?" she asked. "I rang the bell."

"It doesn't work." He took the heap of clothes in his arms, stuffed it into the closet and forced the door shut with his hip. "Wait here. I'll get him."

McNair glanced into the kitchen as he crossed the living room and tiptoed down into the den. He squatted in front of Alan, who was watching TV announcers give the scores of other games. "Someone to see you, Alan."

"Me?"

McNair raised his eyebrows. "A blonde chick."

Alan walked through the living room shaking his head, wondering what this blonde chick was selling—life insurance or magazine subscriptions—and how long it would take him to shoo her out the door. He stopped at the top of the steps and squinted at the woman standing below him. Her face was shaded from the overhead light by the bill of a maroon baseball cap. A blonde ponytail stuck through the back of the cap and fell down to her shoulder blades.

He stared at her with that blank expression a person gets when they unexpectedly encounter someone they haven't seen for a while and don't recognize right away.

"Remember me?" she asked.

Her soft voice and the way she nearly swallowed the "r" when she said "remembah" awakened him to who she was. He breathed her name. "Sara."

The woman who had been sitting next to Alan scurried across the living room and stood beside him. She ran her hand up his back and gripped his shoulder. "Who's your friend?"

"Gia," he said, "this is Sara O'Brien. Sara, Gia Brunetti."

"Hello, Sara." Daggers.

They stuck. "Nice to meet you, Gia. I . . . uh . . ." Sara pulled her lower lip between her teeth. "I was . . . hoping Alan could help us out in the soup kitchen on Wednesday. I think we'll be shorthanded."

"This Wednesday?" Gia pulled on Alan's shoulder. "Eve and I were talking about the four of us going to see *Dr. No* that night. I've heard Sean

Connery is *very* sexy."

"You were?" he said. "Well, I'm not sure, Sara."

Sara scowled at Gia, who retaliated with a wide smile.

"Please?" said Sara. "We could use some help, and everyone would like to see you again."

"I don't think he can," said Gia.

"I'll see," said Alan. "Maybe."

"All right," said Sara. "Bye." She turned and left, stumbling out the door and down the steps with her head down.

Gia tightened her grip. "Who's she?"

"She runs a soup kitchen in Warwick. I lived near there and helped out on Wednesdays when I was in school."

"Kinda scrawny." Gia walked away.

Alan snapped his head toward her and frowned as she went back into the kitchen. What was she trying to do, run his life?

"Come on, come on," said Ollie. "It's started. Come on."

Alan and Ollie watched and cheered as All-American Rod Thorn led the Mountaineers to a 100–97 win over the Colonials. When the game ended, Ollie high-stepped into the kitchen carrying his empty beer can.

Gia followed him. "Ollie, are you and Eve doing anything after work on Wednesday?"

"Eve's spending the day with her brother. He's coming through on his way to Germany for three years." Ollie clicked his heels together and raised his right hand in a salute. "Oberleutnant Jackson Carter reporting for duty, mein Kommandant."

He practiced his jump shot with the can. It rattled around in the corner and dropped into a wastebasket. "Swish! Two points for the Mountaineers." He raised his fists. "Why?"

"I just wondered." Gia picked a dark hair off the sleeve of her sweater. "You know this Sara?"

"That who it was? I never met her. She's a nurse. Alan used to help at a soup kitchen in Warwick. She ran it."

"What else?" she asked, her dark eyes studying him.

"He liked her. She was going to get married, though. To a doctor. Two years ago." He wrinkled his nose. "She married?"

"Huh-unh. No rings."

"What'd she want?"

"She asked him to help her out."

"Really? After all that time." He opened the refrigerator. "He dated her sister for a while. They broke up." He pulled out a slice of bologna and stuck it in his mouth. "What'd she want him to do?"

"She asked him to come and help at the kitchen, but that's not why she came."

"What?"

"She changed her story when she saw me."

He laughed. "How d'you know that?"

"She's after him." Gia turned and left.

Ollie ran a finger across his lips.

If she is, sister, you better watch out.

SARA WAS LATE GETTING to the church on Wednesday. She grabbed a handful of papers from her mailbox on the first floor and hurried down the stairs, through the basement and into the kitchen, where the smell of meat sauce cooking and the moisture from a steaming pasta kettle filled the air. Everyone was working. They had their backs to the entryway when she came through.

"Well," she said, "I guess you don't need me tonight."

The man at the cleanup sink turned around. Sara stood still, her mouth half open. She put a hand on the desk to steady herself. "Alan?"

"Hi."

Everyone else turned around, grinning at her astonishment. She stuck her hands on her hips. "What's going on here?"

"He made us do it," said Mark.

"Sure he did," she said. "Thanks for coming, Alan. Now get back to work, you jokesters."

"Yes, boss."

When the meal had been served and the cleanup was almost finished, Sara leaned on the counter by the sink and faced Alan. "I thought you were going to the movies."

"We weren't."

"But she said—"

"We weren't!"

"All right. Sorry, I'm on edge tonight."

He spoke through grim laughter. "So am I."

"Could you drive me to Mom's after this? It'd save me a long bus ride."

"To Cambridge? I guess so. Is everything okay?"

"Cal's sick. Mom says it's his stomach. Cass and I are going to take care of him and watch the kids so Mom can get some sleep and Mary Clare can go shopping."

Later, in the car, she said, "Why'd you come?"

"What? You invited me."

"What happened to the movies?"

"She made that up."

"You're kidding."

"Huh-unh."

"She was really holding onto you. I'm glad she didn't have a gun."

He blew the horn. "Come on lady, *drive*!" He pulled into the left lane and accelerated past the car in front of them. "Why'd you come to invite me? There were enough people tonight."

"I didn't come to invite you. I came to talk. I called Wednesday and left a message for you."

"Who'd you leave it with?"

"Some guy in a hurry. I heard a car horn."

Chad. I'll kill him. Alan reached across and patted her knee. "Well, I'm glad you came."

"What about her?"

"She wasn't glad."

Sara pushed herself into the corner of the seat and the passenger-side door. "Seriously, what about her?"

"If I were serious about her, I wouldn't be here."

"What about Cass? She still loves you."

He slowed for a stoplight. "Cass and I are over. You know that."

"Is there anyone else?"

"Do you want a list?" he asked.

"Would it be long?"

"No." He pulled the car into the driveway of 386 Concord Avenue. "Is that what you wanted to talk about? The women in my life?"

When she did not reply, he said, "I tried to call you a couple of times, you know."

"I couldn't talk to you. I didn't know what to say."

"And now?"

"I'm sorry, but I'm still not ready. I just can't."

He slapped the steering wheel. "You're putting me through all this to tell me to go away?"

"It's too soon. I can't commit, like Cass."

"You're not Cass." He got out of the car and stood up beside it. The shadow of his head crawled across the roof.

Sara got out. They stood looking at each other over the car. The streetlight made her eyes gleam. "I'm not telling you to go away. Just that I'm not ready."

"What's the difference?"

"I don't want you to go away, but . . ." She studied her reflection in the side window. "I can't explain it."

He walked around the car and took her hands. "What's wrong? What are you doing?" He knelt. "Sara O'Brien, I've loved you since that night at Pokey's when you invited me to Thanksgiving dinner. I have this longing inside that tells me you're the one. I can't explain that either, but it's there."

She pulled her hands away and walked slowly to the front of the car, sliding her feet on the pavement. "I'm . . . impure, Alan. Damaged goods."

He stood and spoke from behind her. "Only one person was ever pure, Sara, and He suffered and died on the cross nearly two thousand years ago. The rest of us fall short. We're all impure. You've been hurt, and hurt again by evil men, but you're not like them. You're as good and pure as anyone can be. We've all been damaged in one way or another. But if all you do is look back at what went wrong, you'll always be unhappy." He stood beside her. "Look ahead—to what you want to be and what you want to have—and take yourself there."

She turned away from him, put a hand on the rim of the headlight and stared at the glass. "I can't get away from what he did to me, Alan. I—"

"Don't say that. Don't let your life be ruined by what someone else did to you."

The bare branches of the red oak tree above them swayed in the breeze, making shadows that swept across their bodies. He walked back and forth through them, waving his arms. "Every time I see you I have trouble staying on my feet. Can't you see that?" He stopped and tilted his head toward her, demanding a reply.

She closed her eyes. "I know."

"Don't you believe me?"

"I have these demons inside me. They keep saying, 'He'll leave you, just like the others.' I can't shut them off. You don't know what it'll be like, living with them, and I do."

"I can live with your demons. I have my own."

She studied his face. "What do they say?"

"No one will love me again. I'll be alone forever." He clenched a fist. "I will *not* give in to them. I will be loved again, and I want it to be by you."

"And if it isn't?"

"I can't think beyond you."

"Maybe you should."

"Sara! If you could love me and you let me go, you'll regret it forever. I'll always be loyal to you. It's in my genes. That's the way we are where I come from—loyal to a fault. I will never leave you."

"Maybe you could be loyal to Cass."

"Maybe I could have. But she can't, so it's over. And the love I had in high school is over." He pressed his palms against his temples. "Do you think you're the only person in the world who's lost anything? Your mother and your sisters are here. Erin and Ryan are adorable kids. They are here for you to love and they love you."

He turned away. "My parents and my sister are gone. I'll never see them again. My home, and the hills I love—I'll never live there again." He pulled on a tree branch and looked into the black sky. "I don't want us to be over." He turned to her, his eyes burning. "But it's up to you."

She put her hands over her face. "I'm so sorry."

He let go of the branch and stepped back, disappearing in the shadow of the tree. His voice came out of the darkness. "I am too, Sara, for what you're doing to yourself. I can't help it that your father ran away, or that Richard betrayed you, and neither can you. But if you want to curl up and wallow in self-pity for the rest of your life, go right ahead." He kicked the tree trunk. "I've had enough. I'm not going to wait outside your door any longer."

He stepped out of the shadow. Sara's hand was over her mouth. She stared at him, her eyes rimmed with moisture. "Please, Alan, I—"

"Goodbye, Sara."

He got in his car, slammed the door shut and drove away.

She doubled over, sobbing. *What have I done?* She watched the red taillights disappear, then she opened the gate and labored up the steps to the porch and into the house. She closed the door and leaned back against it, still sobbing. It was all she could do to keep from sliding to the floor.

"Little one," Cass's voice crept from the unlighted living room, soft as a caress, "why are you crying?"

"He's gone."

Cass came out of the darkness. She put her arm around Sara and led her to the couch. They sat, holding hands.

"What happened?" asked Cass.

"He loves me. But he says I can't love anyone but myself, and he's had enough."

"Can you?"

"I'm afraid. I don't know what I'd do if he—"

"He won't, sweetie. He's not our father, and he's not Richard."

Sara leaned back. "You ought to know."

Cass's eyes flashed.

"I'm sorry." Sara lowered her head. "But he doesn't know, Cass."

"What d'you mean?"

"He doesn't know what I've been through. He can't understand what it's done to me."

"Why d'you say that?"

"He told me to get over what someone else did to me. He doesn't know how hard—"

"Did he tell you about his sister?" Cass's face lost all expression.

Sara pressed her eyebrows together. "He lost her?"

"In a car wreck."

"A wreck? I didn't know—"

"He was driving."

Sara's eyes opened wide.

Cass looked directly into them. "A truck ran their car off the road and she was killed."

Sara touched a cheek with her fingers.

"He'll never get over it, but he's not going to let it ruin his life."

"Why didn't he tell—?"

"He knows, Sara."

15

Ollie answered the knock on the door at 142 Spring Street on a cold January afternoon two Sundays later. A blonde woman in boots, gray slacks and a down ski jacket, said, "Hello, I'm Sara O'Brien. Alan's expecting me."

"Come in, come in," he said, reaching out to usher her into the vestibule. "It's cold out there. Nice to meet you. I'm Ollie. Alan's in the den. Would you like anything?"

She waited for him to breathe. "Tea?"

"I'll make you some. Tell Alan I'll bring him some coffee." He pointed. "Right in there."

Alan stood up and dropped a magazine on the coffee table in front of the beat-up, fabric-covered couch when she came down the steps to the den.

"Hi." Hands in his pockets.

"Hello." Hands together in front.

He waved at the well-used easy chair next to the couch. "This okay?"

She glanced at the chair, then over at him, lowered her eyes and sat down.

He sat on the couch and leaned forward, elbows on his knees, hands clasped. "How are you?"

"Fine."

"Your nickel."

She scanned the ceiling. "I don't know how to do this, Alan."

He tapped his lips with his thumbs.

"I hope—I hope I didn't hurt you too much the other night," she said.

He leaned back. "I'll get over it."

"I know you can."

"I was tough on you, too," he said. "I'm sorry."

"I had it coming."

"No, you didn't. I gave you a hard time when you were hurting. I only thought of myself—my feelings and what I wanted. Not yours."

He studied the floor. She stared into the middle of the room.

The teakettle whistled. Ollie sneezed in the kitchen. Sara murmured, "Bless you." She paused for a second, then turned quickly toward Alan and blurted out, "I wish it hadn't ended up the way it did."

He kept his eyes on the floor. "Yeah, it's too bad."

She closed her eyes. He took a tissue from a box on the table next to the chair, knelt on one knee beside her and dabbed her cheeks. "Come on, kiddo. It wasn't your fault. Richard left you no choice. I know how you must feel."

"Do you?"

He stood up.

Oliver put two cups and saucers on the coffee table, said, "'Scuse me," and slipped out of the room. He stood inside the kitchen and watched them through the doorway.

Alan handed her the cup with a string holding a tag that sat on the saucer. "Your tea."

"Thanks." She pulled the tea bag out of the cup, set it on the saucer and drank. "Good."

He picked up the coffee cup. "How's everybody?"

"Not so good. Cal has heart problems. The doctors say they can't figure out what's wrong. I think it's giving out, but they won't say it. Mary Clare's scared, and Mom's worried about the house. He owns it." She turned her head, studying him. "Cass is in a funk. She's trying to break up with a man who won't go away."

"No kidding."

"From what she says, he's a pretty tough character. Used to getting his way." She gazed into Alan's eyes as if trying to see what he thought.

"What's his name?"

"Tony something. Italian."

He grimaced. "You think he's a mob man?"

"I'm scared to death he is. She's quit talking about it, but she's frightened."

He lowered his head. "God!"

"Trouble, aren't we?"

"You're not trouble. Your sisters don't have a lick of sense between them." He put his cup on the table. "There's only so much you can do. You're not a doctor and you're not a cop. You can help some, but take the advice you gave me. Don't get drawn in."

She stood, put her arms around his neck and raised her chin. "Thank you." She opened her lips.

He pulled her head to his chest and kissed her hair. "You'll be all right."

She looked up and smiled at him, her eyes shining. "Call me sometime. I'll call you back, I promise."

"Sure. I will."

Sara sighed, dropped her arms and stepped back. She lowered her eyes again. "Guess I better go."

"Okay."

They walked to the door. "Thank Ollie for the tea."

He helped her with the jacket. She studied his face. "See ya," she said.

"Good luck."

Ollie was standing in the living room, waiting. "So that's Sara. Cute. Why'd you let her go? I had the bed all made up upstairs. Clean sheets, soft music, low lights. Everything was ready for you."

"You bullshitter!" Alan shoved him backwards with both hands. "We had a spat the other night. She came to straighten things out, that's all. It's over between us."

Ollie laid a hand on Alan's shoulder. "Alan Cottrill, you are one smart fella—with numbers. Today, with that woman, you were blind, deaf, dumb *and stupid*!" He walked into the kitchen, waving his arms and shaking his head. "Jesus!"

———— ✺ ————

CASS CALLED ALAN AT work the following Wednesday. "I'm sure you're busy, my man, but we're having a time at the Top Hat on Friday. One of our senior partners is retiring. I have to be there, but I'll be bored to death. Could you come down for a little while and give us some company? You wouldn't have to stay long."

"I'd like to see you and Ellie again, but I can't get there till eight and I can't stay late. I have to go in to work early Saturday. Will that be okay?"

"That'll be fine. See you then."

———— ✺ ————

WHEN ALAN WENT INTO the Top Hat on Friday, Cass was standing just inside the door. She waited for him stamp the snow off his boots, then spread her arms and slapped his shoulders. "What's doin', my man?"

She took both of his hands, held them low and watched his face. "Sara's here."

"What?"

She kept her eyes on him.

"Sara?"

Cass nodded, let go of his left hand and pulled on his right. "Come on. The festivities have started."

He stayed put. "What's she doing here?"

"She's my sister." Cass pulled harder and he yielded. They threaded through the boisterous after-work crowd at the long bar and into a cluster of men and women in the rear that formed a circle around a gray-haired gentleman who was waving his drink around and saying, "And I remember well the time when I . . ."

Cass put her lips to Alan's ear. "You don't want to listen to Old Man Simpson, do you? He'll go on forever." She led him through the smoke to a table in shadow next to the wall where Ellie and Sara were sitting. "You remember this fella?"

Ellie stood and hugged him. "What's doin', Alan?"

Sara stood and put her arms around him. "Alan." He hesitated, then patted her back lightly with his fingertips. She held herself against him for an extra second, then they sat. Cass ordered a round of drinks. The band began to play "Whole Lotta Shakin' Goin' On." Its pianist pounded the keys, trying to be another Jerry Lee Lewis.

Their drinks came. Cass took a mouthful of her old-fashioned and stood up. "Come on, El, let's dance." The two of them joined the people twisting and swinging their arms on the dance floor.

Alan watched Cass's red hair bouncing above the other dancers, sipped his beer and tried to think of something to say to Sara. What was she doing here? He peered sideways at her. She was studying him.

A hand touched his arm. "Talk to me, Alan?"

He kept his eyes on the dancers. "What about?"

"Us."

"Didn't we already do that?"

"Couldn't we do it again?"

He did not look at her. "I don't know."

"You don't want to."

"I don't know what we have to talk about."

The band took a break. "We'll be back in ten minutes, folks. Don't go 'way." Alan scanned the couples leaving the floor, searching for Cass and Ellie. Where were they?

He heard Sara say, "I've changed since last time."

"Have you?" *Here comes "I'm not ready" again.* He stood. "I have to go."

She grabbed his hand. "Please, Alan." Her voice was quavering. "I'm begging you. Stay just a little longer and hear me out. Please."

"All right." He sat down and pulled his hand back into his lap. "A little longer."

"I'll be quick." She drew a breath. "Alan, I was in such a bad way after what happened with Richard I couldn't think straight. And I couldn't see what I was doing to you. You were being so good to me and I treated you terribly." She watched his face. "I'm not asking you to forgive me, I just want you to know I've realized what I did to you, and I'm sorry. That's why I came tonight."

She closed her eyes. "I did things with Richard I never should have done, and he treated me like a whore. It hurt me—like my father leaving years ago hurt me. They made me afraid of what would happen if I gave myself to another man. That's why I couldn't commit. Not because of you, but because of my fear."

That son of a bitch.

"I don't want that fear to ruin my life." She reached across the table and took his hands. "You said you wanted to take care of me, and I know you would. And I don't want you to be lonely." She squeezed. "We've both lost so much. Couldn't we do more for each other than someone who hasn't lost what we have?" She lowered her head between her arms. "Couldn't . . . we . . . start again, do you think?"

Alan looked at Sara with new eyes. She had been humiliated by the two men she'd loved, and it took a lot of courage for her to make herself vulnerable again—to lay herself out in front of him like this. The wall he'd built within himself to conceal his love for her evaporated as he gazed at her head between her arms.

He put his fingers under her chin and gently raised it. "There's nothing to forgive. You've been going through hell and I've been blind." He pulled her hands closer to him. "After you left on Sunday . . ."

"Yes?"

"Ollie told me I was stupid to let you go. He said he'd fixed a bed for us upstairs. I laughed at him."

She leaned across the table. "I would have done anything—"

Alan stood so suddenly he sent his chair to the floor and pulled her up. He put her hands behind his neck, his arms around her waist and kissed her. After a long minute, she drew her lips away, tightened her arms and put her cheek against his. "I thought I'd lost you."

He raised his head, his eyes closed. "I'd given up, Sara. Forgive me."

She held his head in her hands and gazed into his eyes, hers sparkling. "No more forgiveness talk, y' hear me?"

He nodded.

She patted his cheeks. "Another Bud? It's my turn." She caught the eye of a waiter, made a circle in the air with her hand and pointed to the table. He nodded and headed for the bar.

The band started to play "Let's Twist Again," and the dance floor began to fill up. Sara took his hand. "Come on, Alan-man, let's do the twist."

"I'm no dancer."

"It's not a dance. You stand on the balls of your feet and move everything else." She pulled, and he came behind her. She stopped at the edge of the dance floor, faced him, and began to twist her knees, hips, shoulders and arms in time with the music. "See?" He imitated her, barely twisting at first, but in a few minutes he was shooting his arms out and moving his hips side to side, more or less in time with the music.

The song ended and the band members clapped their hands in rhythm. When the crowd joined in, the leader called, "Come on, everybody, let's do the Locomotion!" and the band blasted out the tune.

"You can do this one, too," she said. "Watch." She slid her feet to one side and then the other while making vertical circles with her elbows and moving her fists and forearms back and forth like pistons.

She stood in front of him. "Here we go—slide to the left—slide to the right." He followed, watching her feet. "Now the arms—good—put some body into it!—left again—now go back—loosen up!" She leaned toward him, sliding and pumping. "Chugga-chugga, chugga-chugga—there, you've got it!" They did the Locomotion, sliding their feet, punching the air with their arms and gyrating around each other until the song ended. She stepped back and applauded. He bowed.

Cass came up behind her. "Who's this dancing fool?"

"A killer, isn't he?" Sara put an arm around him. "I bet he's ready for that beer."

"I sure am."

They went back to the table, dodging the incoming dancers. On the way, Alan saw Ellie walking toward the front door holding hands with a pudgy man in an open vest and loosened tie. Alan caught Cass's eye, and she tilted her head and shrugged. He wondered if that meant she didn't know the man or she didn't know where they were going—or whether Ellie would be coming home that night.

Alan plopped down next to Sara and downed half of his warm beer. "Aah."

Cass ruffled his hair as she went by him to sit down. "Glad you came?"

"You schemer." He put his arm around Sara's shoulders. She scooted her chair closer and leaned into him.

Cass pointed to his nearly empty glass. "Another one?"

"I better not. I have to go in to work tomorrow."

Cass stood up and kissed his forehead. "Time for me to go to the ladies'. See you around, my man."

Alan pulled Sara closer. "I wish I didn't have to go. I'll call you tomorrow."

She tapped his cheek. "You better."

He took her hand in both of his. "Good night, Sara O'Brien. Pleasant dreams."

She pulled his hands up and kissed them. "Good night, Country Boy."

16

Sara was putting on her down jacket and leaving the nurses' station on February seventh when the phone rang. The nurse's aide picked up the receiver. "Pediatric Surgery." She listened. "You just caught her." She held out the receiver. "Sara . . ."

She walked back to the station and took the receiver. "Hello."

"Sara, it's Ellie. Thank goodness, I caught you. Cass has been hurt."

"What happened?"

"I came in and found her on the floor. She's been beaten up."

Sara turned her back to the aide and spoke softly. "Is she breathing?"

"Yes, but she says it hurts."

"Bleeding?"

"I don't see anything," said Ellie.

"Pain?"

"Yes, lots."

"Where?"

"Oh, Sara, it's awful. He hit her. Her face is swelling up."

"Specifics, please," said Sara, keeping her voice calm and looking around the station and the corridor. "Where? I need to know."

"He hit her in the face and side."

"Are you sure she's not bleeding?"

"She's scared to death. She won't let me call emergency or the cops. You've got to help her."

"I'll be there right away." Sara glanced at the wall clock. 11:22 p.m. "Fifteen minutes."

She stuffed rolls of gauze pads and adhesive tape into her purse, then grabbed a stethoscope that was hanging on the wall, pushed it inside her jacket, and ran to the elevator.

Twelve minutes later, Sara stuck her key in the doorknob of Cass and Ellie's apartment, twisted it, put her shoulder to the door and pushed it open. Ellie was standing in the middle of the living room. She pointed to the hall that led to the bedroom. "In there."

"Did she say who it was?" asked Sara.

"Tony."

The bedroom was dark. Cass was in bed, sitting up against the headboard. Sara knelt beside her and took the bag of ice off her face. Dark red bruises extended across her eyes and down her nose and cheeks. Her eyes were swollen nearly shut. She was breathing, and whimpering every time she inhaled.

Sara got up and switched on the overhead light. "Can you see me?"

Cass tried to open her eyes. "Sort of."

"How many times did he hit you?"

"I don't know."

"Two, five, ten, twenty?" asked Sara.

"Ten, maybe," said Cass.

"Where?"

"My face." She touched it. "Stomach, side. It hurts so much!"

"Did you fall or hit anything?"

"He threw me against the wall and I fell on the floor."

Sara held a small light to the right of Cass's face. "Can you see the light?"

"No."

Sara moved the light slowly to the left side. "See this?"

"In the middle."

Sara shined the beam into her eyes. "Do you feel dizzy?"

"Not now. I did when I tried to get up."

"How'd you get in here?"

"Ellie."

Sara got out a tongue depressor. "Open." She peered into Cass's mouth, then put her handkerchief in front of it. "Cough . . . Spit." Cass did, with effort. Sara ran her thumb and forefinger along Cass's nose, then she reached for the stethoscope and pushed its ear tips into her ears. "Lean toward me." She pressed the diaphragm against the front and back of Cass's chest and listened. Cass slumped forward.

Ellie touched Sara on the shoulder. "How bad?" she mouthed.

Sara whispered, "I don't think she has a concussion. Her lungs seem to be all right, and I doubt her nose is broken. She probably has some broken or cracked ribs."

Cass moaned. Sara bent over her. "Cass, listen to me. You may have internal injuries. Bleeding. I can't tell about that. You *have* to go to a hospital."

Cass turned her head away. "No, no! They'll make me tell them what happened. He'll kill me if I tell anyone."

Sara straightened, walked to the window, leaned on the sill and looked down at the alley below. A lamp on the street corner sent long shadows into its dead end. If Cass did not want to go, there was nothing she could do about it. Sara shut her eyes and concentrated on maintaining her professional calm.

She turned to Ellie. "I'm going to wrap her ribs. You hold her up by the shoulders. It'll hurt, so hold on tight." Sara got rolls of adhesive tape out of her purse and wrapped white strands around Cass's rib cage, pulling hand over hand to make them tight. Cass twisted her body one way and then the other, trying to escape the pain. She kept whimpering, "No—please—stop!" When Sara finished, Cass said, "Oh God, Sara, I can't stand it. Can't you get me something?"

"I'll try. It may take a couple of hours though." Sara turned to Ellie. "Have you given her anything?"

"Three aspirin just before I called you."

"Don't give her any more till I get back. If I'm not back in four hours, give her two more, not three. Could you get her some water now?"

Ellie left the room.

Cass mumbled, "How am I?"

"Some of your ribs are damaged. That's what the tape is for. I'm going to the hospital to see if I can get you some strong pain medicine. It may take me a while. You rest. Try not to move around."

"You're my angel."

"I'm your nurse."

"Don't tell anyone," said Cass. "He'll kill me."

"I won't. I promise."

Ellie came back with a glass of water. She held it to Cass's lips.

"Keep putting the ice on her face," said Sara. "Fifteen minutes on, fifteen minutes off." She stuck the stethoscope back in her jacket and hurried out the door of the apartment.

Sara strode from the elevator toward the nurses' station fifteen minutes later. The aide asked, "Did you forget something?"

"No, no," said Sara. "Do you know where Dr. Altizer is?"

"He just went to see the new admission in 426 B."

Sara was standing across the dimly lit corridor from 426 B when Dr. Altizer came out of the room five minutes later.

"Dr. Altizer, may I have a few minutes?"

He glanced at his watch. "It has to be quick."

"My older sister has been beaten up by some thug, and she's too scared to go to the police. Her face is bruised and it hurts to breathe. Her lungs sound all right and there's no bleeding. She probably has some damaged ribs. I wrapped them." Sara held out her hand. "She's in a lot of pain, Doctor. She needs something stronger than I can get for her. Will you help me?"

"How old is she?" he asked.

"Twenty-seven."

"In good health?"

"Very good."

"Has this happened before? A beating?"

"No, Doctor. And I would know if it had."

"Do you know who it was?" he asked.

Sara did not want to answer questions about Cass's assailant. "No, I don't."

"You said it was a thug. Someone she knew?"

"Her roommate told me it was."

He ran the tip of his tongue along his upper lip and studied her.

"You know you can trust me," she said.

"What will happen next?"

"I don't know. It's her life."

"What do you think she should have?"

"Darvocet."

"I'll make the prescription out to you." He took a pad of white paper from his jacket, wrote on it and handed it to her. "You'll have to sign for it at the pharmacy."

"Thank you, Doctor." Her eyes filled with tears. "God bless you."

"Sara, you call me if you need me."

Sara bought a bottle of Adult Tylenol while she waited for the hospital pharmacy to fill the prescription. She signed for it and drove back to the apartment.

The two women were in the bedroom. Cass was moaning and Ellie was sitting on the bed, holding her hand and speaking softly. "Sara's here, Cass. She's back."

"Here's a painkiller for you," said Sara. "It'll help a lot, but you'll be groggy. The walls may move on you, but don't worry about it. Stick out your tongue."

Sara put two pills on Cass's tongue. Ellie took a glass of water from the nightstand and held it to her lips. "Drink some."

"Drink a lot," said Sara. "It'll help."

Cass drank, then sagged back.

"It won't take long," said Sara. "Then you can sleep."

"Thank you, little sister."

When Cass went to sleep, Sara and Ellie tiptoed into the living room. Ellie dropped onto the couch and Sara leaned against the wall. She folded her arms. "What'd she tell you?"

"It was this guy Tony she's been dating a long time. Biggi. He's the man she pushed out the night she came home and found you and me here. The night you saw Richard with what's-her-name."

"I don't remember him."

"She's been trying to get away from him, but he keeps coming back. I don't know how he got her to go out tonight, or if he did. I went out with some friends, and I thought she was going to stay in. When I got back a little before eleven, she was lying on the floor. I almost fainted—I thought it was the Mad Strangler. I was relieved when I saw her move."

Ellie ran her hands through her hair. "I helped her up, got her into bed and made an ice pack for her face. I asked her what happened and she said, 'Tony.' I picked up the phone to call an ambulance and she screamed at me, 'No, he'll kill me! Call Sara.' I tried your apartment and they said you were at work, so I called there and got you."

"What about this Tony?"

"I've only seen him a few times when he came here to get her. He's older, in his fifties, I'd guess. A tough guy. Possessive. You knew she was trying to break up with him."

"Damn her!" Sara stomped into the kitchen, shaking her fists. "My know-it-all sister! Sleeping around like a tramp and calling me to take care of her when she gets in trouble." She leaned back against the refrigerator and glared at Ellie.

"I warned her," said Ellie, "but she kept saying she knew how to handle all the men."

"Didn't she now? Alan throws her over and Tony beats the shit out of her. Next thing you know, she'll come home with something one of her beddy-boys has given her and she won't even know which one of them it was! She won't be able to stay home and sleep that off."

"She says she's careful."

"Careful? She's lying in there with her face smashed in and half a dozen broken ribs. That comes from being careful? Don't make me laugh."

Sara gripped the counter's edge and bent forward over it, her head down. "Sometimes all I want is to get out from under this disaster of a family I have—to go away and forget about it." She pulled her fingers down her face. "But I'm trapped. God, I hate it."

"I know it's hard on you, Sara, but what would Cass do if you weren't here to take care of her?" Ellie stood. "What are you going to do?"

Sara puffed. "What can I do? She's my sister."

"Shouldn't she see a doctor?"

"She should, but it's up to her."

"The police?" asked Ellie.

"She can report the attack if she wants to."

"Shouldn't she?"

"She should, but she's too frightened."

Sara handed Ellie a bottle of pills. "Here's the Darvocet. Give her two more when she wakes up, then two every four hours. The prescription's refillable, so I can get more if she needs it."

She handed Ellie the bottle of Tylenol. "She should stop taking the Darvocet as soon as she can stand the pain or it can be controlled with two of these. Don't give her both." She walked over to the couch where she had thrown her jacket. "Do you want me to stay?"

"I can take care of her," said Ellie, "but what about her work? How long will she be out?"

"It'll be a good two weeks before the bruises heal enough to be covered by makeup." Sara tapped her lips with a finger. "It's flu season. You could call in sick for her. Say she's contagious." She put on her jacket. "Watch her tonight. I think she'll be all right. If there's no bleeding or no more pain in the morning, she can be alone for a while. I'll stop by tomorrow afternoon on my way to work. About two. Call me if you need me before that."

Sara went into the bedroom and closed the door. Cass was sound asleep. Sara knelt beside her, touched her hair and murmured, "Dear God in Heaven, please lay your healing hands on my beloved sister in her time of suffering." She bowed her head. "Amen."

She went back into the living room, said good night to Ellie and went out to her car.

As Sara sank into the driver's seat, an intense wave of sadness flowed through her. *Oh, Cassidy, why do you do this?* She raised her head and tears poured down her face.

She jumped when something struck the window beside her. A policeman's nightstick. His badge and face gleamed in the lamplight. "Are you all right, miss?"

She nodded. "Yes."

"It's not good for a girl to be out at night these days. And lock the doors when you get home."

"I will," she said, and turned the ignition key.

Sara lay in bed that night watching the lights and shadows moving across her bedroom ceiling and thinking about her sister. Cass had always been able to have men on her terms—to hold them as long as she wanted and charm or bully her way out when it suited her—so she did not know what to do when Alan broke up with her and Tony would not go away. What would she do from now on?

—⟨ఠ⟩—

SARA WENT TO THE door of Cass's apartment at one the next afternoon and saw that the locks had been changed. She put her key back in her purse and rang the bell.

"Who is it?" A tremulous voice.

"It's Sara, Cass. Open the door."

Two deadbolts snapped. The doorknob turned. The door opened a crack and Cass's eyes, green and red and surrounded by black and purple, peered out over a heavy metal chain. "Oh." The chain clattered against the frame and the door opened. "Come in. We had new locks put on this morning."

Cass wrapped her arms around Sara. "My angel." She lowered herself slowly onto the couch. "We're going to move."

Sara threw her jacket over a chair and knelt beside Cass. "Un-huh. How do you feel today?"

"Dizzy. What is that stuff?"

"Darvocet. Good for pain, but narcotic. Stretch out the time between pills and switch to the Tylenol as soon as you can."

"I will," said Cass. "I don't like the feeling."

"Have you had lunch?"

"Ellie made me some soup. You want anything?"

"I'll get something at the cafeteria." Sara sat in the easy chair. "Now tell me what happened."

Cass pressed her fingers against her cheeks. "You know I've been trying to get away from Tony. Well, last night he rang the bell about nine and shoved his way in when I opened the door. He wanted to take me to the bedroom but I wouldn't go, and he got mad. I was scared, but I stood my ground. I told him it was time for each of us to move on, and I hoped he would understand."

"He said, 'That's it, then?' I said yes, and he started to turn away. I thought he was going to leave."

She put her hands on her belly and winced. "Then he hit me in the stomach." She doubled over. "I have never been hit like that. I went down and lay there, gagging. I couldn't breathe." She looked up, twisting her face, already painful for Sara to look at, in agony and fear. "He picked me up, threw me against the wall and started slapping me. He grabbed my neck and said, 'You think it's over? Listen, bitch. It's over when *I* say it's over.' I thought he was going to strangle me. He said, 'Now I say it's over,' and let me fall. I curled up like a ball.

"He pulled my arm out of the way and kicked me in the side." She gasped. "He said, 'Be damn glad you don't owe us money, like your old man did.' I was in awful pain, but I'm sure that's what he said. I can still see his face. *Then* he said, 'You better keep your mouth shut. You tell anyone, you'll sleep with ol' Paddy in the harbor.' He kicked me again and left."

Cass dropped her face into her hands. "It hurt *so much*. I was too dizzy to get up. Thank God, Ellie didn't stay out late. I don't know what I would have done without her—or you." Her head and hands collapsed to her knees.

A wave of nausea rose from Sara's bowels to the top of her throat. The color left her face. She sprinted into the kitchen, lunged at the sink and threw up. She raised her head, sucked in air through her mouth, bent again and retched. She turned on the water and stared at the slick brown mess in the sink as it slid down the drain.

She straightened and wiped her mouth. "We knew, didn't we? He had to be gone. But to hear this . . ." She sagged.

"I know he did it to hurt me."

"Poor Dad." Sara swallowed. "It must have been awful."

"He paid an awful price, but he did terrible things to me. I hope God forgave him, I can't."

The two daughters of Padraig O'Brien held each other and wept.

Sara broke the embrace. She wiped her eyes and blew her nose. "You're going to move?"

"I've got to get out of here. Every time the doorbell rings, I'll see Tony standing there and I'll faint." She put a hand on the back of the couch. "Ellie doesn't want to stay here, either."

Sara touched Cass's bruises, examining them. "You're going to be all right." She swept Cass's hair away from her face. "I have to go. Keep eating and putting ice on your face. Drink lots of water and take the pills when you need them. Cough as much as you can. It hurts, but it clears your lungs. And watch your stools. If they're black, call me right away." She took a step back. "I'll call you tomorrow."

"Yes, Mother."

Sara rolled her eyes as she pulled her jacket off the couch. "Do something for me." She stuck her arms in the sleeves and yanked the zipper up. "Think about what we should say to Mom."

Sara stopped in the hallway outside the apartment and examined Cass's door. Changing apartments would be the same as changing locks. If Tony wanted her, he'd track her down and kick the door in.

17

Alan's phone rang when he was at work on Saturday morning, "Cottrill speaking."

"Alan, it's Sara." Her voice was tight.

"Hi, there." He paused. "Are you all right?"

"I need to talk to you. Can I come over tomorrow?"

"Any time after noon. Chad and Bud are out of town, but Ollie may be around." He waited for her to say something. When she did not, he said, "What is it, babe?"

"I'll tell you tomorrow." She hung up.

Alan put the receiver down and wondered what was wrong. Sara had never been that curt with him before. He took off his glasses and rubbed his eyes, then went back to trying to ascertain why the client's receivables had shot up in the last six months. Something was wrong there, too.

SARA WALKED INTO THE vestibule and threw her coat over the hall tree at two the next afternoon. "Hello? Anybody home?" Alan hurried out of the kitchen with his arms open. She fell into them and wrapped her arms around him. "Oh, Alan." He rocked her from side to side and she put her head against his chest. "Make me some tea."

They walked up the steps and into the kitchen, an arm around each other. He took the teakettle from the counter with his free hand, filled it, put it over a burner and turned on the gas. The flame popped on. Still holding her with one arm, he opened a cabinet door, took two teabags from a saucer and put them in mugs sitting on the counter.

He lifted her off her feet, sat her on the opposite counter, pushed his body between her legs and kissed her. She put her arms around his neck. "What are you trying to do?"

"You don't know?" He kissed her again. She patted his back.

The teakettle whistled. She pushed him away and jumped down. "The water's ready."

"Darn." He filled the mugs and handed one to her. "What's happened, babe?"

"Remember the man I told you about? The one Cass was afraid of?"

"The one who wouldn't go away?"

"He beat her up on Thursday."

He stared at her. "Oh, God, no! How bad?"

"He bruised her face and probably cracked some ribs."

"Ah! That's terrible. Did she go to the police?"

"He threatened to kill her if she did."

"Poor Cass." He walked back and forth, hammering the counter with his fist. "Poor Cass. What can she do? Jesus Christ!"

"I think he's through with her. At least he said he was."

"Is she in the hospital?"

"She wouldn't call them, either. She's home. Ellie and I are taking care of her."

"Damn it! Isn't there anything anybody can do? Who runs this town?"

"It's up to her. She doesn't want to do anything and doesn't want anyone to know. You mustn't tell a soul, not even Ollie."

"Yeah. Ollie would tell the world." He picked up his mug. "How bad is it?"

"Pretty bad. Her face is swollen and she's in a lot of pain."

"Anything I can do?"

"Stay away and be quiet about it."

"Poor Cass." They walked slowly into the den, carrying their mugs. "You were afraid he was a mob man." He put his mug on the coffee table. "How long has she been seeing him?"

"A couple of years."

"Why does she do things like that?" Alan threw himself onto the couch. "Y'know, I never understood that woman. I could never figure out what was going on inside. Close as we were, she was always hiding something." He peered at Sara. "Why's that?"

"She won't be dependent on any man. She's been hurt too much."

"By me?"

"Not so much you. Dad."

"Oh? How old was she when he left?"

"Twelve. But he had already hurt her."

He squinted. "What d'you mean?"

She waited, her face darkening.

"You mean he—"

"When she was eleven."

"How d'you know?"

"I saw them one night when I was eight. I didn't know what I was seeing. When I asked her about it, she shrieked and ran away."

"Mary Clare?"

"She doesn't talk."

He bent his neck as far back as it would go. "God in heaven."

"And then Cal."

Alan pulled his head upright. "She told me. I didn't know you knew."

"It was when she was taking courses at Fisher. He loaned her the tuition money."

"He started it, didn't he?"

"Yes!" She glared at him. "Why do you ask, for God's sake?"

"He told me she did."

Sara shook her head. "What a bastard. Poor Mary Clare."

"Does she know?"

"I'll bet."

They sat on the couch and drank their tea in silence.

He pulled her toward him. She sat her mug on the coffee table, put her head on his shoulder and patted his chest. He brushed a strand of hair from her face. She twisted around and lay against him, looking up, and he cradled her body on his arm. She put her hand behind his head, said, "Come here," and pulled him down to her. He lay down beside her and she ran her hands up his back and gripped his shoulders. They kissed, pressing their bodies against each other.

The furnace came on. Radiators cracked as the hot water flowed into them.

Wind rattled the front windows.

His hands moved up her body and covered her breasts. "Yes?"

She took hold of his wrists, raised them and kissed his hands. "No, Alan."

He kissed her some more, then he sat up and smoothed her hair.

"Am I a mess?" she said.

He went to his knees beside the couch. "You're lovely, and you're very sexy."

"Flatterer."

He picked up two rectangular cards from the end table and tapped her head with them. "What are you doing Saturday night? I have two tickets to the Peter, Paul and Mary concert at the Donnelly."

She sat up beside him. "How'd you get them?"

"The firm got them for a contribution to the United Way. None of the partners or clients wanted them. Good seats, too. Second row of the balcony."

"Peter, Paul and Mary! Oh, I love them!" She put her arms around his neck and kissed him. "Thank you."

"You can do better than that."

She clamped his head in her hands and kissed him again, her wet lips over his. "Better?"

"Much."

She pushed herself off the couch and on to her feet. "That'll have to do for now. Mom's making dinner for us." She pulled her fingers down her cheeks. "The O'Brien girls are going to have a heart-to-heart with her tonight, and I'm dreading it."

They walked to the vestibule and Sara put on her coat. "What time Saturday?"

"The concert's at eight. I'll pick you up at six and we can grab a bite before."

"Terrific." She took his rumpled shirt in her hand, pulled him to her and kissed him on the lips.

She smoothed the front of his shirt. "Don't push me, Alan, please. I couldn't stand it."

—————

When Alan drove up to Sara's apartment building on Saturday, she was waiting at the curb.

As she got in, she asked, "Where are we going?"

"There's a restaurant across Mass Ave from the theater. I think it's okay, and we might get a parking spot on the street if we're early. The show's sold out."

Sara was quiet, into herself, as Alan maneuvered through the Back Bay to the theater. As he backed into a parking spot, he said, "You all right?" She did not respond.

He parked parallel to the curb, set the brake and pulled her to him. "What is it, babe? You were going to have dinner with your mother."

"Do we have to talk about that now?"

He kissed her forehead. "Get it off your chest. Then we'll go eat, and then we'll enjoy the show."

"The man who beat up Cass"—she shuddered—"I can hardly say it . . . told her that Dad owed them money—"

"Cass told me that. Loan sharks."

"—and they killed him." She stared out the windshield. "We'd convinced ourselves that the Diocese had called them off or something, but we were dreaming. He owed money to the mob and they found him and killed him. Fifteen years ago. I think, underneath, we all knew something had happened to him. But to hear it like Cass did, right out of that mobster's mouth, hurt her as much as the punches."

She put her clasped hands over Alan's shoulder, rested her forehead on them and spoke softly. "What a monster he must be—to *fuck* the daughter of a man he'd murdered."

She brushed back his forelock. "We told Mom Sunday night. We didn't tell her what happened, just that we'd found out he died a long time ago." She struggled to breathe. "Alan, she was crushed. She'd kept believing he was out there somewhere and she'd see him again. She didn't want to believe us. Just sat there shaking her head. Pale as a ghost."

Sara wiped her eyes. "She didn't say anything. She didn't cry, just stared at us like she didn't know us. Like she was in a trance, like we weren't there—or she didn't want us to be there—or something. After dinner, Mary Clare and I sat with her while Cass cleaned up. She broke two dishes. I think she threw them."

Sara pushed out a stream of air. "Cass stayed over. She was still wearing sunglasses, but Mom didn't say anything."

"Mary Clare?"

"We told her before."

"Cal?"

"He took the kids to the movies. Mary Clare was going to tell him after they went to bed. They'll have to tell the kids something, Mom talked to them about their grandpa." She gripped his arm. "I feel so bad, dumping my family *shit* on you every time we're together. Why do you put up with it?"

"I love you." He smiled. "See, I told you I was loyal."

"Loyal to a fault, you said."

"That's me." Lightly.

"You're wonderful." She wrapped her arms around his neck. "And I'm starving."

A few flakes of snow were in the air when Alan and Sara crossed the street and got into his car after the performance. He started it and they waited for the heat.

"Wow! What a show!" he said. "They had the whole place singing with them."

"They sang everything," she said. 'Five Hundred Miles,' 'If I Had a Hammer,' everything. No one could sit still."

He pulled into the traffic lane. "Tonight, I'm in love with Mary Travers."

"You're a fickle man, Alan Cottrill."

"Didn't I tell you?"

As they drove home, Alan watched Sara out of the corner of his eye. Her face was glowing, and he was suddenly determined to keep her from thinking about her family.

"How long have you wanted to be a nurse?" he asked.

"When I was a little girl I used to hold my dolls and coo over them, telling them I would make them feel better. Then I'd wrap them in Band-Aids and slings, and ask, 'Feel better now?' They always did."

"You love taking care of children."

"There's something wonderful about them. So open and trusting and full of hope, even when they're sick or in pain. They count on me to take care of them, and I always do."

She watched a couple on the sidewalk holding the hands of a little girl skipping between them. The child raised her feet and kicked out, and they swung her back and forth.

"The happiest time is the newborns," she said. "When I bring a new baby into the waiting room and call a dad's name. They start toward me quickly, then slow down when they get near and see their child for the first time. They just glow. They reach out and touch her hair or stroke a cheek with a finger and look at the baby with such love. They stand there, looking down and smiling. Then they say, 'The mother, how is she?' or 'How's my wife?' and I say, 'She's tired and resting,' and they ask again, 'Is she all right?' I say she is, and they stand there, beaming. It's wonderful every time.

"Not all of it's good," she said. "You lose some, and that's sad. So hard on everybody. After a shift where that's happened, I go home and cry myself to sleep. And some of them are born with such defects that they're not going to live long—maybe a few hours, maybe a few years—and nothing can be done about it. They're doomed. I won't stay in the room while the doctor tells them. Doctors are gentle, but they have to be realistic and say there's no hope.

"Sometimes when I come into the room after that, the parents are holding each other and the baby and telling the little one they'll do every-thing they can for her, to give her as much of a life as they can for as long as she's with them. Such wonderful people. Sometimes it's, 'Why has He done this to us?' but other times it's, 'This is God's will and we must do all we can.' I know God is smiling down on them."

The moisture in Alan's eyes blurred the lights going by them.

"I make a difference in those lives," she said. "It's not easy, but that's not important. I can always help people—make things better for them—and that's what I do."

"No wonder I love you."

18

Sara had just finished dressing when Wendy Creighton came to the bedroom doorway and leaned against its frame. Wendy was wiping the sweat from her arms with a gray towel.

"Callie!" Wendy kicked off her running shoes. "Come see Sara."

Callie Hall, a fleshy woman in a bra and panties, stuck her head around the corner. She had a brown bath towel wrapped around her hair. She whistled softly. "Oh, honey. Sex-ee."

Sara smiled at her suitemates. "You think so?" She opened her arms and spun around.

"Black dress and pearls," said Wendy, "and you've got the figure for it."

"The poor man," said Callie. "He doesn't have a chance. He'll give you anything you want."

"Where's he taking you?" asked Wendy.

"Locke-Ober's."

Callie's face disappeared as she scrubbed her head with the towel. Her voice came through it. "Will you give him what he wants?"

Sara rolled her hips. "You never know."

"Give us a dollar and we'll go to the movies," said Wendy.

The intercom buzzed.

"That's him," said Sara. She strutted out the door.

In the vestibule, Sara held out her hands and Alan pulled them around his waist.

"You are absolutely stunning," he said. "Do you know what you do to me?"

She stood on tiptoe to kiss him on the cheek. "Who, me?"

He held the door open. Outside, Sara faced a black Lincoln limousine whose length was accentuated by the glowing sidelights above its windows. The driver, in a black suit, bow tie and billed cap, opened the rear door. "Good evening, Miss O'Brien. My, you are lovely tonight."

"Thank you." Sara's eyes scanned the length of the limousine. To Alan: "Where's your car?"

"In the trunk."

The driver swept his arm toward the open door. "Please." He touched Sara's elbow as she sank into the velour seat. "Comfortable?"

"Yes, thank you." She caressed the plush fabric. Her face and hair gleamed from the soft interior lights.

Alan got in on the other side. Two flutes of champagne sat in the console in front of them. The wine barely quivered as the limousine started to move.

Alan reached for the glasses and handed one to Sara. "The best to you."

"And to you." Glasses clinked. They sipped. Sara leaned back and watched the city lights streaming by. "This is wonderful!"

Fifteen minutes later, they walked under the shield-shaped Locke-Ober sign on Winter Place and into the dim light of Boston's finest restaurant. Sara looked around at the Bohemian crystal chandeliers and wall sconces whose light was swallowed by the walnut-paneled walls. Tall chairs surrounded the tables covered with white cloth and set with candles that made the crystal glasses sparkle. Tuxedo-clad waiters stood with their backs to the walls, overseeing the seated customers and eyeing the incoming ones.

The *maître d'* bowed. "Ah, yes, Mr. Cottrill, and Miss O'Brien. Welcome to Locke-Ober's. William will escort you." He handed two brown folders to the headwaiter, who said, "This way, please."

Sara pulled Alan close beside her. "How'd he know your name?"

"I'm famous."

She squeezed his arm. "Baloney."

"It's our favorite restaurant. We entertain clients here and we always get what we want."

"And what do you want tonight?"

"For you to have a good time."

They followed William up a flight of stairs and down a paneled hall to a waiter standing at attention next to a closed door. "Here you are," said William. "Henry will be serving you this evening." Henry opened the door inward.

Sara walked gingerly into a small room where a table was set for two. Pictures of castles overlooking the Rhine decorated two of the cream-colored walls. A bottle of champagne sat in an ice bucket.

They sat down. Sara said, "Just us?"

Henry lit the candles, popped the cork, poured the champagne and retreated. He closed the door.

Alan raised his glass. "Who else?"

Sara held the glass as though her arm were frozen. She pointed to the closed door. "How will he know?"

"He'll know. Cheers." They drank. Alan refilled their glasses and they drank some more.

Sara blinked. "Champagne makes me dizzy."

"Then let's order." Henry came in, handed them menus and gave Alan the wine list.

"There's a button under there somewhere," she said.

"Mental telepathy."

Sara looked up at Henry. "Should I trust this man?"

"Absolutely, miss. Untrustworthy men are not allowed at Locke-Ober's."

"Well, that's a relief." She opened her menu. There were pages of items—appetizers, soups, salads, entrees—but no prices.

"Our special tonight is Duck à l'Orange, miss. It's rubbed with thyme and marjoram, cooked in a sauce of white wine and fresh orange juice, and served on a bed of brown rice. It's excellent. It comes with one vegetable."

"How much is it?"

"That's for the gentleman, miss."

She grinned at Alan. "I'll have it. And broccoli, please."

"An appetizer, perhaps?"

"Shrimp cocktail."

"Very good, miss. And for you, sir?"

"I'd like the escargot, Henry. Then the Lobster Savanna, a dinner salad and red potatoes."

"Very good, Mr. Cottrill. May I help you with the wine?"

Alan ran his finger down a page of the wine list. "We want a Cotes du Rhône. Do you have a Chateauneuf-du-Pape made from Grenache?"

"An excellent choice," said Henry. "May I suggest the Domaine de Vieux Telegraphe? It's from the La Crau plateau of the southern Rhone. The climate there is ideal for Grenache. A good pairing for Duck à l'Orange."

"Vintage?"

"The fifty-nine has just been released. It's a good vintage. We also have the fifty-three and fifty-five, but . . ." Henry raised his eyes to the ceiling.

"The fifty-nine will do nicely," said Alan. "Thank you."

Ninety minutes later, Sara was soaking up the orange sauce from her empty plate with a piece of bread and Alan was sipping from a snifter of Drambuie. The wine bottle was gone. Henry took their plates from the room and closed the door behind him.

She touched her lips with a napkin. "I've never had a meal like this. The duck, the wine, the service. Thank you."

"You're welcome. It's so good to be here with you."

"As messed up as I am?"

"You're not messed up. Your sisters are. But they're here, and you love each other."

"You don't have that, do you?"

"Not anymore. But I have my memories. Mom and Dad and Connie will always be with me. For now, though, I'm on my own. What happens to me is up to me."

"What do you want to happen to you?"

"I want my own business before too long." He raised his head to drink the last of the Drambuie and put the glass on the table. "I want to have some fun, too. Do some traveling. Since the Army won't take me because of my eyes, I'll have to go with someone else. Any ideas?"

She lowered her head and smiled at him. "I'll try to think of someone."

"What do you want for yourself? Will you always be a nurse?"

"I'll always be a nurse, and I'll work as one till something more important comes along."

"Like . . . ?"

Her face softened. "Children."

"Ah. A houseful?"

"A handful."

He took a deep breath. "I'm so clumsy at this, Sara. I am so much in love with you that I can't think straight when I try to tell you, and the right words don't come out. But I love you with all my heart and I need you in my life if I'm to amount to anything."

"That's not clumsy, Alan."

"There's an emptiness in me, a need. Do you know what it is?"

"Tell me."

"I need to make you happy. You take care of your family and your patients, but you need someone to take care of you." He took her hand. "I'll never be rich or famous, but I'll care for you and I'll be faithful to you for as long as I live, if you'll let me."

He reached into his jacket pocket, took out a small black box and held it over the table. "I need someone who will care for our children, too. And I want it to be you." He opened the hinged box toward her. A diamond flashed in her eyes. She took the ring and rolled it between her fingers and thumb, studying the colors deep inside the diamond.

He knelt beside her. "I love you, Sara O'Brien. Will you marry me?"

"Oh, Alan, I love you so much. Yes. I will marry you, and I will love you forever." She took his hand and they stood up. She held the ring out for him to take and raised the third finger of her left hand so he could slip it on.

He hugged her so hard that he pressed the breath out of her. "You've made me so happy."

The door to the room opened just enough for Henry's head to appear, then it closed.

"Let's do it soon," he said.

She put her hands on his chest and eyed his face. "You mean get married."

He tapped her nose. "That first, then . . . you know . . . right after."

Henry appeared, grinning like the Cheshire Cat. "I see you've had a wonderful evening, miss. May I be the first to congratulate you?" He took Sara's left hand in his and kissed her ring.

19

WEST VIRGINIA

The rains had been heavy in the summer of 1975 so the East Fork River, which was usually the pale color of spent dishwater and smelled like rotten eggs in August, was galloping through Gaines Memorial Park, splashing around the rocks and sparkling in the sun on its way to the Ohio. Graduates of the 1955 class of Washington-Jefferson High School and their families had gathered here to see each other again and celebrate the passage of twenty years since their graduation.

The park was on two levels. The upper one sloped down from the woods to the road that divided the park. It had the picnic facilities—a roofed pavilion, open metal charcoal grills on pipe stands and brick fire pits with chimneys behind them, picnic benches, a paved basketball court and a sand-filled volleyball court. The grass-covered lower level went from the road down to the river.

White-jacketed caterers were covering the long serving tables in the pavilion with white tablecloths and filling them with containers of food and drink carried from gold and blue panel trucks. Boys and young men were running and twisting on the basketball court, calling to their

teammates—"Here!"—passing the ball and jumping to shoot and re-
bound. West Virginia was a basketball state, so they knew what to do
with the ball when they got it.

Women and teenage girls were playing volleyball. They shouted and
laughed when the ball fell into the sand or went into the net. They lost
track of the score and laughed about that, too.

Younger children ran around on the lower level playing tag and Frisbee. Two of them were trying to get a kite in the air, but there wasn't
enough wind and it settled, tail first, to the ground when the boy pulling
it got tired or ran out of space. On one try, when the kite fluttered to the
ground again, a toddler in blue shorts and a white shirt ran to the tail,
squatted, and reached for it.

The kite flyer yelled at him. "No, no. You'll break it!" The little boy
stuck out his lower lip and started to wail.

Sara, in white Capri pants and a maroon Boston College T-shirt,
knelt beside him.

"It's all right, little man," she said. "You wouldn't hurt it, would
you?" The boy dropped his jaw and filled the air with a scream. A man
came from behind her and scooped him up. The boy put an arm around
his father's neck and scowled at Sara as if she were the Wicked Witch of
the West.

His father lifted him in the air. "Now, Mikey, the nice lady was trying to help you." He put the boy on his shoulders. "See? She likes you."
He lowered the toddler to the ground and held out his hand. "I'm Thomas Colombo, and this is Mikey."

"Sara Cottrill." She shook his hand. "He's so cute. How old is he?"

"Twenty-six months," said Thomas, "and spoiled rotten by three
fathers and one mother. His brothers are over there playing Frisbee."

"Are you a graduate?"

"My wife is. I take it you're not, either."

"My husband." Sara pointed to the cluster of people around the beer
keg. "He's over there, talking to his old pals. He'll bring me one sooner or

later." She squatted and smiled at Mikey, who wrapped an arm around his father's leg, put a finger in his mouth, and studied her.

She raised her eyes to Thomas. "Where're you from?"

"San Diego. I'm in the Navy. Is this your husband?" Alan, in a blue and gold West Virginia University T-shirt and carrying two paper cups topped with foam, was stepping carefully through the grass toward them.

"Here he is, the beer man," she said. "Alan, this is Thomas—I'm sorry . . ."

"Colombo. Thomas Colombo. And this is Mikey." Thomas eyed Alan up and down as though trying to take his measure for a competition or recall someone he might resemble. Alan handed a cup to Sara and shook Thomas's hand.

A pair of hands clamped over Alan's eyes. A woman laughed—a low-pitched, rolling laugh. "Guess who." She pulled on his head and laughed again.

"Gina Lollobrigida."

"No, silly."

"Mara!"

She grabbed his shoulders and shook him. "How'd you know?"

He spun around. "I'd know that laugh anywhere."

Sara studied Mara, a petite woman with dark hair and eyes, and wondered if she was the girl Alan had loved in high school. From the way they smiled at each other, it was clear that they had been more than acquaintances. She watched Thomas out of the corner of her eye. He was tossing a sponge ball to Mikey, paying no attention to his wife and Alan.

Mara said, "You've met Tommy." She pulled on her husband's sleeve. "Where are the boys?"

"Over there, by the river, playing Frisbee," he said. "See? TJ just threw it, and Dino is chasing it down." He watched, leaning forward. "There, he got it. Good catch, Dino!" The boy waved the Frisbee and threw it back at the cluster of boys and girls who raised their hands and jostled each other to get to it. It went over their heads.

Thomas said, "The kid's got an arm."

Sara stepped behind Alan and jabbed him in the ribs. "Mara," he said," this is my wife, Sara. We live in Boston."

"They live in San Diego," said Sara. "Thomas is in the Navy."

"He's the ship's fire control officer," said Mara.

"For when it burns?"

"For when it shoots."

"That must be exciting," said Sara.

"Well," said Thomas, "mostly we practice."

TJ and Dino came running up the hill, their dark hair tousled and their shirttails flapping behind them. "Can we eat now? Everyone else is." TJ, the eldest boy, grabbed his father's hand. "Come on."

The seven of them walked up the hill toward the tables of food in the pavilion, the two boys in front. Mikey was straddling his father's neck and holding onto his forehead. They joined the end of the line strung out from the food tables. The boys growled and pushed each other around until Mara said, "Behave, you two." They rolled their eyes at each other, stood with their backs touching and stepped sideways with the line as it advanced.

At the food table, the boys went first, down the right side. Thomas stepped aside, motioned for Sara to follow them, and fell in behind her. Mara and Alan went to the left. They all picked up paper plates and started to fill them, taking biscuits and salads, then vegetables, then meats. The boys piled biscuits, ham and beef on their plates, and Mara made them go back down the line and take some vegetables.

The line on the right side of the table moved more quickly, taking Sara and Thomas ahead of Mara and Alan. Halfway down the table, Mara reached for dinner rolls with her left hand and faced Alan. "Sara is so pretty," she said, "and she's crazy about you." She put a roll on her plate. "Tommy is wonderful—so good to me." She stood still. "And Alan . . ."

"Hmm?" He was studying the desserts.

She touched his arm. Her dark eyes captured his. "He knows

everything. No secrets."

"That's good," he said. "What do you know about—?"

"Nothing. I had to sign away the rights to my child before there could be an adoption. I pray to the Blessed Mother, 'Protect my baby,' every day." She sighed. "Maybe someday my little one, all grown up now, will come to me."

Alan put his hand on her shoulder. "I wish I could do something."

"Mom-ee!" Mikey was on his father's shoulders with his arms out, pulling the air toward him with his fingers.

Mara waved. "I'm coming, buddy." She said goodbye and hurried across the grass to her family.

Sara, who was waiting for Alan, noticed this exchange and did not like what she saw. What were they talking about so furtively? What did she not know about Mara and Alan?

There were no tables with space for seven, and a tall woman standing by a distant table waved and called, "Hey, Alan. There's room for you here." Alan held up two fingers.

"Come on," she said. "There's room."

He caught Sara's eye and pointed to the standing woman. They came at the table from different directions and Alan got there first. The woman hugged him, then pushed back and eyed him up and down. "You've not changed at all. How do you stay so slim?"

Sara thought the woman looked good herself—in tight jeans, a *LaSalle Bank Chicago Marathon 1973* T-shirt and running shoes. She put her arm around Alan's shoulders as he pointed to Sara.

"Barbara Hamilton," he said, "this is my wife, Sara. Sara, meet my best friend from high school." He stopped. "Is it still Barbara Hamilton?"

"It's Barbara Evans."

"Will?"

She nodded.

Alan scanned the crowd. "Is he here?"

"On his way back from 'Nam, and out of the Army after twenty years, thanks be to God. He'll be home for good in a month. The kids can't wait."

"How many kids?" asked Alan.

"Two. William is eleven and little Loie is nine. They've been with my mother in Charleston for two weeks. They'll be spoiled to death."

Barbara sat between Sara and Alan on the bench of the picnic table and put an arm around each of them. "So, you two, tell me about yourselves. Where'd you meet, when were you married, how many kids? Give me the details."

"We met in Boston," said Sara, "at a soup kitchen one rainy night. Alan had an umbrella and walked me to the bus stop. He's been covering me ever since. We were married in sixty-three."

"So were we," said Barbara. "And what do you do, Alan?"

"I have an accounting services business," he said, "and Sara's a supervising nurse at Boston Children's Hospital."

"I have my own business, too," said Barbara. "I'm an interior decorator for the 'richies' in Chicago. And there are a lot of them."

"Lucky, aren't we," said Alan, "to be out of this town."

A man on the basketball court called, "Hey, Cottrill, we need one more. Come help us out."

Sara nodded to him. "Go ahead."

"I'll take care of her," said Barbara. As Alan trotted away, she said, "Quite a guy. He's had it tough, though."

"What was he like in high school?"

"Quiet. A pretty good student and a real straight arrow." Barbara leaned on the table and studied Sara. "A lot of us, me included, had a crush on him at one time or another, but Mara Sabatelli had him all wrapped up."

Sara dipped her head toward Mara Colombo, who was chasing Mikey around their table. He was running stiff-legged away from her, and he shrieked with delight when she caught him and threw him in the air. "Whee!"

"Her?" asked Sara.

"She was something," said Barbara. "And look at her. After three kids she still is."

"What happened?"

"With Alan and Mara? Her family moved away in the middle of our senior year. Old Carmine Sabatelli was one hard-ass Catholic, and I wonder if he didn't move just to get her away from Alan."

"Really?"

"For sure," said Barbara. "Catholics here think they're the only ones going to heaven, and they don't want to take anyone else with them."

Sara thought about Alan and Mara talking softly to each other in the food line. What were they saying? She looked into the trees on the hill above the park. "What'd he do then?"

"He tried to track her down, but he couldn't." Barbara raised her cup and drank. "He was pretty broken up."

"Did he ever see her again?"

"They saw each other at the five-year reunion in 'sixty. She told some of us then she could never marry a Methodist. Since then, I don't know." Barbara peered sideways at Sara. "Why?"

"I just wondered," said Sara. "You had a crush on him?"

"I got over it. We got to be good friends when I was going with Will and he was going with Mara. We had some classes together and were in the choir and some plays, so I got to know him pretty well. Then he went to West Virginia and I went to Marshall because my mother had moved to Charleston, and we lost touch. I worked summers at Torch Lake in Michigan and didn't see him again till the reunion in 'sixty."

Barbara stopped. "Am I boring you? Do you know all this?"

"No, I don't." Sara put on her most charming smile. "I like hearing about him."

Barbara licked her lips. "He'd changed by then. His father had passed away when he was in high school and Mara had gone away his senior year. Then his sister was killed in that awful wreck."

"What happened?"

"A coal truck ran them off the road one night when they were coming home from a drive-in. Connie was in the passenger seat."

"Alan was driving," said Sara.

"There wasn't anything he could do. The truck was in the middle of the road on that curve."

Sara watched Alan pass the ball to a teammate. "He doesn't talk about it."

"He wouldn't talk to me about it, either. He tried to hide how much he was hurting by being the wisecracker. I could see what he was doing, but I couldn't get him to open up and talk to me. It made me sad."

The basketball game had slowed down. Several of the players were bending over, holding on to their knees and gasping. Barbara said, "Looks like it's about over. Let's go watch."

As they rose, she said, "Alan's a lucky guy, Sara. He needed someone to take care of him and I'm glad he has you."

They walked to the court and watched the game for a few minutes, until the player Alan was guarding hit a jump shot that won the game. The other side jumped up and down in celebration while Alan covered his head and his teammates pummeled him with their caps in mock anger. All of them headed for the keg, laughing and pushing each other around.

"Will you be here for the dinner tonight?" asked Barbara.

"I'm afraid not. We're flying back at seven. I have to work tomorrow."

"On Sunday?"

"Yes. Unfortunately, hospitals don't close."

"Well, I'm glad you came. It's good to see Alan again." Barbara paused. "I didn't ask—do you have any children?"

"No, we don't." Sara put on that smile again. "Nice to meet you, Barbara."

Sara was pensive on the flight from Pittsburgh to Boston, gazing out the airplane window at the shoreline, where points of land with houses surrounded by clumps of trees divided the water into inlets and bays, and powerboats moving in and out of them spread wakes that sparkled in the evening sun.

She wondered what would have happened if Mara had not left Alan twenty years ago. Would Mara, Alan and *their* three children be living in Scituate or Newton? Would she be a single nurse like several she knew, living with her mother and Mary Clare in Cambridge and watching her niece and nephew, young adults now, go away and leave the house to her, her aging mother and her silent sister? Would she have married someone else? She couldn't imagine it. She closed her eyes and tried to envision three boys running around their house, but she couldn't. Not anymore.

She wanted nothing to drink. She said no to the stewardess's offer of peanuts.

Alan took hers and opened the package. "Thanks for coming with me. It was good to see everyone again." He popped a handful of peanuts into his mouth.

"I could tell."

He glanced sideways at her.

"You were quite a guy in high school, weren't you?" she said.

"Why d'you say that?"

"All you did there—Honor Society, basketball, choir, lead in the class play—and the girls liked you, too."

"Huh. Too bad I didn't know that." He poured the rest of the peanuts into his mouth and took a drink of Coke. "It doesn't bother you, does it?" He crunched some ice between his teeth. "My goodness, it was twenty years ago. Barb Hamilton was my friend and we had a lot of fun together, but I haven't seen her in fifteen years."

She looked at the clouds streaming by the window. *What about Mara?*

"What's wrong, babe?"

"Nothing."

He sank down in his seat. "C'mon."

She put her head on his shoulder and her hand on his chest. "I'm sorry. I see those happy women, those lovely children, and I—"

"I know." He stroked her hair. "I don't like it either, but we have to have faith that we're here for some other purpose." He kissed her forehead. "And sweetheart, I'd rather have us together than everything else. I love you so much."

She pulled him closer. "What would I do without you?"

"You're never going to find out."

20

BOSTON

"Catch those legs!" said Mike. "Wouldn't you like them wrapped around you? Woo, woo!" The big, barrel-chested man pounded the bar with his palm.

Alan Cottrill, standing beside him, was four inches shorter than Mike. "Did you see her headdress? One hundred percent eagle feathers. It says so on the marquee." He grinned. "Or didn't you notice?"

Princess Cheyenne turned her back to the audience and wriggled her ass at them, tapping her feet and waving her arms, while Roger Pace and the Pacemakers blasted out the theme to "Casino Royale."

The exotic dancer pivoted and strutted to the edge of the small wooden stage, put her hands behind her head and pumped her hips at the businessmen in dark suits sitting at the small round tables that filled the strip club. Their pale faces and hands stood out, almost disembodied, above the black tablecloths in the crowded, semi-dark room. She reached down, grabbed the tie of one of the men near the stage and pulled. His companions yelled, "Go on, Roy! Go, boy!"

He stood up, arms toward her.

Princess flicked the end of the tie. It went over the man's nose and glasses and covered his bald spot. She blew him a kiss, waved goodbye to the audience, sashayed across the stage and disappeared through the black curtains.

The audience stood and cheered. Princess Cheyenne stuck her head through the curtain, blew another kiss and vanished.

The band began to play "In the Midnight Hour." Waitresses in black bras, short skirts and fishnet stockings went among the tables, taking orders. Other women in tight sweaters, high heels and black cutoff pants went from table to table, putting their arms around the seated men, finagling invitations to sit and drink.

Roger Pace took the stage, spinning and jumping as he screeched the words to the song.

Alan stood on his toes, put a hand on Mike's shoulder and spoke into his ear. "This is what you wanted to see," he said, "a club in the Combat Zone. What do you think of it?"

"This whole part of town is one whorehouse," said Mike. "It can't be a secret. Who lets it happen?"

Alan waited until Roger Pace finished the song, then said, "Our city fathers. They think it brings conventions to Boston. One of our state representatives is trying to make prostitution legal in the Zone."

"Unbelievable."

The band took a break. The smoke from a dozen cigars rose to the ceiling of the dark-edged room. The murmur from secretive conversations—proposals, counters, acceptances—drifted along a brick wall to the varnished bar where Alan and Mike stood.

"So, Al," said Mike, scanning the scene in front of them, "what's the name of this place again?"

"The Mouse Trap. And you're the mouse, my friend."

A tall brunette wearing a tight-fitting sleeveless blouse put her arm around Mike's shoulders. "Hey there, big guy," she cooed, "buy me a drink?"

He turned to Alan, who opened his palms. "Your call."

Mike looked the woman up and down. She pressed her breast against his arm and winked. "How 'bout it?"

"Okay."

She called to the bartender. "Over here, Johnny-boy." He brought her a glass full of shaved ice and brown liquid.

Mike laid a twenty-dollar bill on the bar. The bartender took it and brought back a five. The woman snatched the bill from the bar, folded it and slipped it inside her blouse. "Thanks, big guy." She puckered her lips and kissed the air between them.

Mike reached toward her. "Hey, what the hell is this?"

The woman stepped back and put her hands on her hips. "Hands off, buster. You can go to hell." She walked away.

"Did you see that?" said Mike.

Alan patted his client on the back. "You've just been initiated into the Combat Zone, Mister Mike. Relax, I'll buy you one." He raised his hand. "Hey, Johnny-boy, two scotches. Dewar's. Let me see the bottle."

Johnny-boy spun around, grabbed a liter bottle with a picture of the kilted Dewar's Highlander on the label and dropped it on the bar. "What's the matter? Don't you trust me?" He poured the liquor into two ice-filled glasses

"I'm an accountant," said Alan. "I check everything. How much?"

"Twenty."

Alan put a twenty-dollar bill on the bar. Johnny-boy watched him expectantly. "That all?"

"Your lady friend got the tip."

Mike left to go to the men's room. Alan took a sip of scotch—watered-down, and definitely not Dewar's—and listened to Miss Fran, the mistress of ceremonies, introduce Panama Red, "Straight from the dark, steaming jungles of South America, where she wears no clothes, to the Mouse Trap here in Boston's exciting Adult Entertainment District."

Panama Red, a buxom young woman with carrot-red hair and

eyebrows, came through the curtains and pranced around the stage, a red cape flowing behind her supple body. She waved to the clientele. They jumped up, clapped their hands above their heads and cheered.

She's a kid. I'm getting too old for this.

Alan started when someone behind him touched his shoulder. He turned halfway around and stared at a petite girl whose dark eyes reflected the spokes of light from the rotating silver ball in the center of the room.

He felt a hand slide into the pocket of his trousers. "Hi, big fella."

"Sorry, miss," he said, removing her hand, "you've got the wrong guy. I'm just here with a friend, showing him around." He spread his left hand on the bar so his wedding band glistened.

"Please, mister," she said. "You're a decent guy. Your wife is a lady, I know. She won't mind if you buy me a drink or two, will she? I need the money. I have to have it to eat tonight." Her eyes flashed again as she gazed up at him.

He could not turn away. "What'll it cost me?"

"Fifteen. You can afford it." She batted her eyelashes. "Please?"

Those eyes—Dark Eyes. Alan chewed on his lower lip. "How much do you get?"

She hesitated. "Five."

"That's all?"

The girl touched the inside of his upper arm. "Times are hard, mister. Girls are cheap. Five dollars is better than nothing." She held his eyes with hers.

"Can't I just give you the money?"

She scanned the room. Alan saw the reflection of Johnny-boy scowling at her in the mirror behind the bar. "Not here," she said. "Not outside, either. They watch."

"Who?"

"*Them*, mister. Men. They don't fool around." She glanced at Johnny-boy. "Like I said, girls are cheap."

Mike gripped Alan's arm. "Al, for Christ's sake. She'd as soon slit your throat as look at you. Come on, let's go."

The girl said, "Please? Or I'll have to leave," a forced smile on her face.

Alan showed two fingers to Johnny-boy, who put drinks in front of them. Alan put two twenties on the bar. He knew there would be no change. *Oh, well.*

The girl drained her glass with one swallow and bolted along the bar and out the door.

"I guess you've been reinitiated," said Mike.

"Yeah," said Alan, watching the door close. "You'd think she'd at least say goodbye for forty dollars."

Mike said, "Let's get the hell out of here while we still have cab fare," and the two of them headed for the exit. Mike went through the heavy metal door, stepped out on the sidewalk and stopped. A light drizzle filled the air with droplets that floated and spun in the wind. Alan slipped on the wet pavement and bumped up against the big man. "Oops, sorry."

"Look," said Mike, pointing down the street, "there's why she didn't kiss you good night."

The girl was halfway down the nearly empty block, wrapped around a tall blonde woman in a full-length leather jacket, kissing her with an open mouth.

Alan hurried past Mike and ran up to the couple. They separated and the girl, one side of her wet face reflecting the flashing red "XXX" on the marquee of the Pilgrim Theater across the street, glared up at him. "What do you want?"

"Can I talk to you a minute?"

"You fucker," she said. "What do you want for thirty dollars? A blow job? Go home and lick your wife. Maybe she'll give you one."

He held his hand out toward her. "I just want to know where you're from."

She stared at him for a second, a puzzled expression on her face, then she parried his arm away and jabbed his chest with her fingers. "Get out of here. Leave me alone."

The leather-clad woman pulled on the girl's other arm. "C'mon, honey, let's go. It's over for tonight."

Sara was sitting in bed reading when Alan got home, her hair loose around her shoulders. She took off her glasses. "How was it?"

"He got initiated. Dropped a little cash."

"You?"

"Reinitiated." He kissed her on the forehead. "Remind me not to get any new clients that haven't been to the Combat Zone, will you?"

"Go put your suit out for the cleaners and take a shower. You stink."

Later, as he pulled back the covers and lay down beside her, he said, "Talk a minute?"

"Sure."

"Do you remember Mara Colombo? You met her at the reunion."

"Oh, yes. Dark hair. Pretty. Married to that Navy guy." She puffed up her pillow. "Your first love."

"She had an illegitimate child."

Sara lay on her back and stared at the ceiling. The light from the alarm clock on the nightstand outlined her profile. "Yes . . . ?"

"She was raped at the school one night. By a classmate."

"And?"

"Her father sent her to Iowa to have the baby. She gave it up for adoption there."

"What a bastard. What was it?"

"She never saw it. Said that was the saddest day of her life."

"I can imagine." She rolled to her side and faced him, resting her head on her hand. "How do you know this?"

"She came back to the five-year reunion to tell me why she'd gone away our senior year without saying goodbye." He stroked Sara's hair. "No one outside her family knows this, just me and her husband."

"The poor woman. What a cross to bear." She took his hand and kissed it. "So? Why are you telling me this now?"

"Well, I know this is going to sound crazy, but I met a girl tonight who reminded me of Mara."

"In the Combat Zone? You're kidding."

"It was the eyes. Mara has the most beautiful dark eyes. That was my pet name for her. I thought I saw them tonight in a girl at the Mouse Trap. She couldn't have been more than twenty years old, and that's about right."

"How'd you meet her?"

"She propositioned me. I bought her a drink."

Sara wrinkled her forehead. "And?"

"I saw her outside and asked her where she was from, but she pushed me away and went off with her girlfriend. I thought—I don't know—I heard a trace of a Midwestern accent."

"Are you listening to yourself?"

He sighed. "It doesn't matter. I couldn't find her again if I tried."

"You need to stay away from that place. It does things to you." She put her hands behind his neck and pulled. "Come here, Alan-man."

ALAN CAME HOME FROM work a week later and saw their dry cleaning in a brown paper bag hanging from the hall tree. Three pieces of paper were pinned on the outside. Two were red rectangular tickets that had "THE MOUSE TRAP CLUB" printed on them and the date Alan and Mike were there—"Sep 17 1975"—stamped across the letters. The other was a piece of white paper about the size of a business card. It was cut unevenly, apparently from a full sheet by a pair of scissors. On it was printed:

FOR A GOOD TIME
Call
Merry
574-5101

He walked toward the smell of onions and garlic frying in the kitch-en. Sara, in jeans and a maroon Boston College T-shirt, was sprinkling sugar on onions sizzling in a skillet over a gas flame. Two yellow ceramic dinner plates with napkins and silverware beside them sat on the granite kitchen table. A lone candle burned in the center of the table, its flame oscillating in the slight breeze made by the exhaust fan.

He took her by the shoulders and kissed her cheek. "What's cookin'?"

"I've been waiting, and I'm parched." She ran a hand up his back and squeezed his shoulder. "Open a bottle and pour me a glass, will you?"

He took two wine glasses from a cabinet, went to the refrigerator and pulled out a bottle of Hogue sauvignon blanc. He opened it, poured the glasses half full and handed one to her. She raised her glass to him, her eyes twinkling. "See what you left in your suit? Who's Merry?"

"Must be the girl from the Zone. She stuck her hand in my pocket that night."

Sara raised her eyebrows. "And?"

"I pulled it out."

She peered sideways at him. "Her hand?"

He squeezed his eyes shut and laughed. "Oooh, you are *so* bad."

"*I'm* bad?" She gripped his tie just below the knot and shook it. "Grill's ready, master chef. Chicken breasts are on the counter. Go change clothes and get to work out there. I'm starving."

After dinner, they sat at the table, sipping the sauvignon blanc. Alan stared at the flame between them, his eyes unfocused.

Sara poured the last of her wine into his glass. "Psst." She touched his arm. "Bet I know what you're thinking about."

"Bet you do."

"Mara's baby?"

He nodded.

She shook her head. "I don't believe this. Alan Cottrill, CPA and the world's most conservative accountant, chasing a whore around the

Combat Zone. Am I not enough for you?"

Alan reached across the table and took her hand. "Sara, you are all I want. You know that, don't you?"

"Even when I can't give us what we wanted?"

He stood. "I'd rather have you than everything else."

"It's not fair."

"You're right." He lifted her up and held her. "Sweetheart, I'm not going to do anything that'll hurt you. Let's drop it." He wiped her cheeks with a napkin. "She's probably from Indian-noplace, anyway."

Sara put her hands on his chest. "You really want to know, don't you?" She hit his chest with her fists. "You're a jackass."

"Are you just finding that out?"

She pushed him away, easily. "All right. What do you want to do, Mister Jackass?"

"Call her and meet her again. Maybe I can get her to tell me where she's from, how old she is—some kind of a clue."

"What will you do then? It's the oldest canard in the world, you know, the whore with a heart of gold."

"She's not that, and I don't know what I'll do." He put a finger on her chin. "But I have to know, one way or the other."

Sara put her palms on the table. "I hope you know what you're doing, but if that's what you want, call her up. See if she'll meet you. If she will, I'll go along." She cupped her hand behind the candle and blew out the flame.

"Oh, God, no. It's the Combat Zone. Men go there in gangs."

She gave him her mother-to-little-boy look. "You think I've never been there? Anyone who went to BC has been to the Combat Zone." She reached for his plate. "I'll go. And I can tell about her. I know women."

He smiled. "And I don't?"

"And you don't, sweetie. Call her up."

She stacked the dinner plates, took them to the sink and turned on the water.

———∽∾∿—

ALAN AND SARA WALKED into the Mouse Trap at nine-thirty the following Wednesday and took seats at the bar. The band was taking a break,
but women were working the tables. Smoke was curling upward, forming
clouds of blue-purple haze below the vents in the overburdened ventila-
tion system

Johnny-boy came over to Alan. "New girlfriend, huh? What'll
you have?"

"Two glasses of white wine." When they came, Alan put two twenties
on the bar. Johnny-boy looked at him, his face impassive. "Yes?"

"We came to see Merry. Is she here?"

Johnny-boy scanned the room as he folded one of the twenties
around his index finger and stuffed it in his shirt pocket. "She was.
Must've left."

"Go upstairs or out?"

"She's not upstairs."

"Think she'll be back? We were going to meet her here."

"Yeah?" Johnny-boy glanced at Sara. "I wouldn't wait."

As they walked out, Sara said, "Give it up."

"Now we know she's called Merry here, too," he said. "I'll try one
more time."

———∽∾∿—

ALAN CALLED THE NUMBER from his office the next afternoon. Merry answered. "You weren't there last night," he said. "What happened?"

She spoke slowly. "I got a better offer—I thought."

"Miss, I just want to talk to you."

"Was that your wife?"

"Yes."

"What does she do? Clean house? Raise the kids?"

"She's a nurse," he said. "We don't have kids."

"Why not?"

Alan felt the unspoken anger and frustration rising up in him. "We can't."

"Talk—that's bullshit. Men always say that." She paused. "What does *she* want?"

"We both just want to talk to you about who you are and where you're from." He took a deep breath to try to control himself. "What's your real name?"

"Who wants to know?"

"I do, for Christ's sake! Why won't you tell me?"

"What's yours?"

"Alan."

"Alan what?"

"Alan Cottrill. Now it's your turn."

"Mary," she said. "The Virgin Mary. That's me, the virgin."

"Why are you playing games with me? Can we see you or not?"

"Not at the Trap. Want to come to my place?"

Alan thought about that, and said, "No." It would be too risky for him and Sara. There was no way to know who else might be there.

The girl was silent for so long that Alan thought she had hung up. He was about to put the receiver down when she said, "Okay. I'll come to yours."

"I don't know about that."

"Oh, don't worry. I'll be alone, and I'm little."

"Well, all right. I'll pick you up."

"No, no. I'm not getting in another car," she said. "Give me your address."

He did.

"I'll be there Sunday at eleven, okay?" she said. "See both of you. You'll have to miss church."

"How do I know you won't get a better offer?"

"I'm not taking any more offers for a while, asshole." She hung up.

Alan put the receiver down and thought for a few minutes. Then he picked it up, called the Iowa Department of Public Health in Des Moines and spent thirty minutes talking on the phone and writing notes on a pad of yellow accounting paper.

Sara was sitting in a living room chair, still in her uniform and reading *Vogue*, when Alan came home. The late afternoon sun coming in the front window put a red-gold halo around her hair and darkened her face with its shadow. A red *Jimmy's Harborside* mug sat on the coffee table. "Did you get her?"

"I talked to her this afternoon."

"And?"

"She told me she got a better offer last night."

"Nice girl."

"Then she said she wasn't taking offers for a while. What do you suppose that means?"

Sara flipped a page. "No idea."

"She did go somewhere outside the club last night. Maybe she got hurt—roughed up or something." He sat down.

"Hmm."

"Anyway, we'll see her Sunday. She's coming here at eleven."

Sara shot to her feet. "What? Here? You agreed to let that whore into our house? You told her where we lived?"

"I thought—"

"No, you didn't. You *didn't* think." She raised the magazine above her head and flung it to the table. "You call her back and tell her it's off. I am not opening my house to that whore, no matter whose daughter she might be." She glowered at him. "Jesus Christ, Alan, what's to keep her from robbing us once she's inside—or coming back at night with some of her friends from the Combat Zone and cleaning us out—or worse?" She stormed past him into the kitchen and began to unload the dishwasher, slamming doors and throwing plates into cabinets.

Alan stood in the living room listening to the racket. He knew that arguing with Sara when she was this angry would make her even more upset. She would calm down in a few minutes. He paced around the room, studying the carpet, and waited.

Presently, she came to the kitchen door, put her hands on its frame and leaned toward him. "What were you thinking?" She squinted at him. "Just tell me. What were you thinking?"

"To learn anything about her—to get her to talk—we need a quiet place and some time. It can't be done under pressure or with a lot of people around. *Capisce?*"

"Then why did you agree to meet her at the Mouse Trap?"

"That was a mistake. It wouldn't have worked." He paused, waiting for a reaction.

"Go on."

"I didn't want us to go to her place."

"So you told her she could come here."

"She's tiny. I doubt she weighs a hundred pounds. And she's coming alone. If someone's with her, we won't let them in."

"You're obsessed with this, you know that?"

"I know, and I want to get rid of it." He closed his eyes. "I need you to help me. You'll be able to tell about her." He opened them. "I'm not sure I can."

Sara walked back into the kitchen.

"If she gives us trouble when she's here, we'll call the police. They'll come right away." He peered into the kitchen. "But I don't think she will."

Sara put her hands on the counter and frowned at him. "Why not?"

"She won't give us any trouble in this neighborhood, where we can get help and she can't." He waited again. "Can you see that?"

"I guess."

"So we only let her in if she's alone and we lock the door behind her. If she doesn't like that, she can leave." He held his hands out toward her, palms up. "And if there's trouble, we call the police. All right?"

"All right, Mister Jackass."

21

The girl, wearing black—knit leggings with knee-high side zippers and a long-sleeved turtleneck—walked slowly down Salem Street toward the Old North Church, stepping carefully on the rough sidewalk to avoid catching the heels of her boots on the uneven surface. She passed a real estate office and a delicatessen where customers stood in line for their Sunday morning coffee. The wall clock above the counter said 10:30. She stopped across from the iron rail fence by the church and looked up and down the street, ready to cross.

A blue and white Boston police car came down the street, cruising slowly. It stopped, and the driver, a bareheaded, blue-uniformed officer, stuck his hand out the window and waved for her to cross. She lowered her head and scooted across in front of the car, glancing sideways at the two policemen watching her. She stepped onto the sidewalk and stared at the cruiser as it drifted down the street, flashed its signal, made a right turn at the next intersection and disappeared behind the row of townhouses.

As he turned the wheel, the driver saw his partner watching her. "Recognize that one, Sarge?"

The sergeant grimaced. "Sure do."

"She was going to Twenty-one. Want to go back and check?"

"Nah. She'll be all right." They drove on.

The girl walked quickly across the sidewalk to a townhouse with "21" above the door. She took a deep breath, rang the doorbell, stepped back on the concrete stoop and stared at the corner where the cruiser had gone.

Sara, in sandals, jeans and a white polo shirt, opened the door part way and studied the girl staring down the street. She was petite—about five feet tall—with dark brown eyes and solid blue-black hair. Sara could not imagine anything hidden in her pants or turtleneck. *So young! How'd she come to this?*

She opened the door wide. "Hello. Merry?"

The girl peered at her. "Did you call them?"

"Sorry?"

"The cops. Did you call them?"

Sara spoke slowly. "No, why?"

"They just went by. They waved at me. Why did they do that?"

Sara shook her head. *She's frightened.* She stepped out on the stoop and looked down the street. "I didn't call anybody. I don't know why they went by. Probably on their way to the Dunkies for a coffee break. They get it free there."

The girl stared at the corner again. "Free. Yeah. They like free."

Sara held the door open. "Come on in. Alan went to the bakery to get some pastries. He'll be back in a few minutes. I made some coffee."

The girl walked past Sara, looking into her eyes as she went.

Sara said, "What should I call you?"

"Mary. With an 'a' in it."

"I'm Sara."

Mary nodded, almost imperceptibly. "Okay."

Sara said, "To the left," as Mary walked into the hardwood-floored side hall of the townhouse. She looked back at Sara when the deadbolt closed.

Mary stepped gingerly into the carpeted living room. The large front window and a lamp in the far corner lighted the space. The smell of just-brewed coffee drifted in from the kitchen. She looked around at the dark purple couch and two easy chairs, then strode to the window, going between the chairs and the fireplace across from the couch. She stood there, chewing a fingernail and staring out at the empty sidewalk and street.

Sara watched her. "Are you looking for something?"

"Cops."

"Oh, they're gone," said Sara. "Anyway, they won't bother us."

Mary spoke quietly, still facing the window. "They won't bother *you*. But what I do is not allowed out here. They can run me in, and they'd like to do it. They like to get me—then I'm free." She turned. "You don't know what I'm talking about, do you?"

Sara murmured, "No."

"Cops protect you. They watch out for you so you can walk to the store and home from the T. So kids can wait on the street for the school bus."

Mary turned back to the window. "They see me here, they ask, 'What are you doing here?'" She put her hand on the window. "They ever ask you that? What are you doing on your street?"

Sara shook her head.

"They ask me that on any street. You tell them I'm here to see you, they believe it. They think they know why I'm here, but they believe you. I say I'm here to see you, they tell me I'm lying. You get robbed tonight, they come after me tomorrow. They know where I live. They ask where I was last night, I say with Sally, they say I'm lying. Sally says I was with her they say she's lying." She faced Sara. "They ever tell you you're lying?"

Sara shook her head slowly.

"They run me in. Put me in a holding cell. Alone. They walk by, grinning at me like I'm a piece of raw meat. Ask me questions. Tell me I'm lying. Slap me around. Shake me, maybe. Soften me up. What can I do? I'm a whore. They put me in a little room with one-way windows, so they can watch. I have to give them blow jobs to get out. Act like I like it.

Tell them they're big men. Lie to them." She pushed out a hard, mirthless laugh. "They believe me then."

Mary sat down on the couch, pressing a hand against her side and wincing as she lowered her body. She leaned back, her dark eyes piercing the air between them. "You afraid of anything like that?"

Sara opened her mouth. *Dear God.*

Mary straightened, her face full of pain and resignation. "That's what cops do for me."

Sara forced herself to look at the girl. All she could think of to say was, "They won't bother you here," in a soft, unsteady voice.

Mary took a deep breath and puffed air out of her mouth as if trying to exhale her fright. "Okay," she said. "Okay."

"Can I get you something? I've made some coffee and tea, and we have soda. What would you like?"

Mary stared at the floor, then up at Sara. "Some water? And . . ."

"Yes?" Softly.

"Do you have any Tylenol?"

"We do. How many?"

"Three would be good. Strong ones."

Sara went to the kitchen and took three Tylenol Extra Strength capsules from a bottle in an upper cabinet. She filled a glass with water and poured herself a mug of tea, put the capsules in a napkin and brought them to Mary. "Here you are."

Mary popped the capsules into her mouth and drank the water. "Thanks."

Sara sat in a chair across the coffee table from Mary, holding the mug with both hands. "I hope you feel better."

Mary put the glass on the table. "You can't have kids?"

Sara stiffened. "What? Who told you that?"

"He did. Why not?"

Sara's face hardened. "That's none of your business."

"You or him?"

Sara sat back, too angry to speak. *Damn him!*

After several seconds, Mary said, "Why should I tell you anything?"

"You know," said Sara, keeping her voice soft and speaking slowly to control her anger, "I don't care if you tell me anything or not. Alan thought you might be related to someone from his past. But if you won't talk about it, there's nothing we can do. And I'm getting to a point where I don't care."

The deadbolt clicked and the front door burst open. Alan, who had been pushing it with his rump, stumbled backwards into the hall, coming in only far enough to see Sara. He was carrying a bag from Parziale's Bakery.

"The whole North End was in line for goodies this morning. I've never seen a line that long. And then they ran out of"—he saw Mary— "Oh, hello. Sorry I'm late."

He looked from one to the other. "Oh, heck. Am I *too* late?"

Mary shifted her gaze to Sara, who said, "I think you are."

Alan said, "Shoot," and plopped down in a chair. "Now who's going to eat this cannoli I stood in line for?" He tapped the side of the bag. "Nice and fresh." He took a ricotta-stuffed pastry shell out of the bag, held it up in its wrapping and twisted it in the air, eyeing the stone-faced women in front of him. "Come on, ladies, you gotta help me here."

Sara studied him for a second, then stuck out an open hand. "All right, baker boy, I'll have that one, unless Mary wants it."

Alan handed her the cannoli. "There's plenty more in here. Mary?"

"Okay."

"Terrific! I'll have one, too." He jumped up and tramped into the kitchen. "And some coffee. I'm starving."

Mary said to Sara, "Is he always like that?"

"Only when it'll get him what he wants."

Alan came back carrying a mug and a fistful of napkins, dropped them on the coffee table and sat down slowly. "Now, where were we?"

"I don't know," said Mary.

"Nowhere," said Sara.

Alan pursed his lips. "Mary, do you know why we want to talk to you?"

"You think I might be related to someone you know."

"That's right."

"Does she want me back?"

Sara straightened and stared at her.

Alan kept his face expressionless. "She doesn't know we're doing this. And we don't know who you are."

"What do you want to know?"

"Can you tell us where you were born? Your birthday?"

"I grew up in Chicago. My birthday is December fifth."

"What year?"

"Nineteen fifty-five."

"Do you know where you were born?"

"Chicago, I think. No?"

"I don't know. Do you have a birth certificate?"

"I know she didn't want me," said Mary. "Does that mean I don't have one?"

Sara put her hands over her face.

"No, it doesn't," said Alan. "Everybody has one." He stood up and walked around the coffee table to the window, holding his hands behind his back.

"Mary," said Sara, "what about your parents?"

"They live in Chicago. Been a while since I saw them."

"A while?"

Mary studied her fingernails. "A couple of years."

"That's a long time."

Mary snorted. "They threw me out."

"Why?"

"They got tired of coming to school to get me. Didn't want to pay my bills."

Alan squatted down, forearms on his knees. Sara leaned forward, toward Mary.

"I was seventeen," she said. "I didn't have to go back. They didn't want me, I didn't want to go."

"The school?" asked Alan.

"Yeah. They didn't want my fat belly in their classes. Wanted to send me to a home."

"And your parents?"

"Said my mother was no good, either. A tramp. She didn't want me and now they didn't. They only wanted their real daughter."

"Their real daughter?" asked Sara.

"Danuta—little Dannie." Mary's voice softened. "She would sneak into my room and kiss the tears off my face. Then she would pat me to sleep." Mary touched her cheek. "I didn't want to leave her."

"What did you do?"

"Got someone else to pay my bills and got myself fixed."

Alan was afraid to ask, but he did. "What do you mean, fixed?"

Mary and Sara glared at him.

The mantel clock chimed the half hour.

Sara asked, "What about the father?"

Mary lowered her head. "We were going to run away and get married." She pressed her eyes shut.

Silence.

"And . . . ?" said Sara.

"He said he wasn't ready. Ran away and joined the Army."

"What did you do then?" asked Alan.

Mary eyed Sara. "Why should I tell you? You don't tell me anything."

Sara stared at the dust motes drifting upward in the shaft of sunlight slanting through the window and brightening half the room. She stood and faced the fireplace, her arms folded. "What do you want to know?" she cried. "I'm the reason we can't have children." She turned to Mary. "Me!" She struck her chest. "Not him. Is that enough?" She sagged back into the chair.

They waited.

"Who is she?" said Mary, her voice resonating. She turned her eyes to Alan. "My mother. Who is she?"

Alan's knee cracked as he stood. "We don't know. We don't know who she is."

"Not the person you know—your friend? How do you know she isn't? How can you tell? I think she is." Mary clutched her thighs. "You're lying! You won't tell me because I'm a whore." She threw her head back, crying, her tears sliding into the collar of her turtleneck. "My mother would want to know! She'd love me. She'd help me, but you won't let her."

Mary looked at Sara. "Why? Am I not worth anything? Am I not a person in trouble? I want something better, can't you see? That's why I came."

Alan leaned back against the wall. "Mary, the woman I knew a long time ago was never in Chicago. Her child was born somewhere else, a long way from there. I'm sorry about this, but she is not your mother. She can't be."

Mary fell to her knees before Alan. "Please, Mr. Cottrill. *Please.* I don't know where I was born. Maybe it's where she was. How can you know?" She put arms around his waist, holding him tightly as her body shuddered. "Let her decide. Aren't there tests or something? Let me meet her. She'll know. I'll know. She'd want you to do that for her daughter. You're her friend, aren't you? You can help her."

Alan squeezed his eyes shut and lowered his head.

Outside, a car horn blared.

Mary's tears stopped, but she was shaking and gasping for air like a small child exhausted from crying. Alan put his hands under her armpits and started to lift her up, but she shoved him away and rose on her own. She sat, carefully again, on the couch, still shaking. Sara handed her some tissues. Mary looked up at Sara, but did not speak. She was sure they wanted her to leave so they could forget about her, just like her other clients when they were finished with her. She ran her hands over her forehead and through her hair. "I get it," she said. "I'll go." She got up and ran through the hall and out the front door, leaving it ajar.

Alan went to the door and watched her trot away, her head bowed. She broke into a stiff-legged run, tripped and fell, got up slowly and scurried north on Salem Street until she was out of sight.

He closed the front door and went back to the living room where Sara was standing. She spoke quietly. "I have to know something. Could she be your daughter?"

"No." Solemnly.

"No chance?"

"No chance. Mara and I didn't . . ."

"Fuck."

He winced. "That's a terrible word."

"It was the rape, then."

He looked at the floor, then raised his eyes to her. "If I'd been the father, I would have married her. If she'd told me about it at the time, I'd have wanted to marry her then."

Sara sat down on the couch and pulled legs under her body. "What are you going to do now? She could be, you know. She looks a lot like Mara."

Alan paced the floor with his hands clasped behind his head. "We don't know for sure. We have no proof, just an age and a resemblance. We know she was adopted, but that's not enough. If I call Mara, the first thing she'll say is, 'Are you certain?' I'll be asking her to mess up her family when we don't have proof. I can't do that." He closed his eyes. "I've messed up enough lives already."

"You said it. How do you get proof?"

"Go to Iowa and search records, I guess. Mara said she gave her baby up for adoption in Iowa City."

"We can't do that."

"We could pay someone."

Sara glared at him. "*We?*"

"Well, you know—"

"No, I *don't* know." She got up and turned her back to him. "That girl is not your daughter—I know that now—but what is this hold Mara has on you? Is she the one you're chasing in all of this?"

"Sara—"

"She's the one who can give you what I can't, isn't she? Wouldn't you rather have her? Dark eyes, big tits and three boys?" She faced him, tears falling from her cheeks and disappearing in the carpet. "I'm sorry, Alan. I am *so sorry*, but I don't have those tits and those eyes"—she inhaled—"and I can't give you boys." She fell on the couch and curled up, shaking, hands hiding her face. "Go away." She waved at him. "Go away."

Alan walked out the door and around the block, thinking. Why had he done this? Why hadn't he thought ahead before plunging into a situation he did not understand—especially this one, so full of evil? He had wounded that poor girl, and sent her back to a miserable life.

He looked up at the sky full of roiling dark clouds. Could he and Sara help her get out?

He ran his hand along the gray stone wall beside the sidewalk.

Sara was sitting on the couch, hands on her thighs, when Alan came back. She jumped up, ran to him and wrapped her arms around him. "Alan, I am so sorry. How could I do this to you? I know you would never be unfaithful to me."

She put her head against his chest. "It's not you, it's *me*. I can never give you children, and sometimes it hurts me so much I can't stand it, and I take it out on you. I know you want so much to have your heritage go on. It's the finest thing you have, and it will die when you do."

She tightened her hold on him. "We'll never have a baby for me to hold and feed, never feel little fingers around ours and have her toddle between us holding our hands or grow up and get married and have our grandchildren." She raised her head. "I'm a curse! Nothing of you will be left behind, and it's all because of me."

"Sara." He walked her to the couch, sat down and pulled her onto his lap. He wiped her tears with his handkerchief. She dropped her head to his shoulder.

"Do you remember what you told me about the families who gave birth to infants that were doomed?" he asked.

"What was that?"

"They would be holding the little one and saying, 'This is God's will for us, and we must do all we can.' Remember?" He put his hand on her temple and pressed her head to his chest. "What's happening must be God's will for us. Since we can't have our own, we're being called to do all we can for someone else's child."

She put her arm around him. "What can we do?"

"Get her birth certificate. If it says she was born in Iowa City in December of nineteen fifty-five, she's Mara's child."

"Would you tell Mara, then?" she asked.

"I would. Then it would be up to her and Thomas, but I'm sure they'd help her. Maybe move her to San Diego where she could start over."

"And if she's not?"

"We could help her get another start, here or someplace else," he said.

"How would we do that?"

"I don't know. But there have to be places here that give refuge to people like Mary—runaways, abused women and children." He took in a breath and exhaled. "Who would know?"

She raised her head. "Father Lloyd?"

"I thought he'd retired."

"I think he's still working in the diocese office. Mom will know. He calls her once in a while."

"See if you can find him."

"I'll call Mom tomorrow."

22

Sara made an appointment with the O'Briens' former priest, the Honorable John Mark Lloyd, for 2 p.m. on the next Thursday. Father Lloyd was now the Retired Bishop Suffragan in the Episcopal Diocese of Massachusetts. He remembered them, and said he would be delighted to see Sara again.

———✎✎✎———

A WOMAN NAMED AMY greeted Sara and Alan in the lobby of the Diocesan building on Tremont Street and ushered them into Bishop Lloyd's office.

Full, dark bookcases ran down the right-hand wall, across from the walnut desk that faced the door. One chair sat next to the bookshelves in the back. A large-eyed teddy bear holding a sign that said "Decaf is for sissies" filled another, to the left and in front of the desk. Diplomas and plaques of recognition hung on the back wall. A worn paisley couch sat to the left of the door. The odor of pipe smoke sat in the air.

Bishop Lloyd came around his desk and took Sara's hands "My child, my young woman. It's so good to see you." He put a hand on Alan's shoulder. "My memory fails me. How long has it been?"

"Twelve years, Father," said Sara, "since you married us in Saint

Mark's. Twelve wonderful years."

"August, wasn't it?" he said. "As I recall, it was hot that day."

"We didn't notice," said Alan.

"Of course not, of course not." The priest put his arm around Sara and looked sideways at her. "He's pretty thin. Are you feeding him enough?"

"I do my best, but he stays thin."

"She's a wonderful cook," said Alan. "It's always tempting, but I try not to eat too much."

"We all must avoid temptation," said the cleric, "no matter how sweet it may appear." He went back around his desk. "Sit down, sit down, and tell me about yourselves. I'm frightfully out of touch in this damn— excuse me—administrative position. Sometimes I think all I do is fill out forms and shuffle paper. I'd rather be listening to people and helping." Sara and Alan sat on the couch across from his desk.

He sat, selected a Meerschaum pipe from the wood rack on his desk, tamped tobacco in the bowl and took a lighter from his vest pocket. "Twelve years! My goodness!" He looked at Sara. "Children?"

"We've tried, Father. Alan's count is good, but for some reason I'm not able to conceive."

"The best specialists in Boston haven't been able to help us," said Alan. "We've seen them all."

Sara lowered her head. "It never occurred to me that I couldn't have children."

The bishop lit his pipe. The smoke curled behind his head and rose to the ceiling. "I'm sorry. You would be good parents. Have you considered adoption?"

They said "Yes," in unison, then Alan said, "We don't want to raise someone else's child."

Bishop Lloyd puffed. "Very well. What can I help you with today?"

"We've come to you for advice," said Sara. "We are in a situation we don't know how to handle. We don't know what's right, and we need your counsel."

"Go on."

"Twenty years ago in West Virginia," said Alan, "my high school girlfriend was raped by a classmate. When her family found out she was pregnant they moved to another state and sent her to Iowa to live with her mother's sister and give the child up for adoption. She never saw her baby."

Bishop Lloyd tapped his pipe on the rim of an ashtray and relit it. "A sad story. A Catholic family?"

"Yes."

"And?"

"Last month I ran into a young woman who reminded me very much of that high school girlfriend."

"What was the mother's name? That will make it easier for me to follow you."

"Mara."

"And the young woman's?"

"Mary."

"You said you ran into her," said the bishop. "Where?"

"A place called the Mouse Trap. It's a—"

"I know what it is. What were you doing there?"

"Entertaining a new client," said Alan. "He wanted to see the Combat Zone."

"He told me he was going," said Sara.

"Shame on you, Alan. But go on."

"I was so taken by the possibility she might be Mara's child that I agreed to have her come to our house," said Alan.

"I didn't like it, but I went along," said Sara. "He was obsessed and it wasn't going to go away till he knew."

Bishop Lloyd leaned back in his chair and studied the ceiling. He puffed.

"When she came," said Alan, "she told us she'd been adopted by a family in Chicago. She got in trouble there."

"She loved a boy who promised to marry her, but he ran away when she told him she was pregnant," said Sara. "Then she was kicked out of school and out of the house by her parents. She was seventeen."

"Did she give birth to the child?"

"She had an abortion," said Sara.

"And now?"

"She lives somewhere in the Combat Zone," said Alan, "with a woman named Sally."

The priest stuck his chin on the heel of his palm, curled his fingers over his mouth and spoke through them. "In hell."

"When she was at our house," said Alan, "I told her I thought she might be related to someone from my past."

"She might have thought we were her parents," said Sara, "until I told her I couldn't have children. Now she may suspect that Alan is her father."

Bishop Lloyd eyed Alan.

"I'm not," he said.

"You're sure?"

"Positive. Mara and I didn't . . . ."

Bishop Lloyd closed his eyes. "So what does she want now? Mary."

"She's desperate to know who her mother is, and she thinks Alan knows," said Sara.

The gaze of the priest shifted to Alan again. "Do you?"

"I'm not sure. Mary's birth date is about right, and there's an uncanny resemblance . . ."

"But?"

"I don't know where she was born, or her mother's name," said Alan. "If we could get a birth certificate from her adoptive parents—"

"They don't always show the mother's name."

"I know," said Alan, "but if it shows Mary was born in Iowa City where Mara gave her baby up, and her birthday is in early December, she's probably Mara's child. If not, then she isn't."

"Can the state help you?" asked Father Lloyd.

"I talked with the Iowa Department of Health before Mary came to see us. A child given up in a blind adoption there has to be twenty-one before she can try to get the name of her birth mother. Mary's twenty. And the state doesn't keep track of the mothers."

Another tamp. Another flame. Another cloud of smoke. "Have you told this child who her mother might be?"

"No," said Alan. "I can't do that."

"Well, that's one thing you've done right." Father Lloyd studied the surface of his desk. "What do you want from this, Alan?"

"I want to know if Mary is Mara's daughter. If she is, I'll tell Mara."

"Where is Mara now?"

"In San Diego," said Alan. "Happily married. Her husband is an officer in the Navy. They have three boys."

"We saw them at Alan's high school reunion last August," said Sara. "Before all this happened."

"I see. And if she's not Mara's daughter?"

"We want to help her," said Alan.

Bishop Lloyd ran his curled index finger across his lips. "Excuse me." He pressed a button on a brown box on his desk. A voice came through its speaker. "Hello?"

"Becca, will you come in, please?" He pressed the button again. "Rebecca Harding is our Director of Social Services. Her mission is to help us care for the poor and unfortunate. Your Mrs. Harris retired a long time ago."

In a few seconds, the office door opened and a stout woman with dark hair in a pageboy cut wearing a white blouse and a gray skirt walked softly into the room. "Yes, Father?"

"Rebecca Harding, these are two of my former parishioners, Sara and Alan Cottrill. They are here for advice about how to rescue a lost soul who is separated from her natural mother, her adoptive parents, and the Lord.

The woman is a twenty-year-old prostitute in the Combat Zone."

He paused. "They want to help her but don't know how. They know a woman who might be her birth mother, but they aren't sure. They want to help the young woman get out of there, even if they don't locate her mother." He turned to Alan. "Is that about right?"

"Yes."

Rebecca sat upright in the leather chair beside the shelves, hands folded in her lap. "Some questions?"

"Please," said Alan.

"How did you come in contact with her?"

"I met her in a strip club in the Combat Zone. She propositioned me. She looked so much like my high school sweetheart that I thought she might be her daughter."

"Just when you think you've heard them all." Rebecca shook her head. "What else? Surely there's more than a resemblance."

"Her age is about right," said Alan, "and the girl knows she was adopted, but nothing more than that. It was a closed adoption."

"She's desperate to find her mother," said Sara.

Rebecca put her elbows on the arms of the chair and her chin in her hands. She gazed at the floor for a few seconds. The sound of another puff on the pipe filled the room. "How well do you know this woman?" she asked.

"I met her once, Alan met her twice," said Sara. "The three of us talked for maybe an hour one day."

"So all you know about her is what she told you?"

"Yes," said Sara. "About how she had been deserted by the boy who made her pregnant, kicked out by the couple who adopted her, and abused by the police."

"Did she say why she was in Boston? How she got here?"

Alan and Sara exchanged glances. "No."

"Do you believe her?"

"Yes."

"Uh-huh." Rebecca folded her arms. "You need to be careful. I don't doubt your intentions, but I must tell you that women in these circumstances are very good liars and skilled manipulators, especially of people with good intentions." She leaned forward. "Did she ask you for money?"

"No," said Alan.

"Did you give her any?"

"No, we didn't."

Rebecca's eyebrows went up and down. She smiled at the carpet. "I wasn't there," she said, "so I don't know. I'm not saying you shouldn't help her. Just be careful."

"What should we do?" asked Sara.

"You can only help her if she wants to change her life," said Rebecca. "You can't change it for her. And it's hard for a prostitute. They become so desensitized, so detached from the people they encounter, that having any kind of a caring relationship is difficult. Doing what they do, they learn to be disengaged from the act, as if they were observing it from a corner of the room. And acceptance back into society . . ." She tightened her lips. "How many men can love a woman who has been known—the biblical term—by a thousand others?"

"A thousand?" Sara put her hand to her chest. "No!"

Rebecca's eyes were cold. "That's three a night for one year. They all do more than that."

"No!" said Sara. "God, what hell that must be. I can't imagine . . . Oh!" She stood, faced the wall and leaned her head against it. "Ah!" She pushed herself away and spun around, her face contorted. "Alan, we have to do something. Whoever she is, we can't leave her there."

"You can help her if she wants out." Rebecca turned to Bishop Lloyd. "Maybe Peg can help them, don't you think?"

"Yes," he said. "Thank you, Becca."

Rebecca shook hands with Sara and Alan. "Good luck. Let God guide you." She left the room as quietly as she had entered.

The bishop said, "Let's see if I can get you some help." He picked up the phone and pushed a button on its console. "Amy, will you see if you can get Margaret Walsh for me, please?"

He hung up the phone. "Mrs. Walsh is the executive director of the House by the Side of the Road. It takes in and supports young women who've been abandoned or abused, or both, and prepares them for reentry into society." He relit his pipe. "She's been doing that for a long time, and she's—"

The phone rang. "Hello? Thank you. . . . Peg! How are you? And Bill? . . . We're fine, thanks. Colin graduates this spring. Yes, Jean's boy." He winked at Sara and Alan. "Thank you, I will." He put his pipe on the ashtray. "Peg, I have a couple in my office—former parishioners of mine, I married them—who need your help." He listened. "That's right. They want to rescue a poor child from a life in the Combat Zone. Becca and I have talked to them about it. They want to save her but they don't know how. When do you suppose you could meet with them?"

Bishop Lloyd listened, then turned to Alan and Sara. "Tomorrow?" They shook their heads. "Monday?"

"Tuesday afternoon," said Sara. "I'm off at one." Alan nodded.

"How about Tuesday at two? All right? Wonderful! Their names are Sara and Alan Cottrill. They're good kids. I'm grateful to you, Peg. Bye."

He took a slip of paper from a small leather box and began writing. "Her name is Margaret Walsh. She and I go back a long way. As I said, it's the House by the Side of the Road. Peg calls it 'the House.' They're on West Street. Here's the address and phone number."

He studied the slip, then handed it to Alan. "Peg's a wonder."

"Thank you very much, Father," said Sara, "for being so good to us again. I don't know where my family would be now without you."

"You're a wonderful story," he said. "An example for others." Father Lloyd tapped his pipe on the ashtray. "You're doing a good thing for that child. It won't be easy, but with God's help, you just might save her."

23

Early Tuesday afternoon, Alan and Sara walked down West Street to a brick building that had empty, taped display windows on both sides of a narrow entryway. They went up to the cracked glass entrance door and peered down a narrow corridor.

"What kind of a place is this?" asked Sara. She stepped back and looked up and down the street. "Are you sure this is it?"

Alan unfolded the note from Father Lloyd. "It's the right address. Let's go in and see."

The corridor ended at an open doorway to a dim room. A woman sat at a metal desk along the far wall, typing. Cardboard boxes stacked two and three high sat around the periphery, the top ones with their lids askew or leaning against the stack. Piles of papers—flyers, brochures and blank forms—covered a table beside the door. A doorway in the left wall led to a room of metal shelves that held more boxes.

The woman did not stop typing. "Yes?"

"We're here to see Margaret Walsh."

The typist opened her mouth and sucked in air. Her chest, already large, swelled. "Peg!"

A voice from the room of shelves said, "Be right there." The type-writer hammered away.

Sara and Alan waited, studying the posters taped to the walls tell-ing of church festivals, bike races, job openings and offers to give Greek lessons. They were perusing the offers when a tall, full-bodied woman in a white headband and a blue jumpsuit came through the doorway. She wiped her hands on the backs of her legs. "Hello, hello. You're the Cot-trills, aren't you? I'm Peg Walsh." She held out her hand. "Come in."

They followed her into a small office off the storage room. It had another metal desk with two file cabinets beside it and a row of book-shelves along the far side. Peg slid between the desk and the wall behind it, brushed off the desk chair and threw the dust rag to Alan. "Wipe off the couch, put that stack of paper on the floor, and take a seat." They sat down carefully on a sagging wicker couch with wrinkled green pillows.

Peg sat down and leaned on her elbows. "Father John said you want-ed to rescue a child from the Combat Zone. A woman, I'm sure. Tell me about her."

"She's a twenty-year-old prostitute," said Alan. "She might be the daughter of a girl I knew in high school who went to Iowa and gave a child up for adoption there in nineteen fifty-five."

"What's the mother's name?"

"Mara Colombo. She's married and living in San Diego."

"What does she know about this?"

"Nothing," said Sara. "Alan met the girl here in September."

"The girl's name?"

"Mary," said Alan. "She's living in the Combat Zone with a woman named Sally."

"Tell me about her." The typist came to the door. Peg said, "No calls for a while."

"She was raised in Chicago," said Alan. "She told us her parents threw her out when she was seventeen."

"A boy she loved made her pregnant, then he deserted her," said Sara, "and she was kicked out of school because she was pregnant. She had an abortion and became a prostitute after that."

"When did she come here?" asked Peg.

"We don't know," said Alan.

"Where does she work? Around?"

"I met her in the Mouse Trap," said Alan.

"Huh," said Peg. "I won't ask what you were doing there."

"I knew he was going," said Sara.

"Un-huh," said Peg. "Why do you think she may be this woman's child?"

"There's an amazing physical resemblance," said Alan, "and the girl's birthday is about right. And she knows she was adopted."

"So she told you," said Peg.

"So she told us, unprompted," said Alan.

"That's not enough."

"I know," said Alan. "But if we can get her birth certificate and match it with the one from the hospital where she was born, we can find out. If she was born in Iowa City in November or December of nineteen fifty-five, then she almost has to be Mara's daughter."

"Iowa City," said Peg. "Do you know the adoptive parents?"

"She'll have to tell us," said Alan. "If she does, can you get her birth certificate?"

"We've done it before," said Peg, "but let's not get ahead of ourselves." She leaned back. "When you look at her, what do you see? In her eyes."

"Sorry?" said Alan. "I don't understand."

"Are they empty? Is there anything behind them?" Peg twisted her lips to one side. "These women reach a point where there's nothing inside them. They've been destroyed. They're soulless beings, existing only to be used by others for their purposes or their appetites."

"No," said Sara, "she's not that. She's desperate to find her mother and get away from here."

"She's told you that," said Peg, "but you have to be careful. It might be hard for her to leave the predictability of her life in the Combat Zone. She may believe she can't cope with the outside world. Think about how it's treated her—abandoned at birth, impregnated and deserted when she was in high school, kicked out by the school and her parents. She's run away and found refuge in this woman—what's her name?"

"Sally," said Alan.

"Wanting to know who her mother is and reunite with her is a positive sign *if* Mary wants to get out. If she wants to take advantage of her mother—and she may want to do that—then a reunion will be a disaster. And it can't be undone."

"So we have to play God here," said Alan.

"Someone may have to do that," said Peg.

"There is some spirit left in her," said Sara.

"I'm glad to hear it," said Peg, "but I'll have to see her before I can commit to anything."

"I understand," said Alan. "When can you do it?"

"Any day next week." Peg opened a drawer and took out two small white cards. "Give her one of these and have her call me." She handed the cards to Alan. "Will she come by herself?"

"I think so," said Alan. "Or we'll bring her and leave."

"That'll be fine."

As they walked out, Alan asked, "What d'you think?"

"She'll take her," said Sara, "because of Father Lloyd."

ALAN CALLED MARY'S NUMBER the next day and asked the woman who answered to have her call him. He left his work number.

His telephone rang just as he was leaving for the day. "Cottrill speaking."

He heard coins dropping into a pay telephone. "It's Mary."

"Where are you?"

"What do you want?"

"Sara and I have found a place for you to stay while we try to find your mother—if you want us to."

"Where is it?"

"Downtown, on West Street. It's the House by the Side of the Road. The woman in charge wants to talk to you about staying with them for a while."

"I know where it is. What will they do for me?"

"Give you a place to stay, feed you," he said. "Give you work to do while you're there."

"Why are you doing this?"

"You said you wanted a better life. We want you to have one."

"Why?"

"Sara and I think you can have a better life, and we want you to have it."

"Yeah?"

"Yes!"

The telephone buzzed. Through the static, Mary said, "My time's up. Don't call me at that number any—" The line went dead.

Alan slammed down the phone. "Crap! All that for nothing!" He pounded his desk. "Nothing!"

When he told Sara that evening she said, "Wait a day or two. She'll call you."

24

At nine a.m. the following Sunday, Sara, in curlers and a fluffy white bathrobe, was sitting in the living room reading the *Globe* and sipping from a mug of tea, waiting for Alan to come back from his run.

The doorbell rang.

Forgot his key again.

She smiled and pulled the door open. Mary, wearing a starched white blouse, a knee-length gray skirt and saddle oxfords, was standing on the stoop. A small duffel bag hung from her clasped hands. "Hello, Mrs. Cottrill."

Sara stared at her.

"Can I come in?"

Sara looked up and down the street.

"I'm alone," said Mary. "A cop car went by, but I'm not afraid. I know they won't bother me up here." She looked past Sara. "Is Mr. Cottrill here?"

"He'll be back in a few minutes." Sara was still in shock.

"Can I wait?" Mary lowered her eyes.

"Of course, Mary. Come in. He's out running and getting pastries."

Mary walked into the hall. She stopped at the entryway to the living room and turned around. "You can lock the door."

"Oh, no. He probably forgot his key." Sara walked slowly into the living room. "Sit down, please. What can I get you?"

Mary sat on the couch. "Some water."

"Anything else?"

"Not this time."

Sara went to the kitchen, filled a glass and put it on the coffee table. "You look nice."

"Thank you."

"Younger."

Mary studied her feet. "I'm pretty young." She raised her eyes and forced a smile.

Sara held out her arms. Mary stood up, and Sara pulled the girl to her. "I'm happy to see you," she said. "Do you want to talk now, or would you like to wait?"

"Wait for him, if it's okay."

They sat back down, Mary on the couch and Sara in the easy chair across the coffee table.

Mary brushed her thighs. "I have to quit, Mrs. Cottrill. I can't face my mother if I'm a whore. Maybe she'll understand if I tell her I've quit and I'm doing something else. I have to tell her, don't I?"

"Yes," said Sara. "Do you have any money?"

"I've saved some."

"Where is it?"

"With me," said Mary. "About a thousand."

"You don't have a bank account?"

"No. I hide it."

"I can help you open one. It'll be safe."

"Okay." Mary closed her eyes. "Does he know who my mother is?"

"Let's wait. He'll tell you what he knows."

"Does he?"

"He'll tell you what he knows, but he doesn't know everything."

Mary drank half of the water. "I'm sorry you can't have kids."

"So am I."

"I can't either. I'm all fucked—I'm sorry, Mrs. Cottrill—all messed up."

The door creaked open and slammed shut. Alan came in, carrying a paper bag from Parziale's Bakery. He looked from Sara to Mary, his eyebrows high. "Hello! You look nice."

"She thinks so, too."

"Okay," he said, "something we agree on." He sat and handed out cannoli from the bag. "One for you, Mary, one for Sara, two for me. My reward for running four miles." He stood. "Anybody want anything?" They shook their heads.

He went into the kitchen, drew a glass of water and gulped it down, then poured himself a mug of coffee and came back. "How are you, Mary?"

"I told her—I can't face my mother if I'm a whore. If I quit, maybe she'll understand."

"Let's hope so."

"Who is she?" asked Mary.

"I don't know for sure. I wish I did." He leaned forward. "Here's what I do know. In nineteen fifty-five—"

"I was born then."

"—a girl I knew went to Iowa to live with her aunt because she was pregnant."

"You?" asked Mary.

"Someone else."

"Where is he?"

"He died a long time ago," said Alan. "She gave the child up for adoption. It was a closed adoption. Do you know what that is?"

Mary shook her head.

"She never saw her baby or the people who adopted it. She doesn't even know if it was a boy or girl."

"Is she in Iowa now?"

"If she's your mother, I'll write to her and ask if she wants to see you," said Alan. "If she does, you'll meet her."

"When?"

"We have to be sure she's your mother first—and she may not be." Sara refilled Mary's glass.

"To do that," said Alan, "we need your birth certificate."

"I don't have one."

"The couple that adopted you must have it," said Alan.

"Shit."

"Who are they?" asked Sara.

"Bolek and Agnes Jawonsky. They live on Thirty-First Street in South Chicago—or they did."

"What did they name you?"

"Mary Ann. Mary Ann Jawonsky." Mary lowered her head. "They won't give it to me."

"We'll help you get it," said Alan. "We know someone who does that for people."

"When?"

"As soon as we can."

Mary hugged herself and twisted her body back and forth. "Please, soon," she said. "Real soon."

"We have a question for you," said Sara. "What if the woman Alan knows is not your mother, or she is and doesn't want to meet you? What will you do then?"

"Would she do that? To me, her daughter?"

"We don't know," said Alan. "But what if she's not your mother and we can't find out who is?"

Mary slumped. "There won't be anything left of me if I don't get out."

"I told you, there's a place downtown where you can go," said Alan. "They'll take you in, give you a place to sleep, maybe a job, until you're ready to go out on your own."

"Here? In Boston?"

"When you're ready, you'll want to go someplace else to start over, won't you?" said Sara.

"I will," said Mary. "What do I have to do?"

Alan handed Margaret Walsh's card to Mary. "Call Mrs. Walsh and make an appointment to see her. She expects you to call, and she wants to help you. She knows how, Mary, and we don't."

"We'll stay in touch," said Sara, "and help when we can. But you have to put yourself in her hands."

Mary studied the card. "Will you come with me? I'm scared."

"We can take you there," said Alan, "but she wants to talk to you alone."

"Okay," said Mary. "Can I call her now?"

"Not on Sunday," said Alan. "Tomorrow."

Mary murmured, "I need a place to go."

Two men in garish clothing—white fur and orange—walked past the living room window. A few seconds later, they strolled back from the other direction, reading house numbers.

Mary cried, "No!" She bolted from the room, through the kitchen and into the bedroom.

"What was that about?" asked Sara.

The doorbell rang. Startled, Alan and Sara exchanged glances. Alan said, "I don't know. You go to Mary. I'll get the door."

A mid-sized man wearing a black suit, ruffled tuxedo shirt and a white bow tie was standing at the door when Alan opened it. His hands were in the pockets of an open, full-length white fur coat and his legs were spread apart in a fighter's stance. Another man wearing solid orange—shoes, suit and fedora—was standing on the sidewalk with his wide back to the door, looking up and down the street and slapping the concrete with a long, flexible cane.

Alan looked into the cold eyes of the man facing him. "Yes?"

"We want to see Mary."

"Mary who?"

The man shook his head. His long hair swirled.

"There's no one named Mary here," said Alan.

"Yes, there is."

Alan took in a mouthful of air, trying to swallow his fright. "Who are you?"

"Friends of hers."

"Really?" Alan's pulse pounded in his ears.

"I'm Walter. Tell her we're here for her."

"I told you, there's no Mary here."

"I tell you there is."

"What makes you think so?" Alan clenched his fists to keep from trembling.

"Quit stalling. Tell her to come here."

Alan took a step toward Walter, clutched the lapels of his fur coat and shoved him backwards. "Get out of here!"

Walter snarled, grabbed Alan's arms and swung him around. Alan held on and they fell to the concrete. They scrambled to their feet and Alan lunged at Walter, but he backed away and Alan fell to all fours.

Walter stood over him, sneering. "Don't fuck with me, boy." He was standing between Alan and the open front door.

A police cruiser skidded to a stop in the street and the passenger door flew open. A bareheaded sergeant jumped out and stepped quickly to the sidewalk, a nightstick in his right hand. The name badge on his shirt said "McCarran." He looked from one man to another, ending with his eyes on Walter. "What's going on here?"

McCarran's partner got out, walked around the front of the cruiser and took up a position in front of the door, holding his nightstick in front of him by its ends.

"We were just talking with Mr. Cottrill," said Walter. He took a step backward.

Alan stared at Walter. *He knows my name.*

McCarran flipped the nightstick on its sling. "I didn't see anyone talking."

The man in orange started toward the sergeant, pointing the cane at him and flexing it. "Listen, you—"

McCarran drove his nightstick into the man's stomach, forcing the air from his lungs out through his mouth and doubling him over. Standing over him, McCarran raised a fist and pounded the big man's back between the shoulder blades like a sledgehammer striking a spike, sending him to the ground.

Walter screamed like a little girl.

McCarran shook the nightstick under Walter's chin. "I coulda killed him if I'd wanted to. You want some a' that?"

Walter froze. His head twitched. "No, no."

"You only fight women, don't you? Coward." McCarran stepped back, still brandishing his stick. "Walter, you better not make trouble up here. You make trouble for me up here, I'll make trouble for you down there. Have the boys run in your girls. Make 'em post bail to get out." He hitched his belt. "You might have to miss a payment on your Cadillac. You wouldn't want that."

"No."

"Mr. Cottrill gets hurt, I'll know you did it, Walter. You and I'll have a little visit."

"I wouldn't do that."

"You better make sure nobody else does." The sergeant glared at Mr. Orange, who was slowly getting to his feet. "You understan' that?"

Mr. Orange held his hand out toward the policeman. He lowered his head. "Yes, sir."

"You got anything else to say to Mr. Cottrill, Walter?" Alan folded his arms and clutched his elbows to stop shivering.

Walter looked at Alan, his eyes blank. "I guess not."

The two men shuffled to the sidewalk and around the corner of the building, looking back with hatred burning in their eyes.

"I'm watchin' you, Walter." The sergeant turned to Alan. "That girl in there. Is he her pimp?"

Alan had to get control of his throat before he could speak. "I—I don't think she has one."

"He's after her, then. If he gets her, it's over."

"What d'you mean?" asked Alan.

"He's a Jonas. Did you see the cane? He'll beat her till she's his. After that, if she tries to get away, he'll kill her."

"Just like that?"

The sergeant wiped his nightstick with a handkerchief. "Just like that."

"Will he get away with it?"

"If anyone finds the body, they won't recognize it. An' no one will talk."

Alan closed his eyes and exhaled through his mouth. *My God—Mary.*

"I don't know what you're doing with her, Mister Cottrill, but whatever it is, you keep her outta there from now on. I can't help her down there. You, either."

"My wife and I want to help her get out." Alan narrowed his eyes. "You've been watching her?"

"Saw her come here two-three weeks ago. Couldn't figure out why."

"Had you seen her before that?"

"Not up here." McCarran smacked his palm with the nightstick. "I know she was pulled in a coupla times down there. Those sons a' bitches kept her till they were through with her, then they let her out. No charges."

He knows.

"Pretty little girl. You know how old she is?"

"Twenty."

"Mine woulda been twenty-one in April." The sergeant took out a thick black wallet and handed Alan a business card. "Mr. Cottrill, if you see either of those men around here, you call me." He tapped his chest. "Me. You understand? Whatever you do, don't talk to 'em." He put the wallet back in his pocket. "I don't think they'll be back, but if you see 'em, you call me."

"I will." Alan blew out his tension. "Thank you, Sergeant."

Alan stumbled into the bedroom and braced himself on the foot of the mattress. "The police came. They're gone."

Mary was in Sara's arms on the bed. "Don't make me go back," she whimpered. "He'll beat me to death. That's what he did to Libby. Brought his girls in to see them beat her up and watch her die. I'll kill myself first."

"Why does he want you?" asked Alan.

"Sally sold me."

"*Sold* you?" said Sara. "How could she sell you?"

"To Walter. She says I'm his now."

Sara stroked Mary's hair. "She has to stay here tonight. We'll take her to Peg first thing tomorrow."

When the two men were well out of sight and earshot, Walter stamped his tasseled loafer on the sidewalk. "Fuckin' McCarran! I paid good money for that cunt and I want it back, with interest." He put his hand on Mr. Orange's shoulder. "Cap, you go get Sally and bring her in. If she doesn't have it, you and I'll have a private conversation with her in our special room. When we're finished she'll be glad to take little Mary's place."

25

Alan called Peg the next morning. "Mary's in trouble. She spent last night with us and now she needs some place to go."

"What kind of trouble? With her friend? Susan, wasn't it?"

"Sally. Mary says she sold her to a pimp. Can you imagine—?"

"I can imagine anything happening down there," said Peg.

"Two of them came here yesterday and tried to get her."

"To the North End? No, sir!" Alan heard her exhale. "What happened?"

"A police car came by, and a sergeant ran them off."

"Huh. What was his name?"

"McCarran."

"McCarran," said Peg. "He had to know something. Who were the pimps?"

"He called one of them Walter."

"Whoo. I know that one. Mary's a lucky girl. Bring her down." She paused. "Are you driving?"

"Yes."

"Well, be careful. I bet Mac left a patrol, but you lock the doors."

Alan, Sara and Mary were sitting in Peg's office half an hour later.

Mary sat against Sara on the couch and Alan sat in a folding chair Peg had dragged in from the storage room. Alan told Peg what had happened the day before.

"You're a lucky girl, Mary," said Peg.

Mary's eyes widened. "Don't let them get me, please." Sara put her arm around the girl.

"Any chance of that?" asked Alan.

"They won't mess with our girls," said Peg. "If they hurt one of them I'll have it on the front page of the *Globe* the next day, and they know it. I'd raise so much hell that those good-for-nothings in City Hall who pull in money from the misery down there would have to face the press and say things to placate the so-called decent citizens who patronize the place. Our city fathers might even have to do something—run in some girls, raid a few clubs, maybe arrest some pushers. They'd have to lay low for a while down there. Bad for business."

She sat back in her chair. "So you'll be safe here, Mary. Now here's what we expect from you."

"Yes, Miss Walsh."

"Call me Peg. Everyone here goes by their first name." She leaned forward. "We need you here to help us serve and clean up after meals and do housekeeping and laundry. You'll sleep in the dorm with the other girls. All of you have had a hard time, but you'll treat everyone with re-spect and you will *not* crowd them. Do what you're told and don't make trouble for anyone. If trouble starts, walk away. Even if they hit you. If you don't, we'll send you back outside."

"I will, Peg. I promise."

Peg stood up. "Loretta!" A young black woman with an Afro and wearing a tan jumpsuit came to the door. "Loretta, this is our new guest, Mary Ann Jawonsky. She'll be with us for a while. She's not to go outside unless I'm with her."

"Right, Peg." Loretta held out her hands. "Welcome, Mary Ann. I love that name. Grab your bag and come with me. I'll show you around and introduce you to everyone. Then we'll do some paperwork." She made a wry face. "Yuck."

Mary stood slowly and picked up her duffel bag. She turned to Sara. "Will you come with me?"

"Of course." Sara got up and put her arm around Mary's shoulder. They followed Loretta out the door.

Alan and Peg watched them go. "I sound tougher than I am, to put a little fear of God in them," she said. "But I have to be careful, she's fragile right now. If there's trouble, we straighten it out here. We talk to them before we do anything. We don't want to throw anyone out and we almost never do. Only the hardened ones who have to rule or those who just won't get along. I don't think we'll have trouble with Mary but if we do, I'll call you. And I won't send her out. If she has to leave, I'll turn her over to you and she'll be yours from then on. Do we understand each other?"

"Yes."

"Good. We'll have her examined by a doctor in a day or two. We want to be sure she doesn't have anything that can be passed around and she's free of any sexually transmitted disease."

"What are the chances?"

"No way to tell. There'll be tests after the exam, so it'll be a week or so before we know anything. I'll call you when we do."

Peg walked to the door, put her hands on the frame and leaned through it. "Callie," she called, "will you ask Bobby to come here, please?"

The typist's voice bellowed, "Bob-EE! Peg wants you."

A squeaky voice called out, "In a minute."

"Our intercom," said Peg. She went back to her chair.

"You know McCarran," said Alan.

"Mac used to work in the Combat Zone. It's tough for the boys down there. Our city fathers won't admit it, but they know what's going on and some of them profit from it, so they look the other way. That means the cops can only do so much, and the good ones don't like it. They know that whores mean pimps and pimps bring gangs and gangs corrupt everyone, even them. They can only operate around the edges, arresting girls and pushers, not the kingpins because they're connected downtown."

"I had no idea . . ."

"Mac wouldn't go along with that. When a Jonas named Harley beat one of his girls so badly he crippled her and no one would do anything about it, he came down one night, pulled Harley into a dark alley and beat him to a pulp. Mac was out of uniform but everyone knew who did it and they're all afraid of him. For good reason."

"McCarran told Walter if I got hurt he'd pay him a visit."

"That's what he meant." Peg tapped the desk with her pencil. "Well, someone downtown got wind of what Mac did, and he was transferred. Probably a good thing for him."

"He talked like he'd lost a daughter. Said she would've been twenty-one soon."

"I don't know anything about his personal life."

A short, pudgy boy of about twenty waddled into the room. Black hair in a bowl cut and round dark-rimmed glasses gave him the appearance of a fat little owl. He was wearing a gray T-shirt, dungarees and open sandals and carrying a spiral notebook. He stopped just inside the door. "Yeah?"

"Bobby, this is Alan Cottrill." Bobby nodded to him. "His wife, Sara, is here with Mary Ann Jawonsky, who's just joined us. They need to get the birth certificate for Mary, who will be with us for a while. Alan can tell you about her."

Alan told Bobby what he knew about Mary, and gave him the name and address of Mary's adoptive parents. "We think she was born in Iowa, but we're not sure. The certificate her adoptive parents have will tell you where she was born, and—"

"I know how that works," said Bobby. "The state certificate will show names for the child and the birth mother, but they may not be their real names." He wrote in his notebook. "And the state may not tell us anything, but I'll ask."

"Sometimes I can help with that," said Peg. "Anything else?"

"What about the mother?" asked Bobby.

"The woman who may be her mother left high school in the spring of 1955, her senior year," said Alan, "and went to Iowa to have the baby. She told me she gave it up for adoption in Iowa City."

"Iowa City." Bobby wrote in his notebook again. "She didn't graduate?"

"Right. She didn't."

"See what I can do." Bobby slapped his notebook shut and marched away.

Sara came back. "She likes Loretta."

"Everyone does," said Peg.

Alan told Sara about his conversation with Bobby.

"How long will it take?" she asked.

"At least a couple of months," said Peg. "It'll depend on the cooperation of the Jawonskys and how long it takes to get what we need from the state."

"Iowa's law says the child has to be twenty-one to petition," said Alan.

"Well," said Peg, "we may have to do it informally. Sing a sad song and beg. Sometimes that works."

"And if it doesn't?" asked Alan.

"We'll try something else." Peg stood. "I have to go. I have a meeting with our board and some donors. I'll call you next week."

Peg called the next Friday and told Alan that Mary had passed all the tests. "No diseases, but she's had an abortion."

"She told us."

"And the doctor says she probably can't conceive. He's told her."

"She told us that, too."

"We called the Jawonskys," she said. "He wanted a letter from us requesting a certified copy of the birth certificate. We sent it to him yesterday."

"Did he ask about her?"

"He didn't. I think he wanted to wash his hands of her."

"How could anyone do that to their daughter?" asked Alan.

"Oh, he made it clear she's not their daughter. But that doesn't matter now."

"Do you think he'll send it?"

"Probably. Another washing of the hands. I'll call you when we have anything."

PEG GAVE ALAN WEEKLY updates on Mary. Her first reports were that Mary was doing well—following instructions, doing her tasks willingly and getting along. As weeks went by, Mary opened up with Peg and told her the story of her life.

Mary had been a rebellious teenager. The Jawonskys were upset with her for several years before she was impregnated by a boy they had ordered her to stay away from. When she told them she was pregnant by him, they ordered her out of their house.

A man named Jared paid for her to have an abortion and forced her into prostitution to repay him. He kept claiming that she was not repaying him fast enough to offset the interest on the loan and what she was costing him, trapping her in sexual slavery. After a year of this bondage, she met Sally and accepted her offer to come and live with her in Boston, though she knew nothing about Boston or Sally.

Sally was another, though gentler, Jared. At first, Mary had to pay Sally so much for moving her and for room and board that she could not save anything, but she quickly learned how to beg men for extra money. Sally told Mary that life on the "outside"—away from the Combat Zone—was not a safe place for her, that she would be captured and abused by the rich people in Boston, as she was by the police in the Combat Zone.

"I saw Mary and Sally kissing like lovers one night," said Alan. "Could Mary be a lesbian?"

"I'm sure she isn't. She's wary about men, though. They've all mistreated her. She's toughening up here, getting her feet under her. Taking classes to get her GED. She can make it outside, but she'll need help for a while. Some nurturing. She's determined, though. I don't know where she got it."

"Maybe it's in her genes."

"She's keeps asking about her mother. I tell her we're trying, but we don't know anything."

"What do you know?"

"Bobby's been sick. I'll call you when we have anything."

—◦◦◦—

ALAN WAS EXPECTING THE usual update when Peg called him in late March, but she asked for him and Sara to come to her office. "We've dug up some things you need to see."

"Is it good news or bad?" he asked.

"You'll have to tell us. When can you come?"

"Sara gets off at five. We could be there by six, if that's okay."

"We'll see you then."

Sara met Alan on West Street outside the House by the Side of the Road at 5:45. "What's this about?" she asked.

"They've dug up some things they want me to see."

The lights were out in the entryway, but Bobby and Peg were waiting in her office. Bobby was sitting, cross-legged and barefoot, on a stack of boxes beside Peg, holding his notebook and a sheaf of papers.

"Your show, Bobby," she said. "Take them through it."

He took a pencil from his mouth. "The Jawonskys' adoption papers say that Mary Ann Jawonsky was adopted on December fourth, 1955, and that she was born at Sisters of Mercy Hospital in Iowa City. In Iowa they wait four days after the birth before adoption is finalized, so she was born on December first."

Alan grabbed Sara's hand. "She's Mara's."

"Slow down," said Peg. "Listen."

Bobby studied his notebook. "I called the Bureau of Vital Statistics in Des Moines with the registration number on the Jawonsky certificate, but they wouldn't tell me anything. They said the child had to be twenty-one to apply through the courts and that would take months. So I told Wonder Woman here." He tipped his head toward Peg. "She called some high mogul at the Bureau and sang the sad song of Mary's life—how she'd been mistreated, where she was now, and how only her mother could save her from the men who were after her. The woman told Peg they'd talk about it and call her back."

"I was lucky," said Peg. "She's a mother. She called two days later and said they couldn't send us anything in writing, but what was it we wanted to know?" She winked at Bobby. "I learned later that she'd called the Department of Public Welfare to check on me."

"Ah!" said Alan. "I can't stand this. What did you say?"

"I told her all I needed was the baby's name and the name of the mother on the Iowa birth certificate."

"And?"

"She said, 'Baby Jane Doe, and Angelina Spadafore.' Does that tell you anything?" Peg shifted her body sideways and studied Alan.

"Angelina is Mara's middle name. Mara Angelina Sabatelli."

"There's more," said Peg. "Bobby?"

"While I was at it," he said, "I called two local high schools and asked if an Angelina Spadafore was there in 1955 or '56. The principal at the second one, Iowa City High School, knew the name because Sophia Spadafore has taught Latin there for the last thirty years. He went through their records and found that Angelina Spadafore graduated in 1956."

Alan put a hand over his mouth. "It's her." He bowed his head. "Thanks be to God."

Sara touched his arm. "What, Alan? Talk to us."

He took a deep breath. "Mara told me she went to Iowa to live with her Aunt Sophie while she was pregnant, and she gave her child up for adoption in Iowa City. She said Aunt Sophie was a schoolteacher. Mara must have put Spadafore on the birth certificate because she was living with Sophia Spadafore and going by that name."

"Or for some reason she couldn't use her own name and she wanted to leave a clue," said Peg. "But why she did it doesn't matter, does it? She's Mary's mother."

"No doubt," said Alan. He turned to Bobby. "Thank you so much for all you you've done to uncover this. I hope you know what you've done for Mary and her mother. This'll bring them together." Bobby waved his notebook in the air.

"Peg," said Alan, "how should I tell Mara? Write to her?"

"I wouldn't write," said Peg. "A letter would sound too cold and you wouldn't be there to explain anything when she opened it. It's best to call. You'll know what to say if you're talking to her."

"What about Mary?" asked Sara. "Should we tell her?"

"The mother first," said Peg. "We won't tell Mary till we know what her mother is going to do." She pointed the pencil at Alan. "So call Mara and let me know what she says. Then we'll figure out what to do next."

26

"Hello, Colombo residence, TJ speaking."

"Hello, TJ, my name is Alan Cottrill. I met you in West Virginia last summer at your mother's reunion."

"Yes, sir."

"Do you remember me?"

"No, sir. Would you like to speak to my father?"

"I'm calling for your mother. Is she there?"

"No, sir."

"Will she be back soon?"

"No, sir. My father's right here."

"Hello?" A commander's voice.

"Thomas, this is Alan Cottrill. I'm calling for Mara."

"Yes, Alan, I remember you. You were Mara's boyfriend in high school."

"Yes!"

"Before she went away."

Alan did not know what to say.

"I know she told you," said Thomas. "Mara's in Ohio for her father's funeral. She'll be back on Saturday. I'll be talking to her this afternoon.

Can I give her a message?"

"Well . . . I don't know . . ."

"What is it, Alan?"

"It's about"—he inhaled—"the child."

There was a pause. "Yes?"

He'd started, so he might as well go on. "She's here, Thomas. In Boston. Her name is Mary Ann Jawonsky."

"Good God. A girl. She must be—what—twenty now?"

"That's right."

"In Boston."

"She's at a shelter for abandoned young women," said Alan.

"A shelter. How did she get there?"

"She came here from Chicago a year or so ago."

"I mean to the shelter. Did she run away?" asked Thomas.

"Well . . . not really."

Another pause. Then, softly, "What happened, Alan?"

"Sara and I got her to move there from a bad section of Boston. She was living with a woman there." Alan closed his eyes and waited.

"Mother of God." Alan heard a long release of air. "How is she?"

"She's in good shape, Thomas. She looks a lot like Mara."

"What does she know?"

"She knows she was adopted and she wants to find her mother. From what I've said to her, she suspects I'm her father."

"About Mara?"

"Nothing. I wanted to be sure before I said anything."

"What about her . . . health?" asked Thomas.

"She's clean, if that's what you mean. The shelter had her examined. She has had an abortion."

"Hm. How do you know she's Mara's child?"

"Her Iowa birth certificate. She was born on December first, 1955, in Iowa City. The mother's name on the hospital certificate is Angelina Spadafore. Mara was living—"

"I know. How did you meet her?"

"In a bar. Nothing happened. I was with a—"

"It doesn't matter. How do you know she's in good health?"

"I can get a copy of the exam if you want it. Do you want to wait?"

Quickly. "Oh, no. I'll call Mara. Give me your number."

Alan did. "What do you think she'll do?"

"She prays for the child every day. She'll call you."

27

"Alan! She's alive!" He held the phone away from his ear. "My baby was a girl and she's alive!"

"Mara—"

"How did you find her? Is she there? Can I talk to her?" She squealed. "My daughter, alive after twenty years! When can I see her?" The pitch of her voice lowered. "You said she was staying someplace. A shelter or something. Are they taking good care of her?"

"Yes—"

"What does she look like? Is she pretty?"

"Very pretty. She looks like you."

Mara squealed again. "She looks like *me*?"

"A little smaller, and she has your eyes."

"Oh, Alan, you don't know—you couldn't—how much I've thought about my baby since she was taken away from me. She is always in my heart. I pray for her every day. I wanted her to have a good life with a good mother and father."

"She's had a hard life, Mara."

"Tommy told me. He was so choked up he had a hard time talking. I was in my stepmother's bedroom screaming and jumping up and down when he was telling me. My baby is alive and Alan knows her. It's a miracle!"

"You went to your father's funeral?"

"Frankie called me. He said Papa was dying and he'd asked to see me. I got to talk to him and hold his hand his last day. He said he was sorry and I told him I loved him. I showed him pictures of the boys. His wife and her children have been so good to Frankie and me. They all loved him. He was at peace."

"I'm glad, Mara. For both of you."

"Thank you. Now, tell me about my daughter, Mary Ann." She paused. "You are sure, aren't you?"

"The mother's name on her birth certificate is Angelina Spadafore. And Sophia Spadafore still teaches Latin at—"

"Aunt Sophie! I can't wait to tell her! She'll be so happy! I'll call her right now. No, I don't have her number with me."

"Mara—"

"When can I see her? Tomorrow? No, I can't come tomorrow. I'm going home tomorrow." She stopped. "This is Thursday, isn't it?"

"It's Wednesday."

"Oh, yes, Wednesday. Well, I don't know . . ."

"Do you want to talk to Thomas about it?"

"About what? We'll come."

"Maybe he can make the arrangements while you're flying home."

"Yes! He always does that. I'll call him right now, goodbye—Wait! Are you still there?"

He chuckled. "Yes."

"I can't thank you enough, Alan. You're my hero. You found my baby! I love you."

—⚬⚬⚬—

THOMAS CALLED THE NEXT afternoon. He had arranged for Mara to fly from Defiance to Boston on Friday instead of returning to San Diego.

He was able to get a seat on a Military Air Transport Command flight from San Diego to Boston with some officers flying to Boston that day. He and Mara would spend Friday night with one of Thomas's Annapolis classmates. "It's the price of my ticket," he said. Mara and Thomas would come to 21 Salem Street on Saturday morning.

Alan told Thomas he would arrange for Mary to come there that afternoon.

Thomas had made reservations for the three of them to fly back to San Diego late Saturday. "We want to get her out of Boston."

Alan hung up and left a message at the House by the Side of the Road for Peg, who called him the next morning.

"Mary's mother and her husband are coming to get her," he said. "They'll be here Saturday."

"Saturday?" asked Peg. "Next week?"

"Tomorrow, Peg."

"You're kidding. How can they get here tomorrow?"

"Mara's been in Ohio for her father's funeral. She's coming from there, and her husband is coming to Boston on a military flight from San Diego. They'll be here late tonight and stay over with one of his Annapolis classmates."

"And . . . ?"

"They want to take Mary back to San Diego with them tomorrow."

"Do you have any idea what you're doing? They can't just waltz in here tomorrow and whisk her away to San Diego. That's a formula for disaster, and I won't let it happen!"

"Oh, Peg, I'm sorry. What have I done?"

"Made a mess," she said. "Let me think." After half a minute she said, "Okay. Do this. Call the husband—what's his name?"

"Thomas."

"Call Thomas and tell him you know they want to do right by Mary, but they need to spend some time with me to learn about her—her life, what it's done to her, and the condition she's in now. It's not going to be easy for them, and they have to know what they'll be dealing with. It's not at all like raising a child from birth."

"How do you want to do that?"

Peg was silent for several seconds. "They're flying into Boston to-night. Suppose I meet with them tomorrow. Noon, say. Someplace where Mary won't see us."

"You could come here."

"Good. Then I can bring Mary over there to meet her mother on Sunday." Another pause. "Yeah, that'll do it. So tell them to stay over Saturday night and plan to fly home with her late on Sunday."

"What will you tell Mary?"

"I'll tell her you and Sara want her to stay with you for a few days, and I'll bring her over Sunday whatever happens."

"You won't tell her?" asked Alan.

"Not till I see what happens on Saturday."

"Why?"

"They could change their minds. Sometimes the euphoria wears off when they see how hard it will be to stick a new person into their family and they back out."

"You're kidding!" he said.

"It's happened. I'm not going to take any chances."

Alan called and talked to Thomas before he left for the airport.

Thomas understood. "We only have one chance to get this right, and we don't want to mess it up." He said he would arrange for him and Mara to stay over Saturday and fly to San Diego late Sunday.

28

Sara opened the door of 21 Salem Street as Mara and Thomas, hunched over in the wind that bounced pellets of sleet off of them, hustled up the sidewalk. She hugged Mara and then held her at arm's length, marveling at how much she resembled Mary.

"Welcome!" said Alan. "It's nice to see you again."

Thomas pushed the door closed. "Man, I'm not used to this. San Diego has thinned my blood." He slapped his chest. "Brr." He and Mara took off their light jackets and gave them to Sara.

Alan led them into the living room where Peg was sitting in the far easy chair. A thick folder sat on the coffee table in front of her. She was dressed formally today, in a tan sweater and a full-length pleated skirt. She stood and started toward Mara and Thomas.

"Peg Walsh, this is Mara and Thomas Colombo," said Alan. He turned to them. "Peg has run the Boston shelter for runaways and abandoned girls for the last ten years. She's been caring for Mary since October. She's here to tell you about her and what it will be like to have her living with you."

"Bless you," said Mara, taking Peg's hand, "for showing kindness and mercy to our loved one."

"We can't wait to hear about her," said Thomas. He and Mara sat together on the deep purple couch and Peg went back to her seat across the coffee table from them.

Sara put a tray with a thermos pitcher of coffee, five mugs and a plate of apple and cheese Danish on the table. Everyone helped themselves. Sara and Alan sat in the tan fabric-covered chairs across from the Colombos. Morning light slanting in through the side window brightened the table and the carpet beside it.

Peg looked around the table. "I've never seen anything like this," she said. "Alan knows Mara, he recognizes Mary, and now Mara and Thomas are here for her. It's almost a miracle."

"It *is* a miracle," said Mara. "God answered my prayers to the Blessed Mother. He sent Alan to find my baby."

"Thanks be to God," said Alan. He turned to Peg. "What do we do now?"

"Let's start at the beginning," said Peg, "and ask Mara and Thomas to tell us about themselves." She picked up her mug. "Mara?"

"I was born and raised in Hartsburg, West Virginia." said Mara. "My father owned a butcher shop there. He sent me away in 1955 to live with my aunt in Iowa because I was pregnant." She looked across the table. "I left Alan and my high school that spring without saying goodbye to anyone. I couldn't face them."

She lifted her mug. "My baby was born in December that year. I finished high school in Iowa the next year and lived there till I married Tommy." She sipped some coffee.

"Alan was your boyfriend," said Peg. "He isn't the father?"

Mara pressed her lips together. "I was assaulted by a classmate that March. I didn't tell Alan about it till I saw him five years later." She put her mug on the table and gripped Thomas's arm. "This is so hard." He patted her hand.

"How did you and Thomas meet?"

"I went to San Diego in 'sixty-three to visit my brother in the Navy," said Mara. "Tommy was his commanding officer. He joined us for dinner at a restaurant one night." She gave his shoulder a friendly punch. "I still think Frankie set that up." Thomas shook his head. "Anyway, we met there and we hit it off. We were married in 'sixty-four and we've lived in San Diego ever since. Tommy's a lieutenant commander now."

"We have three sons," said Thomas. "Eleven, eight and three."

"We're blessed," said Mara.

"How do you get along with your family now?" asked Peg.

"I lost my mother in 'fifty-seven," said Mara, "and my father passed away on Monday. I went to see him just before he died and we made up after all those years. My brother, Frankie, is my buddy."

"What a week you've had," said Peg. "Thomas?"

"My brother Angelo teaches high school in Chicago, where we were born. My mother lives with him and his family. We get along fine."

"Can you tell us about Mary Ann now?" said Mara. "I'm about to bust open."

Peg took a drink of coffee. "Your daughter—"

"I didn't know my baby was a girl till Tommy told me," said Mara.

"She was adopted by a childless Chicago couple named Jawonsky," said Peg. "They named her Mary Ann. Two years later, Mrs. Jawonsky gave birth to a daughter. When Mary Ann was a senior in high school, she was seduced by a boy who promised to marry her, but he ran away when she told him she was pregnant. The Jawonskys kicked her out when she told them, and the school was going to send her to a home for unwed mothers."

Sara refilled Peg's cup, and she continued. "So there she was, seventeen years old, out on the street with nothing but the clothes on her back, and four months pregnant. She met a man named Jared at a homeless shelter and he talked her into having an abortion. He paid for it, and then told her she'd have to pay him back, so he had her where he wanted her. He forced himself on her, then one of his so-called friends, then another, then another, and so on.

"He kept all the money, telling her she owed him more and more, and that she had to keep working to pay him back. Of course, she never could. He had her, and pretty soon she found out he had other girls, too."

Sara leaned forward. "Mara, we knew nothing about the awful world Mary lived in till we met her and tried to help her get out of it."

"The world is full of evil people, most of them men," said Peg.

"Chicago," said Thomas, softly. "Do you know where this Jared is now?"

"I don't," said Peg. She reached for a cheese Danish. "A client helped her get away from Jared. He gave her a good bit of money, but he was married and couldn't support her indefinitely. Jared had her school ID and driver's license, so she couldn't get any regular work." Peg nibbled at the pastry.

"Couldn't she go to the police?" asked Alan.

Peg swallowed. "She was afraid to. Jared told her he'd paid them off and they'd beat her up—and worse—and then give her back to him. And remember, she had no ID."

"How'd she get out of Chicago?" asked Thomas.

"She met a woman named Sally somewhere—a bar or a brothel, I'm not sure. Sally got her a driver's license—it was probably forged—and brought her to Boston a year and a half ago."

Peg stretched her arms and put her hands on top of her head. "Sally was cleverer than Jared. She pretended to be Mary's friend while she held onto the license and pressured her to work to pay off the debt from that and the cost of the trip to Boston. Mary worked the bars in the Boston's red light district, and Sally watched her like a hawk. Mary did squirrel away some money. She had about eleven hundred dollars when she met Alan."

"Is this Sally a lesbian?" asked Thomas.

"She is, and she forced Mary into that too. She says it makes her sick," said Peg. "She slipped away from Sally when she came here to see Alan and Sara. She really believes that Alan is her father. She asks me all the time, 'Why else would he be doing this?' I can't convince her he's not."

"I can," said Mara. "He's not her father. A boy named Bucky Connor was."

"And he's—?"

"Gone. Killed in a hunting accident a long time ago."

"Mary told Sally she was adopted and she wanted to find her mother," said Peg. "When Mary started getting calls from Alan, Sally became suspicious. She thought he was her father and knew who her mother was. Sally must've thought she couldn't hold on to Mary, so she sold her to a pimp named Walter." Peg rubbed her chin with her fingers. "A real SOB, that one. He's beaten women to death when they tried to leave him."

Peg turned to Alan. "Somehow, again, Mary got away and came here before Walter could get his hands on her. I swear, Alan, someone was watching out for her."

"Sergeant McCarran?"

"Maybe," said Peg. "But it's a miracle she got to you before Walter and his thugs caught up with her. Then Mac ran them off." She inhaled through clenched teeth. "I wouldn't want to be in Sally's shoes right now."

She stood up. "That's Mary's life before she came to the House. I'll tell you how she is now in a minute, but I need a break."

"The bathroom's down there," said Sara, pointing.

Thomas and Alan stood up and stretched. Sara refilled the thermos pitcher. Mara sat still, staring into the fireplace. "My baby." She closed her eyes. "My baby."

Sara studied Mara's face and wished she could relate to her—how she felt last week when she learned that the child she had given up was alive and then today when she learned about her daughter's miserable life. Would Mara feel responsible for what happened to Mary? Sara's stomach felt queasy. She covered her mouth.

Alan squatted beside her. "You all right, babe?"

"I'm okay."

"You sure?"

Peg came back into the room. "The first thing I want to say about Mary is that she's not been destroyed by what she's been through. She's a good little girl, but she's been badly traumatized, and she's fragile. She needs help and support by professionals as well as your love, and she can get that help in San Diego."

Mara's eyes widened. "She can live with us, can't she? We have a room for her."

Peg walked around to her chair and sat. "It would be better if you introduced her to your boys and had her stay with you for a few days, but then take her to a place that knows how to care for her. For a month or two. She won't like to go, but you can assure her she'll live with you after that, and you should visit her as often as you can."

"I'll go see her every day," said Mara.

"Do you know a place?" asked Thomas.

Peg touched her folder. "I'll give you the names of some places that can take her in and help her along."

"Good."

"Mary has been betrayed and abused by almost everyone she's trusted," said Peg. "She'll suspect any man she meets is out to take advantage of her. That suspicion and fear is subterranean. She may not realize it's there or what it's doing to her."

"I don't understand," said Thomas.

"She'll be skittish any time she's alone with a man. She won't show it—she may not even know why she's frightened—but any man could spook her. So you mustn't be alone in a room with her. If you are, she may defend herself by tempting you, or she may lose control of her emotions. Don't reach for her, touch her, crowd her or stand over her. She won't be able to stand it."

Peg paused. "Thomas, have you ever driven past a place where you were in a car accident?"

"I have."

Sara glanced at Alan. He closed his eyes and rubbed his forehead.

"Didn't your palms sweat?" asked Peg. "That's how she'll be. The bad things done to her will live inside her for a long time. She'll react badly sometimes, even to good things, and she won't know why. You mustn't expect her to be rational or predictable all the time, and don't come down on her when she behaves badly. Calm her down and get her to talk about how she feels. When she understands what's happening inside her she begins to heal. She's done some of that already."

Peg turned to Alan. "You're the exception. She loves you more than she realizes. Like a father. She loves Sara and me, too, but that's different. You found her and saved her. Even then, she has a residual fear of being abandoned. Anyone who's been abandoned like she has will carry the fear of it happening again for the rest of her life."

Peg put her glasses on the table and rubbed her eyes. "Mary will be very volatile. She'll blow up or cry over things you don't understand. Remember that she doesn't understand what's going on either, so whatever you do, don't think it's your doing, or her fault. She'll think it is sometimes, and you'll have to console her. Make sure she knows she isn't to blame."

"What about the boys?" asked Thomas. "They're expecting a long-lost sister. I think TJ understands what happened, but the others are too young."

"I run a harem," said Peg. "I don't know much about boys. But I do know that having Mary in the house will disrupt their lives. She'll cling to Mara and compete with them for her time and attention. There'll be problems, but it might be worse if you had three girls. Boys don't cling as much."

"I'm not worried," said Mara. "They'll be nice to her."

Thomas put his hands on his thighs and leaned forward. "I'm not worried about how they will treat her. How will she treat them? They didn't grow up together. Does she know how to be a sister?"

"Mary was part of a family for her first seventeen years," said Peg. "Her parents were tough on her and she rebelled, but her family was not dysfunctional like the ones my girls come from. And she gets along with everyone at the House."

"What's her attitude going to be toward other men?" said Thomas. "Will she be hungry for them?"

"She'll avoid them," said Peg. "Her fear will make it hard for her to have a loving relationship with a man. She won't be sexually attracted to one for a long time."

Thomas folded his arms. "And she's not a lesbian."

"She's a survivor. She's done what she had to do when she had no way out. She believes she had no choice and she's probably right. She learned how to get along in that awful world and saved herself by separating her spirit from the things she was forced to do." Peg put her glasses on. "She couldn't have done that with Walter. He would have beaten the spirit out of her if he didn't kill her."

"And not diseased?"

"Tommy," said Mara softly, "what's wrong? What are you worried about?"

"I'm wondering if it wouldn't be a good idea to have her stay here a little longer and be treated by the people who know her," he said. "She could stay with Peg until she's straightened out. We could pay for that and come back later to get her."

Peg stood, stepped slowly to the fireplace and put her hand on the mantel. "You could do that." She lowered her head and stared over her glasses at Mara. "But if you do, you'll have to go back to San Diego without seeing her. You can't meet her and leave. She'd think she was being abandoned by her mother again, and I think too much of her to let that happen."

Peg drummed the top of the mantel with her fingernails. "And if she stays here, sooner or later her past will get out. Someone who comes to us for help or someone who sees her on the street will recognize her and talk. We won't tell anyone, but it will get out. And once it does, she won't be safe here."

Sara eyed Thomas up and down. Was he serious? Did he really want to leave Mary here? Would he let Mara come back for her if they did? She saw Alan leaning back in his chair and staring at Thomas in disbelief. What was going on between Thomas and Mara?

"Tommy," said Mara, "I *know* it will be hard. Mary will cling to me and the boys will be upset sometimes. But they're good boys. TJ is our little man. He'll help me. And Dino will do whatever his big brother does, you know that." She touched his chest. "I know you're thinking about me and the boys because you love us so much, but I know we can do this."

She put her arms around his neck and gazed into his eyes. "She's my daughter, Tommy. My blood. They took her away from me and look what happened. I can't let her go again. We have to save her *now*. I have to do it, Tommy." She ran a hand over his hair. "And I can't do it without you."

Thomas put an arm around Mara. "Peg," he said, "how do we know she'll stay with us once she gets to San Diego?"

"The first thing she needs is love and acceptance as a person," said Peg. "She's been nothing but a body used to satisfy appetites for sex or money for three years. She believes she's more than that, and she needs someone who will treat her like she is." Peg furrowed her brow. "Is that clear? She needs to know who she is and that she's a worthwhile person. She needs a family."

"She'll have that with us," said Mara.

"And after that?" asked Thomas. "She'll have to go out on her own sooner or later."

"Like the boys will someday," said Mara.

"She'll be ready," said Peg. "She'll want to go out on her own and take care of herself. She should get her GED first. Then she can go to work, or school, or both. You can help her be sure an employer doesn't take advantage of her."

"Take advantage?" asked Thomas.

"By overworking or underpaying her, or anything else. She'll need guidance, especially at first. You'll be able to tell when she's unhappy, and she'll come to you when she's uncertain."

"Like the boys?" asked Mara.

"They'll be more confident when they go out on their own," said Peg. "It'll be easier for them to say no than it will be for her. But a girl will be more likely to share confidences with her mother." She chuckled. "Listen to me, the expert on raising boys *and* girls. But I think that's what it'll be like."

"So you think it'll be all right?" asked Thomas.

Peg stood and walked to the side window. She looked across the street at the iron rail fence around the grass courtyard of the Old North Church. "I know your boys are good kids, but they'll resent her after a while, and they may challenge her right to be a member of your family—make her feel guilty for coming in when she did. If that happens, Mary could see herself tearing up another family like she did the Jawonskys, and that could drive her away again."

"That's what happened to me," said Mara.

"But you had your Aunt Sophie to go to, and Frankie," said Alan.

"Mary will have to feel she's wanted, especially when things aren't going well," said Peg. "You'll have to keep telling her she's one of you, that disagreement and tension happen in all families and you can get through it together. She's not been able to get through it before. She's either been kicked out or she's run away when things got bad, and you can't let that happen. She has no Aunt Sophie to go to."

"Could she come back here?" asked Sara.

"Don't even think about that," said Peg. She turned around and leaned on the windowsill. "Thomas, Alan told me you went to Annapolis."

"That's right."

"What was your plebe year like?"

"It was hell."

"Were you ready for it?"

"I had no idea what it would be like," he said. "Halfway through that year I asked myself what in God's name I was doing there. All the work and all the harassment was about to do me in. I thought I was tough, but I didn't know what tough was till I got to the Academy." He drew himself up. "But by then I had too much invested in it to give up. And I was *not* going to come home and tell Mom and Pop and Angelo that I'd quit. It would've broken their hearts."

He pushed his glasses higher on his nose. "I decided then and there that the only way they were going to get me out was to pick me up and throw me out. And I wasn't going to go without a fight."

"And you made it," said Mara.

"By the skin of my teeth."

"This is going to be like that," said Peg. "There'll be times when you wonder if you'll ever get through it." She sat down. "You can do it, but you'll have to be as tough as you were when you were a plebe, and as Mara was after she gave up her baby."

Alan was on the edge of his chair, about to speak. Sara cleared her throat, and he noticed. She shook her head so slightly that no one else saw it. She knew that Thomas and Mara had to talk this out themselves. He sat back.

"She needs us now," said Mara.

"Yes," said Peg.

"I see that," said Thomas. He put his arm around Mara's shoulders. "We have to do it. I'm ready." He looked at Peg. "What's next?"

Peg picked up the folder. "Here's what I have on her. Birth certificate, adoption papers, high school transcript, our counselor's report and recommendations, which you've just heard from me, her physical exam and a release from the Jawonskys that allows you to take her to California. Legally she's still their daughter, but they won't contest a request for an adoption if you apply for it. You don't really need to, she'll be twenty-one in December, but you can if you want to."

She held up two glossy brochures. "Here's information about two places in San Diego that can help her. The county-run Women's Resource Center and a private one called Little Creek Ranch for Women. They both help women deal with the problems that come with sexual abuse and abandonment. I think Little Creek would be better, but you should visit them both and decide."

She tucked the brochures back in the folder. "Mary needs counseling as much as she needs love. A good counselor will be objective about where she is on her path to recovery and will help her—and you—see what she's struggling with, and will help you all work through it. Mary will need counseling off and on for a long time. When things come up that you don't understand and can't handle, get someone to help."

Peg leaned toward Mara. "I've talked to Hallie Carson, the director of Little Creek. She'd like to see you and Mary."

Peg looked at the ceiling for several seconds, then lowered her head. "If there's anything I can do—or you think there might be—call me. She's a dear little girl who's been horribly abused for the last three years, but she *can* come out of it. Let me know where you are taking her and I'll stay in touch with them."

Peg pushed the folder across the table to Thomas. "She had no police record in Chicago. She was pulled in here a year ago but wasn't charged."

Thomas took the folder and tapped the table with its edge. "What else?"

"That's all you need," said Peg.

"No, it isn't," said Mara. "Where is she? When can I see her?"

"I'll tell her the Cottrills want her to spend a few days with them starting tomorrow," said Peg. "I'll bring her here around one."

"Our flight's at six," said Thomas. "We'll have to leave by four."

"The three of us," said Mara.

Sara tapped her lips. "I'll have lunch delivered at two."

"Anything else?" said Peg. She waited a few seconds. "All right. We'll see you tomorrow." She stood. "I won't tell Mary anything about today. She'll expect to see Sara and Alan."

Peg smiled at Mara. "You're going to love your daughter. And I'm going to miss her."

Mara's eyes filled with tears.

IT WAS QUIET TIME in the House by the Side of the Road that evening. Everyone had done their chores for the day and was taking it easy. The stainless steel serving counter in the kitchen and the pots and pans that hung over the island behind it were glistening in the overhead lights. The plastic tablecloths in the dining room were streaked with small beads of water from being cleaned. The tables were set for Sunday's breakfast, with silverware and white napkins along the sides and salt and pepper shakers in the center.

Two girls were sitting at a table in the middle of the dining room, whispering to each other. Mary was at a corner table playing solitaire. The irregular *flick* of her cards carried across the room.

The older girl tipped her head toward Mary. "She's a whore."

"No shit?"

"Five bucks a flop, I bet. She ain't worth no more'n that. Too little to take it all."

"Ya think?" The other girl, a teenager with a face full of acne, twisted her chair around and stared at Mary. "How d'you know?"

"I seen her once, at Good Time Charlie's." The older girl gave out a breathy whistle. "Hey, whore!"

Mary kept dealing cards and playing them.

"I'm talkin' ta you, whore."

Acne-face gasped. Peg was standing behind her companion. She grabbed the girl's collar, twisted it and pulled. Peg's eyes were blazing with anger, but her voice was soft. "On your feet. One more like that and you're out of here." She spun the girl around and shoved her toward Mary, who had not looked up. "Now you go over there and apologize to her."

The girl shuffled over to Mary's table. "Sorry," she said. Then she murmured, "I bet you're used to it," and walked out of the room.

Peg glared at the seated girl until she got up and left, then sat down beside Mary. "I could wring her neck."

A knowing look passed between them.

"I'll do it if you want me to," said Mary. She went back to playing her cards. "That one's a chicken with a mouth."

"But you're so little."

"I know how to fight."

"You are something."

"I like it here. No one bothers me 'cept her, and she doesn't matter." Mary laid her handful of cards on the table. "Anything about my mother?"

"The Cottrills would like to see you. Could you stay with them for a few days?"

"I guess so. When?"

"I'll take you there tomorrow after the service," said Peg. "Pack a bag with some clothes. I don't know how long you'll be there."

"Don't they both work?"

"They're going to have some company and Sara's not feeling well. They thought you could help them out and then stay over."

"Oh. Well, sure." Mary picked up the queen of hearts and snapped it with one hand. "Do they know what she has?"

Peg grinned. "I don't think they do."

Mary swept up the cards and shuffled them as Peg walked away.

29

The last hymn of the service the next day was "Just as I Am." When it ended, the stylishly coiffured middle-aged woman at the piano dropped the cover over its keyboard and slapped her hymnal shut. She stood up straight, brushed the wrinkles from her flowered dress and strutted like a fashion model to the rear door, her heels clacking on the hardwood floor as she went. The congregation, listless women in dark, shabby clothes, filed out the other door that led to the kitchen.

Mary stayed behind. She had collected and shelved the hymnals and straightened the rows of chairs when Peg came into the room. "Ready?"

Mary brushed off the front of her blouse and skirt. "Do I look all right? I wore this the last time I was there."

"You look nice. They'll be glad to see you."

"I'll get my stuff."

Outside, Mary opened the door and threw her duffel bag onto the back seat of Peg's five-year-old Vega. Peg turned the ignition key. "Come on, come on." The engine sputtered and coughed, then started. Peg took her foot off the clutch and the car lurched into the street. "One day I'm going to drive this darn thing into the bay."

"Not today, I hope." Mary fastened her seat belt. "Is Mrs. Cottrill going to be all right?"

"Oh, yes."

—◦◦◦—

"WHERE IS SHE?" MARA walked down the hall and looked around the living room of 21 Salem Street. "Is she here?"

"*Sta' calmo, signora,*" said Thomas. "We'll have some time to talk."

"She's not here yet. Would you like some coffee?" Sara went into the kitchen and filled two mugs with steaming black liquid. "Cream?"

"Please," said Mara. Sara poured cream into one of the mugs.

"Not for me," said Thomas.

Mara and Thomas sat on the couch. Alan and Sara took two easy chairs on the other side of the coffee table.

"Alan," said Mara, "I want to know how you met her. Tell me everything."

"It was last September," he said, "at a strip club in a bad section of Boston."

"And what were you doing in a strip club?" asked Mara.

"He had a new client who wanted to see it," said Sara. "He was stunned by how much Mary resembled you. He had to find out if she was your daughter." She told Mara about the encounter with the pimps and the police.

"Thank God for Peg Walsh and the House by the Side of the Road," said Alan. "They took her in, protected her, and found out that your name was on her Iowa birth certificate."

"That's when you called," said Thomas.

"Yes," said Alan.

"Stop it," said Mara. "When will she be here?"

"About one," said Alan.

Mara looked at the mantel clock. "It's twenty after. Are you sure she's coming?"

WHEN THEY GOT OUT of the car at 21 Salem Street, Peg motioned to Mary to go ahead of her. "I'll bring your bag."

Sara opened the door. "Come in, Mary. Alan's in the living room."

Mary walked through the hall and into the living room. The first person she saw was a woman standing in front of the coffee table, facing her. She was a little taller than Mary, with dark hair and eyes. Alan was sitting in an easy chair and a man she didn't know was sitting on the couch. They were all watching her. She peered at the woman. Who was she?

"Mary," she said, "I'm your mother."

Mary collapsed to the floor like a puppet whose strings were cut.

Alan and Thomas knelt beside Mary, picked her up gently and laid her on the couch. Peg slipped a pillow under her head, took a vial from her pocket, twisted its top off and held it under Mary's nose. She jerked her head from side to side to get away from the acrid smell.

Peg beckoned to Sara. "Come here. She should see someone she knows." Sara leaned over Mary's face. Her eyes fluttered, then opened wide.

She stared at Sara. "Mrs. Cottrill, I just had a dream. I saw a beautiful woman. She said she was my mother. I didn't want to wake up."

Sara stepped aside. Mara leaned over Mary, touched her and spoke softly. "Mary, it's not a dream. I'm your mother."

"My mother." Mary held out her arms. Mara bent down and put her arms under the girl. They looked into each other's eyes—the same eyes—and embraced. Mary was sobbing, and the more her body shook the tighter Mara held her. "My baby, after all these years, my baby." She helped Mary to her feet and the girl buried her head in Mara's chest.

Mary kept saying, "My mother. It's not a dream. My mother."

They rocked back and forth in each other's arms, crying in their happiness.

After several minutes, Mary sniffled and pulled back, holding on to Mara with one arm. "Who *are* you?"

"My name is Mara Colombo. I live in San Diego."

"Your friend?" Mary asked Alan.

He nodded.

"Why didn't you tell me?"

"I had to be sure."

"My father?" asked Mary.

"Died a long time ago," said Mara.

Mary pointed to Alan. "Not him?"

"Not him."

"Who's he?" asked Mary, looking at Thomas.

"My husband," said Mara.

"Your husband. Do you have kids?"

"We have three boys," said Mara.

"Three boys," said Mary. "Wow."

Thomas got up and put his arm around Mara's shoulders. "We want you to come home with us, Mary. The boys want to meet their sister." Mara kissed Mary's cheek.

"Go *home* with you? Where?" asked Mary.

"To San Diego," said Mara, "and meet your brothers."

"Brothers," said Mary. "How old?"

"Eleven, eight and three," said Mara. "Good boys."

Mary spoke to Thomas, almost whispering. "But aren't you worried about me? I'm older and—you know." She lowered her eyes.

"We know you've had a hard life, and we know you want to leave it behind," said Thomas. "But if something goes wrong, Mary, you'll have to leave us."

Her gaze was steady. "I've had enough go wrong." She wrapped her arms around Mara. "No more."

The others watched the two women, mother and daughter, holding and kissing each other.

The doorbell rang. Sara said, "I'll get it," and went to the front door. "Come in. It goes in the dining room." A teenage boy wearing a white cotton jacket that had "Polpetta Italiano" on the front and carrying three large white paper bags came tentatively into the room. Sara said, "In here," and led him through the kitchen and into the dining room.

The two of them bustled around, Sara getting out plates, glasses and silverware while the boy took out trays of food—pasta, meatball sandwiches and green salads—and put them on a side table. Sara poured iced tea into the glasses at the end of the table where the plates were stacked and called, "All right, everyone. Lunch is ready."

Thomas reached for his wallet. "Can I help?"

"It's taken care of," said Sara. The boy thanked her and left.

Everyone lined up along the wall to get plates and fill them. Mary stood behind Mara in the line and kept touching her as if to be sure she was real. Sara watched the movement from a corner.

Alan said, "Your turn now, babe."

"In a minute."

Mara patted the chair next to her and Mary took it. Everyone at the table dug in except Mary, who stared at Mara. "Mother," she said, "why did you leave me?"

"I didn't leave you," said Mara. "They took you away from me. It was the saddest day of my life."

"Took me away? How could they do that?"

"I was seventeen," said Mara. "When my mother saw I was pregnant she took me to the doctor and then our priest. When she told him I was pregnant, he scowled at me and told me I had sinned against my parents, the church and God. When I told him I'd been raped, he said the boy wouldn't have done it unless I'd tempted him."

"He said you *tempted* him?" said Sara from the doorway. "He *raped* you." She stepped out of the room.

"Father Basile asked me if I wanted to marry the boy and I said no, I didn't love him," said Mara. "He asked me if the boy was Catholic and I said no to that, too. Then he said, 'You shouldn't marry him anyway if he's not a Catholic.' Mama asked about Alan. She said he was a good boy, but he wasn't a Catholic. Father Basile said my husband would have to be a Catholic man who would adopt the child or the marriage would not be accepted by the church.

"Then Mama asked him, 'What do you mean, not accepted by the church?' and he said, 'If she keeps the child and doesn't marry a Catholic man, the child can't be baptized into the church. It will be condemned to purgatory when it dies.' When I heard that, I got hysterical. I screamed, 'No! Not my baby!'

"Mama asked Father Basile what I should do, and he said the best thing for the child would be to give it to a good Catholic family. Then it could be baptized and not spend eternity in purgatory." Mara put a hand to her throat. "I almost threw up."

"That's horrible," said Alan.

"Mama said, 'You mean adoption? She should give up the child?' and he said 'Yes.' He told us it would protect my family's reputation, and I would get over it before very long."

"You never have," said Thomas. "I've watched you carry the burden of losing your child for as long as I've known you."

"We went home after that and Mama told Papa," said Mara. "He went crazy. He said, 'How could she do this to us?' He cursed me. I heard my father curse me. He wanted to send me to a Catholic home for unwed mothers but Mama, for the first time in her life, stood up to him. She said no, that I needed to be with someone who loved me, not some mean old nuns. That made Papa madder, but Mama would not give in. She said she would take me to live with her sister in Iowa till my baby was born.

"Papa finally agreed, but only if I would give my baby up for adoption. I didn't want to, but I had no choice. My father and the Church took you away from me." She put her arm around Mary and pulled her close. "I've thought about you every day since you were born."

Mary hugged her. "My mother."

Alan got up and walked quietly into the bedroom. Sara was closing the door to the bathroom. "Are you feeling okay, sweetheart?"

"I'm all right. Just not hungry."

He held her arm. "You'll feel better if you eat something."

"I guess." She went into the dining room, put a few pieces of pasta on a plate and sat at the end of the table.

Alan poured her a glass of iced tea. "There you go."

Thomas was saying, "Tell her about bringing TJ home."

"We fixed up a nursery for the baby," said Mara. "We painted and decorated the walls with flowers and bunnies, put up a crib and bought a changing table and blankets, everything the baby would need. After TJ was born, I would not let go of him. Every time the nurse came for him, I was terrified, thinking she would take him away like they did my first baby.

"When they brought him to me to take home, I held him so tight that he screamed. But Tommy held out his arms and said, 'Let's take our son home,' and I wasn't scared anymore. No one would ever take Tommy's son away from him."

Mary turned to Thomas. "I wish you'd been there when I was born."

Sara left the room again. While she was gone, Peg and Alan collected the silverware, plates and serving dishes and piled them on the kitchen counter.

Alan said, "We'll clean up later." He went around the table refilling cups.

Sara came back into the room and stood close to Alan.

Thomas glanced at his watch. "Mary, we're flying back to San Diego tonight. I have a car coming for us at four, so we have half an hour. Do you have everything you need?"

"Me?" asked Mary. "You're taking me?"

"Yes," said Mara. "To be with your family."

"I love happy endings," said Peg. "There aren't nearly enough of them."

"It couldn't have happened without you," said Alan. "You and Bobby."

"And this guy," said Sara. "I called him a jackass, but look what he did."

"You were kidding, weren't you?" said Alan.

A car horn blew outside. Thomas went to the window. "There's our car. He's early, but we might as well go now." He gripped Alan's shoulder. "We'll always be grateful for what you've done for us, Alan. You've saved Mara's baby." They embraced, slapping each other on the back. "We'll keep in touch."

Mara hugged Alan and kissed him, her eyes glowing. "Goodbye, my hero."

"Goodbye, Dark Eyes."

"Time to weigh anchor, ladies," said Thomas. "American Airlines waits for no woman." He hugged Sara, then put an arm around Peg and kissed her on the cheek. He picked up Mary's duffel bag and the suitcase he and Mara had brought and started toward the door.

Mary threw her arms around Sara and Peg and squeezed them as hard as she could. Then she ran to Alan with her arms open. He held her to his chest. "Goodbye, Mary. Be a good girl."

"I will, Papa."

"I'm not your father."

"I know, but you will always be my papa." She stood on her tiptoes to kiss his cheek. "You found my mother and you saved me from Walter. I love you."

Mara put an arm around Mary's waist. "The car's waiting, Mary. It's time for you to come home." Alan kissed Mary's forehead and let go of her. The two women walked out to the car with their arms around each other.

Thomas dropped their bags into the trunk and got in the back seat beside Mara. The driver closed the doors. The three in the car leaned forward and waved to the three standing on the stoop and waving to them. The car pulled away.

Sara grasped Alan's hands and shook them. "Alan Cottrill, you've done a wonderful thing. Mary's going to be someone you can be proud of."

"She sure is," said Peg. She put her hand on Sara's back. "How're you feeling?"

"Is something wrong?" asked Alan.

"I haven't felt right lately, but I didn't want to bother you with it," said Sara. "I have an appointment with Doctor Sullivan tomorrow."

Alan stepped back and took hold of her shoulders. "What do you think it is, babe?"

"I don't know," said Sara. "I'll find out tomorrow."

"Tell me what the doctor says," said Peg. "I'm sure there's nothing to worry about. And let me know when you hear anything from San Diego. I'm invested in that little girl." Peg wiped her eyes. Then she stuffed the tissue in her purse and winked at Alan. "Goodbye, Papa."

——◊◊◊——

ALAN'S SECRETARY SLIPPED INTO the meeting room at two the next afternoon and whispered in his ear, "Sara needs to talk to you."

He sprinted from the room and down the hall to his office. What had the doctor told her? "Hello? How are you, sweetheart?"

"Are you sitting down?"

"What's wrong?" he asked.

"Sit down, please."

"Okay." He did. "What is it?"

"It's wonderful news. I'm pregnant!"

The room spun. It was a few seconds before he could pull in enough air to speak. "Are you . . . sure?"

"Doctor Sullivan is. He laughed when I told him I couldn't be. He says both of us are fine. . . . And Alan, I'm the happiest woman in the world—you're going to be a father."

ACKNOWLEDGMENTS

This book originated with a short story that Dr. Liza Weiland of the North Carolina Literary Review suggested might be expanded into a novel.

John Harten and Michelle Dias edited the manuscript, Christine Le-Porte proofread two editions, and Melissa Schropp formatted the manuscript for publication. I am indebted to the four of them.

My friend Ed Rose informed me about women rising to partnerships in large accounting firms in the 1960s, and my sister, Janet Richards, shared her knowledge of nursing practices in hospitals during that decade. Both of them contributed to the authenticity of the novel.

Mary Ann Grossman, Kate Marple, Dale Olbrich, Martha Rainbolt, Lisa Stroud and the late Jane Munro read and gave comments on earlier versions of the manuscript.

Chapters were critiqued by two North Carolina writing groups, the Phoenix Writers of Chapel Hill and the Mugs Coffee Group of Charlotte.

I grew up in a town in north central West Virginia in the 1940s and 1950s. There I witnessed the attitudes, beliefs and prejudices in that part of the state, especially with regard to young girls who became pregnant, that shaped this novel.

Two books were especially helpful. *The Girls Who Went Away* by Ann Fessler (Penguin Books, 2007), helped me understand the plight of young women who became pregnant and how it affected their later lives. *Paid for – My Journey Through Prostitution* by Rachel Moran (W.W. Morton and Company, 2013), informed me about the life experiences of a young prostitute.

This book would not have been written were it not for the help and encouragement of my wife, Nancy Marple. She is the *sine qua non* of this novel.

I am responsible for any errors.

Made in the USA
Middletown, DE
21 January 2018